Raincoast Chronicles 23

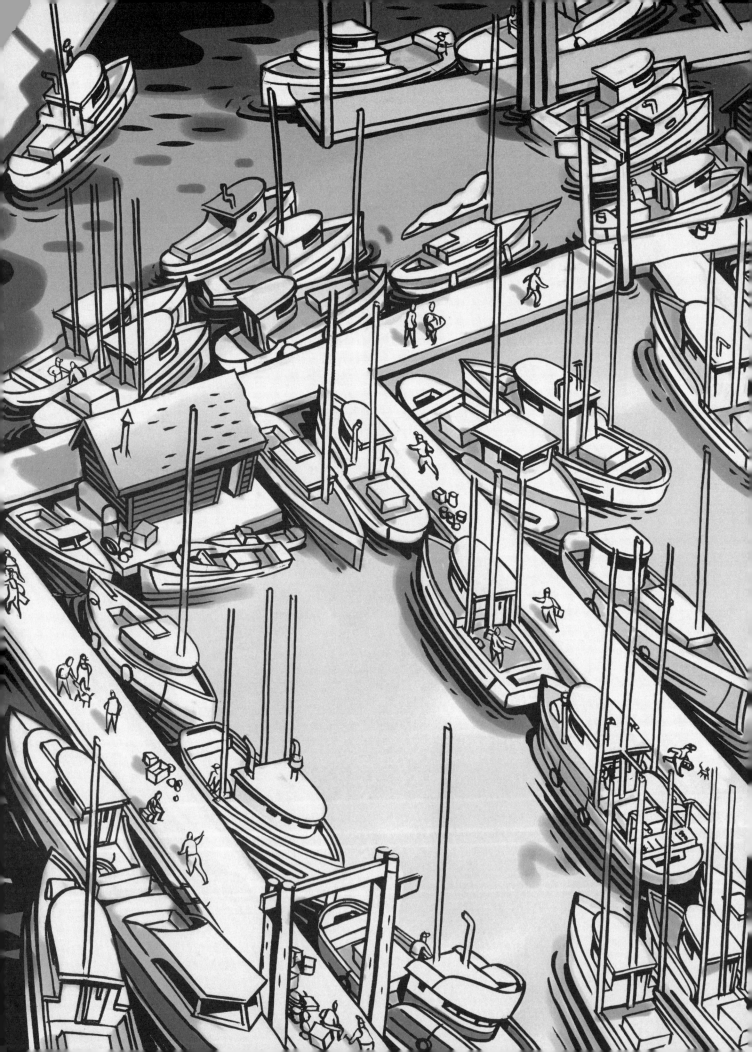

Harbour Publishing 40th Anniversary Edition

RAINCOAST
Chronicles 23

STORIES & HISTORY OF THE BRITISH COLUMBIA COAST

Edited by PETER A. ROBSON

with an introduction by HOWARD WHITE

HARBOUR PUBLISHING

Harbour Publishing Co. Ltd.
P.O. Box 219, Madeira Park, BC, V0N 2H0
www.harbourpublishing.com

Edited by Peter A. Robson
Copyedited by Lucy Kenward
Indexed by Brianna Cerkiewicz
Cover and title page art by Kim La Fave from *Fishing with Gubby*
Cover design by Anna Comfort O'Keeffe
Text design by Roger Handling
Printed and bound in Canada
Printed on chlorine-free FSC certified paper

Harbour Publishing acknowledges the support of the Canada Council for the Arts,
which last year invested $157 million to bring the arts to Canadians throughout the
country. We also gratefully acknowledge financial support from the Government of
Canada through the Canada Book Fund and from the Province of British Columbia
through the BC Arts Council and the Book Publishing Tax Credit.

Cataloguing data available from Library and Archives Canada
ISBN 978-1-55017-710-7 (paper)
ISBN 978-1-55017-711-4 (ebook)

CONTENTS

POETRY

INTRODUCTION

By Howard White

The year 2014 marked the fortieth year that books bearing the Harbour Publishing imprint have been flowing out into the world from our headquarters in Pender Harbour, BC.

My wife, Mary, and I actually bought our first printing press in 1969, started our newspaper in 1970 and published the first issue of *Raincoast Chronicles* in 1972, but it wasn't until 1974 that the first actual book with the first actual Harbour Publishing imprint appeared, so that's what we decided to use as Harbour's official start date. Our very first book (*A Dictionary of Chinook Jargon*, 1972) and the first issues of *Raincoast Chronicles* didn't have any imprint on the spine because we didn't know they needed one. When a concerned reader pointed out the omission, we decided to call ourselves Harbour Publishing because every business in Pender Harbour was Harbour this or Harbour that—Harbour Motors, Harbour Grocery, Harbour Barber. There was also a Harbour Pub and for years the freight truck delivered our books to them, which we might not have minded if they delivered the pub's beer to us, but somehow that never happened.

The Harbour Publishing imprint burst upon the scene with three books in 1974 and nobody can now remember which was first, *Build Your Own Floor Loom* by Steve Lones or *The Dulcimer Tuning Book* by Randy Christopher Rain (a.k.a. Randy Raine-Reusch). These were quickly followed by *Between the Sky and the Splinters*, a book of logging poems by Peter Trower that helped establish a distinguished literary career and became a classic of its kind.

My approach to starting a publishing operation was conditioned by my background in isolated BC coast logging camps where if something wanted making you made it yourself. My first move had been to get a bulldozer and clear a piece of land. Then I tore down an old building supply building in Vancouver and used the lumber to build a print shop on the cleared land. Then I bought a press and learned how to print with it (sort of). Only then did I start looking around for a likely book to publish. And only after the book was printed and bound did I begin to wonder if anybody might want to buy it. I know, I can hear the wiseacres muttering that my approach hasn't changed much. Luckily I am now surrounded by a brilliant and dedicated staff, some of whom have actually studied modern publishing methods in university, and they do their best to compensate for my atavistic habits.

I don't suppose many onlookers, watching Mary and I pulling armfuls of spoiled paper from our antique press late into the nights of those first years, would have given our enterprise much chance of surviving, but four decades and some 600 books later, here we are.

The years went by in a blur. Once we hung out the Harbour Publishing shingle, the stories poured in from all corners of BC, and we were swept away in the tide. We never had time to stop and ask ourselves if this was how we wanted to spend our entire working lives. But any time we have doubt, we find much reassurance in thumbing through the volumes that crowd the bookshelves of our home and next-door office— books like *Now You're Logging* by Bus Griffiths, *Spilsbury's Coast* by Jim Spilsbury, *Fishing with John* by Edith Iglauer, *Grizzlies and White Guys* by Clayton Mack, *Marine Life of the Pacific Northwest* by Andy Lamb and Bernie Hanby and yes, *The Encyclopedia of British Columbia* edited by Dan Francis, to name only a few. Those are the kind of BC-born-and-bred books Harbour has become known for and the kind in which we take the greatest satisfaction because if Harbour hadn't been here to coax them into life, perhaps that whole corpus of regional literature might not exist.

To mark the occasion we have decided to conscript this issue of *Raincoast Chronicles* to reprint some of the more memorable passages from Harbour's forty years of books. It is only a taste, but we think it conveys the unique flavour Harbour has brought to BC's cultural life. We hope you enjoy reading it half as much as we enjoyed creating it.

ON MEETING EMILY CARR

Excerpted from Haunting Vancouver *(2013), by Mike McCardell.*

This book was written by McCardell using the voice of an imaginary immortal, Jock Linn, a former sapper with the Royal Engineers who came to BC in 1859. Linn needed an eternal job so he decided to become a reporter and interview some of the province's most notable persons. —Ed.

Nutcase. The first time I met her I knew I was not dealing with an ordinary, boring woman. She was a nutcase.

When I walked into her home she was pulling a rope attached to a pulley in the ceiling with the other end of the rope going down to the back of a chair, and the chair was rising.

"I don't like reporters," she said.

I have met many people like that. I don't blame them. After knowing reporters all my life, actually all my lifetimes, do you think I would trust them? You tell them something and you have to put your faith in someone you don't know to tell the story back as you told it.

Come to think of it, I don't know how I have ever found anyone to talk to me. "May I sit down and talk?" I asked.

There was nothing, absolutely nothing, in the life of Emily Carr that might be considered normal, including her pet monkey, Woo.
Image I-61505 courtesy of the Royal BC Museum, BC Archives

"Only if you can fly. Can you fly, Mr. Linn?"

"What do you mean?"

She pointed to the chair now hung near the ceiling. "There is your chair."

Okay, at that moment I was in love. I must clarify that. It was not the kind of love that I had for Pauline Johnson, with whom I wanted to snuggle. Pauline was beautiful, and in the way boys and girls have been behaving since we were creatures in the sea I was attracted to Pauline. Then we could make more little Paulines.

Emily was different. I loved her mind. I hate to say that but it explains it all. I did not want to snuggle with her mind but, for goodness' sake, her furniture was hanging near the ceiling and I loved the mind and the woman who would do that.

I also liked her paintings, though they all looked the same to me. One tree, two trees, one totem pole, two, etc.

"I see you looking at my paintings. You don't like them, right?" she said to me.

I said I liked them.

"You are full of crap," she said. "I can tell a liar when I see one." Then she took a long drag on her cigarette.

"They did not like this when I taught school," she said.

"I heard that was your problem."

"What was my problem?"

"You smoked in school when you were teaching."

"So what? And I cursed the bad attitudes. I cursed them with curse words. You have a problem with that?"

"No, ma'am."

You see, that is why I liked her, in a platonic sort of way. Poor Emily. By the time I met her she was a washed-up artist. Those were her words.

"No one is ever going to buy my work."

"Maybe," I said. "There will come a time when people see the original inhabitants in a different way. They might even like them."

If you want to be an artist, study the life of Emily Carr—rejected, lonely, despairing and then "discovered" at the very end. Take up running a boarding house instead. She did.

Image D-06009 courtesy of the Royal BC Museum, BC Archives

She shook her head, which was covered with a skull cap that she wore all the time.

"Are you crazy? They see them as savages and they will always see them like that."

This was true. The government was snatching the Native children from their parents, which really was kidnapping, and forbidding the potlatch, which was like forbidding Christmas and Easter to a Christian, and not allowing the children to learn their own languages. In a word, the government would erase the savage from the savages, though they did not say it that way.

When I'd thought about that I said, "You're right. So why are you painting totem poles?"

"I like them."

That is the problem with artists. They are out of step with government edicts.

Then she reached out for her monkey, which was her pet, and it climbed on her arm and sat on her shoulder.

You can see why I said she was a nutcase. But she also lowered the chair so I could sit on it.

"You are not so bad," she said. "Not good, mind you, but your face looks like one of those on the totem poles, so you can sit."

Her life in short: She was raised by a Victorian father who transplanted Victorian life to Victoria—high ceilings, pictures of Queen Victoria on numerous walls, slipcovers on the chairs and the couch that covered the legs of the furniture because it would be obscene to see exposed legs, even those of a couch.

Emily did not like that. That upset her father so Emily disliked it even more. Her father went out of his mind. Emily did the only thing she could. She became an artist.

Now being an artist in those days meant that she would paint landscapes, and her father agreed. It was called dabbling in the arts and a daughter should be allowed to do that.

Then her father died. It happens. Her guardian, chosen by her father, said she could go to California to study art, so long as it was landscapes.

She went, but then she got on a freighter going to France. Sometimes kids do the craziest things and you want to kill them. It is a good thing they are faster than you.

She learned amazing ways of painting things, close up and personal and far away and still attached. It had nothing to do with Victorian painting.

Emily came back to British Columbia and painted totem poles far up the coast, in the Queen Charlottes before the name was changed to an aboriginal name. No one wanted her work.

She was broke—that happens to artists—so she quit painting. If she could not make a living of art she would run a boarding house. That was her way of saying "Screw you" to the world and to herself.

But there was income in renting rooms to folks who did not want to be homeless, so she did that for twenty years.

Can you imagine giving up everything you love and want to do for two decades?

This is where the historian and the journalist fail. They say she gave up art for twenty years and ran a boarding house but it was not twenty years, not in the beginning. As with all of us it was one month that became six and became twelve and is it Christmas already? And then two years became six and those became ten.

"I can't believe I have been doing this for ten years. Once upon a time I painted pictures. That's a joke."

We all say that.

And then ten years more and thoughts of a brush and canvas and paint were a distant memory. "I once thought I could paint trees. Now I use the sawdust to keep a fire going so the guests won't complain."

She said that to a mirror.

And then what happens? She becomes famous overnight. The Group of Seven— that was Canada's artists to the world and they all lived in Ontario—got to see Emily's paintings of trees.

"Magnificent. Wonderful. Just what we are trying to do," they said.

Just as an aside, every time a reporter writes "they said" I wonder if they said it

Emily Carr grew up in a staid Victorian home. When she left that, she travelled with her friends and animals in her caravan named "Elephant." Her life was as much her art as her art was her life.

Image B-09610 courtesy of the Royal BC Museum, BC Archives

all at once. Imagine the Group of Seven together in a room looking at Emily's trees. "Okay, the official word is, now, all together, 'Magnificent. Wonderful. Just what we are trying to do.'"

"Oh, come on. Someone didn't say it. Let's try again."

Anyway, Emily was made an honorary member of the Group and she was suddenly famous, while she was still running a boarding house.

How the heck did this happen? Out of the blue the famous men with brushes decided that a woman on the West Coast who lives with a monkey was pretty good. Why did it not happen sooner? You only get angry when you think about it, or disappointed, or disillusioned. No, life is not fair.

Anyway, she was closing in on sixty when her fame came. But of course fame at home does not naturally follow. She was closing in on seventy when the Vancouver Art Gallery had a one-woman show of her paintings. The gallery was then a small building on Georgia next to a movie house.

"Totem poles? Trees? Why are we looking at these?" some patrons of the art of Victorian landscapes said.

Three years later she was too sick to paint any longer, and four years after that she died.

The Vancouver Art Gallery now has a permanent display of her trees and totem poles. When it moves to a new and larger building it will have an even larger permanent display. And the Emily Carr University of Art + Design has graduated thousands of students, most of whom look at things in strange and challenging ways.

The only difference is none of them are allowed to smoke in class. Emily would have probably lit up anyway.

THE STORY OF PRINCESS LOUISA INLET

Excerpted from The Sunshine Coast: From Gibsons to Powell River
(1996, 2011), by Howard White. Photos by Dean van't Schip

Jervis Inlet, which zigzags deep into the Coast Range like a forty-mile lightning bolt between the Sechelt Peninsula and the Powell River side, is a classic coastal fjord, shadowed most of its length by mile-high mountain walls. It is very deep and includes a 3,000-foot-deep hole known as the Jervis Deep. However, the feature that sets Jervis Inlet apart from its sister inlets occurs ten miles from the head on the east side. There the mountain walls unexpectedly part and let into a four-mile side inlet—Princess Louisa—surrounded by such precipitous bluffs the effect is like looking up at the sky from the bottom of a colossal and extremely gorgeous cavern.

"There is no use describing that inlet," Erle Stanley Gardner once wrote, before proceeding to ignore his own advice. "There is a calm tranquility which stretches from the smooth surface of the reflecting waters straight up into infinity. The deep calm of eternal silence is only disturbed by the muffled roar of throbbing waterfalls as they plunge down from sheer cliffs. There is no scenery in the world that can beat it. Not that I've seen the rest of the world. I don't need to. I've seen Princess Louisa Inlet."

I won't fall into the trap of trying to describe Princess Louisa except to say few

A trip to Princess Louisa is an experience that won't ever be forgotten.

Sunshine Coasters would deny it is the Hope Diamond of the area's scenic jewels. It is the place we take those special visitors we want to hook on the coast, the one experience guaranteed to jar the most jaded soul into a full-blown state of awe. I have been visiting Princess Louisa regularly since I was a kid and it never seems enough. Despite going in many different weathers, moods and ages, it has never failed to send me away with a renewed sense of life's promise.

The inlet's rare magnetism draws remarkable people to it and inspires them to extraordinary exertions. Legend has it that it was avoided by the Sechelt people after a small village at the head was buried by one of the inlet's periodic rock slides, but band elder Clarence Joe claimed his people used to visit it for recreational purposes just as the white man would later.

Early on, Princess Louisa was ignored by the more development-minded settlers because its only substantial resource was beauty, which didn't readily lend itself to being canned or milled. This was a challenge inventor Thomas Hamilton would apply himself to later.

Herman Casper just wanted to wake up in the morning and see it. Casper was a deserter from the German army who homesteaded the only decently flat land in the area, the peninsula down at the inlet mouth by Malibu Rapids, in 1900. When he wasn't blacksmithing for local handloggers, Casper whiled away his days spoiling his twenty-six cats and composing songs in praise of the magnificent surroundings, which he was happy to perform with his zither for visiting boaters:

Looking out at the entrance to Princess Louisa Inlet. Fortunately, the inlet was mostly ignored by those seeking to extract resources because its only substantial resource was beauty.

> Beyond Mount Alfred, in ze vest
> Where ze sun goes down to rest
> It draws me dere, I don' know vy
> S'pose it is ze colour in ze sky.
> For zey are purple, mauve and pink
> Howeber it makes me vunder, look and t'ink.

Casper was followed by Charles (Daddy) Johnstone, a towering mountain man from Daniel Boone country who kept edging west ahead of civilization until he and his family of six landed up at Princess Louisa around 1909. There they threw together a one-room split-cedar shack, lived off the land and had three more kids. The Johnstone gang may have succeeded in getting closer to the inlet's soul than anyone since the Sechelt in the days when they had it to themselves. As part of their education, sons Steve and Judd were sent up on the snowy plateau above Princess Louisa without jacket or shoes and with only matches, salt and a jackknife for survival. They would live by their wits for weeks at a time, and explore miles into the interior of the province. After World War One, Daddy began to feel even Jervis was too cramped and carried on to Alaska, where he became famous as a pioneer. But Steve and Judd returned to British Columbia and passed the rest of their days in homage to the fabulous Jervis landscape that had been so deeply imprinted on them in their formative years. Their names became synonymous with the inlet's wild spirit, and Judd in particular became famous for his tall tales of pioneer times.

Judd married Dora Jeffries from Egmont and they stayed up Princess Louisa, sixty miles from the nearest family, through the birth of their first three girls. The sun would disappear behind the inlet crags for two months in the depths of winter, and it would get so cold the salt water would freeze from shore to shore. To get anything that couldn't be obtained from the bush, Judd would have to drag the boat across two

Below left: The beauties of Princess Louisa Inlet defy description, though many have tried.

Below right: The sheer walls of Jervis Inlet can take your breath away.

James (Mac) MacDonald devoted his entire existence to being the inlet's chief admirer, protector and ambassador to the world.
Courtesy of the Princess Louisa Society, W.A. Stenner photo

The interior of Mac MacDonald's log cabin.
Courtesy of the Princess Louisa Society

miles of sea ice and row to Pender Harbour, a hundred-mile round trip. He was always a welcome sight at Portuguese Joe's bar in Irvines Landing and never had to pay for a drink. All you had to do was ask him how things were going.

"Could be worse. Had a hard blow and a cedar tree come down on the shack is all."

"Very big?"

"Naw, only about six foot on the butt."

"Good God, Judd. Didn't it do a lot of damage?"

"Naw. Fell crost the bed right where the old woman was sleepin', but it hung up on the stove before it could git 'er. Tore the roof off is all."

"That's terrible, Judd!"

"Naw. I just took a couple blocks off the end and split up a mess o' shakes. Old woman bin after me fer a new roof anyways."

"What about the rest of the tree. How did you remove it?"

"Didn't bother. It was pointin' in the stove anyways, so I jus' lit the fire and stuck the Gilchrist jack on the other end. Every time the old woman wanted some exter heat, I just hollered at the kid to go out and give a few clicks on the jack. It was auto-feed, like."

"So it wasn't so bad after all."

"Hell no. I got a new roof and a whole winter's heat without once havin' to leave the shack."

I sometimes wonder if it was due to Judd Johnstone that the entire Jervis Inlet–Nelson Island area seemed to become such a prime bullshit-producing zone. When I was growing up there, it seemed you couldn't get a straight answer out of anybody.

Certainly you couldn't get one out of James (Mac) MacDonald, the globetrotting American playboy who fell under the Princess's spell in 1919. "After travelling around the world and seeing many of its famous beauty spots, I felt I was well able to evaluate the magnificence of Princess Louisa," he wrote in one of his more sober utterances. "This place had to equal or better anything I had seen."

Like many another wealthy American who no sooner spied a thing of beauty in a foreign land than he had to have it, MacDonald promptly applied to the BC government to purchase the inlet head, and the government turned out to be eager to unload it. Their appraisal of the 292-acre site, which would come to be called "The Eighth Wonder of the World" and attract 20,000 gawkers a season despite its inaccessibility, was that only 42 acres were flat enough to be of any use, so MacDonald could have the whole thing for $420, if that wasn't asking too much. He took possession in 1927.

Through absolutely no fault of its own, this turned out to be the best thing the government could have done. Within a few years MacDonald would be turning down $400,000 offers from hotel chains and preserving the area for public use with a determination the government would not come to appreciate until 1964, when MacDonald finally had the satisfaction of seeing his beloved charge consecrated as a Class A marine park.

Rich, eloquent and handsome, "Mac" MacDonald could have had his pick of successful careers, but from his fateful encounter with the Princess in the prime of his life until the day he could no longer hobble around on his own, he devoted his entire existence to being her chief admirer, protector and ambassador to the world. He got married in 1939, but the new wife made the mistake of forcing him to choose between the Princess and her, and a Mexican divorce quickly followed.

Mac left the inlet only during the winter months, when the weather becomes much harsher than the coastal norm. At first he rented a *pied à terre* in Pender Harbour from his friend Bertrand Sinclair, and later he established regular winter digs in Acapulco. From May to October he was back at Princess Louisa, continuing his endless study of her moods, cataloguing her wonders and expounding on them to visitors. In time every feature in the inlet, from Chatterbox Falls to Trapper's Rock, came to be known by a name Mac gave it. He became a walking encyclopedia of inlet history and lore, most of it unreliable, but all of it highly entertaining.

MacDonald's presence became an attraction in itself, compelling regulars like John Barrymore to return year after year to pass long evenings sitting on the afterdeck of his splendiferous MV *Infanta*, where Mac would tell stories and point out faces in the rock formations of the bluffs. (Barrymore claimed to have discovered Napoleon, though Mac later speculated you had to be drinking Napoleon brandy to see it.) Hollywood types seemed to take a particular shine to Mac. At various times he entertained the likes of Ronald Colman, William Powell and Mack Sennett, complete with his entourage of bathing beauties, who filmed part of a movie called *Alaska Love* in the inlet, but MacDonald was equally attentive to locals and kids, reputedly turning down dinner with Arthur Godfrey so he could keep a storytelling date at the youth camp. This is all the more notable considering Mac's legendary appetite for free grub. It is said that from the time the first yacht showed up in the spring to the time the last one left in the fall, he never ate his own cooking.

MacDonald was a great admirer of Judd Johnstone and, after Judd moved south to Hardy Island, of his brother Steve, who stayed up-inlet all his life. He was also a great fan of old Casper. During one of his winters south, MacDonald hired some professional musicians to make a record of Casper's songs, which proved a great hit among inlet fanciers and netted the old smithy a rare spot of cash. MacDonald was outraged in 1940 when Thomas Hamilton talked Casper into parting with his beloved acreage for $500 so the aviation tycoon could build a luxury resort called Malibu Lodge. Mac cheered when Malibu went broke in 1947 and was taken over by Young Life, a non-denominational church group offering low-budget vacations to city kids.

MacDonald was particularly attentive to Muriel Blanchet, the adventuring Victoria widow who cruised the inlet with her five children in the 1930s. With the help of

Hubert Evans she recorded her experiences in the coastal classic *The Curve of Time*, which has a lengthy passage describing Mac as "the Man from California," which of course he wasn't.

Under the inlet's influence MacDonald became one of the most ardent apostles of the creed that humanity was placed on the Sunshine Coast "not to be doing but to be." He even went so far as to dedicate himself formally to "the satisfying state of loaferhood."

"The world needs ten million full time thinking loafers dedicated to the purpose of bringing this cockeyed life back to its normal balance," he declared in his five-point manifesto of loaferdom.

Of course it helped to be the favourite son of a Seattle grocery heiress, a fact Mac-Donald made no bones about, advising would-be loafers: "Before birth, look the field over and pick out a family in which some member has misspent his life in amassing sufficient do-re-me to permit you to dodge the squirrel cage." In this he differs from the Johnstone boys, who would argue that you could enjoy the best the coast had to offer with no more accumulated assets than a jackknife and a box of matches.

I remember Mac as a pleasant old man with a crown of luminous silver hair who used to keep his houseboat, the *Seaholm*, in Madeira Park while he waited for the inlet to thaw in the spring. I had a paper route, and while it was a bit of nuisance to paddle

Above: A quiet forest trail, part of Princess Louisa Marine Park.

Right: Chatterbox Falls provides a focus for the breathtaking scenery at the head of Princess Louisa Inlet.

over to where he was anchored, it was always worth seeing what nonsense he would come up with. One spring he launched into a big production about a new sport which had taken Acapulco beaches by storm that season, and ceremoniously produced this wonderful innovation he'd smuggled back just for my benefit. I was excited by the buildup but disappointed by the actual item, which looked like the lid of a small garbage can. He said you flicked it so it sort of hovered like a flying saucer. He made me practise it with him until I had the knack, then commanded me to go off and spread the fad among my friends. That was how Madeira Park became the first Canadian beachhead of the Frisbee craze, way back in 1957. To a twelve-year-old, Mac seemed like nothing so much as a great big overaged kid, which I am sure is a judgment he would have been most delighted to accept. The only thing you had to watch was that he didn't lure you inside his cabin and try to make you play chess. As a chess fanatic he was known for his willingness to play with anyone, no matter how incompetent, but I am sad to say even his legendary patience was checkmated in my case.

Mac died in a Seattle rest home in 1978. His ashes are planted inside a boulder at the head of Princess Louisa, beneath an inscription which reads "Laird of the inlet, Gentleman, friend to all who came here."

Kids get a chance to experience the wilderness at Malibu Club. Originally a luxury resort for Hollywood movie stars, the property now serves as an affordable summer youth camp operated by Young Life, a non-denominational Christian organization.

PILING BLOOD

by Al Purdy

It was powdered blood
in heavy brown paper bags
supposed to be strong enough
to prevent the stuff from escaping
but didn't

We piled it ten feet high
right to the shed roof
working at Arrow Transfer
on Granville Island
The bags weighed 75 pounds
and you had to stand on two
of the bags to pile the top rows
I was six feet three inches
and needed all of it

I forgot to say
the blood was cattle blood
horses sheep and cows
to be used for fertilizer
the foreman said

It was a matter of some delicacy
to plop the bags down softly
as if you were piling dynamite
if you weren't gentle
the stuff would belly out
from bags in brown clouds
settle on your sweating face
cover hands and arms
enter ears and nose
seep inside pants and shirt
reverting back to liquid blood
and you looked like
you'd been scalped
by a tribe of
particularly unfriendly
Indians and forgot to die

We piled glass as well
it came in wooden crates
two of us hoicking them

off trucks into warehouses
every crate
weighing 200 pounds
By late afternoon
my muscles would twitch and throb
in a death-like rhythm
from hundreds of bags of blood
and hundreds of crates of glass

Then at Burns' slaughterhouse
on East Hastings Street
I got a job part time
shouldering sides of frozen beef
hoisting it from steel hooks
staggering to and from
the refrigerated trucks
and eerie freezing rooms
with breath a white vapour
among the dangling corpses
and the sound of bawling animals
screeched down from an upper floor
with their throats cut
and blood gurgling into special drains
for later retrieval

And the blood smell clung to me
clung to clothes and body
sickly and sweet
and I heard the screams
of dying cattle
and I wrote no poems
there were no poems
to exclude the screams
which boarded the streetcar
and travelled with me
till I reached home
turned on the record player
and faintly
in the last century
heard Beethoven weeping

From Beyond Remembering: The Collected Poems of Al Purdy *(2000),*
selected and edited by Al Purdy and Sam Solecki

THE SIMPLE JOY OF RAIN

3

Excerpted from A Walk with the Rainy Sisters: In Praise of
British Columbia's Places *(2010), by Stephen Hume*

I'm not a guy who faithfully scans newspaper travel sections for winter getaway deals. I don't line up at the airports for a break in Hawaii or Fiji or Palm Springs or some Mexican beach in the Baja and then return with tales of iguanas, golf and too many green swizzles.

Nor am I that guy's gloomy alter ego, hunkered down and complaining about the dark, dank, insufferable months of January and February on the soggy, dreary, dismal West Coast.

What's to complain about?

A little damp is the price I pay for living amid the wonders of North America's temperate raincoast.

All things considered, it's a small price compared to what I fork over to the government to pay for wars in Afghanistan, a retractable roof for Vancouver's football stadium, temporary digs for speed skaters or the latest city hall facelift.

Complaining about winter rains on the West Coast makes as much sense as complaining that the sun rises too early in the morning. Things are what they are. This is a marine climate. It rains.

As for me, I love rain. I love it even when it saturates the slope we're on and we get a surfeit of it seeping into our deepest sub-basement, as it does every so often when downpours escalate to monsoons.

I love the subtle gradations of grey and the filtered light and the ever-changing sky. I love the gossamer drift of fine drizzle and halos around street lights and wraiths of water vapour drifting over depths in which the luminous globes of jellyfish pulse. I love the faint scent of the tropics that sometimes arrives with the Pineapple Express.

I love a shower's dimpling hiss across the still, glassy surface of a woodland bog and the drumming of raindrops on elephant-sized leaves of skunk cabbage. I love the splash and clatter of coho in a seething fall freshet to announce winter's imminent arrival and the massed trilling as the March rains bring out spring peepers to sing winter away.

Suzanne Boyer photo

My own winter mornings are always a surprise. Bands of fog layering the horizon in patterns that are never the same from one dawn to the next, with snow-clad mountains rising out of the sea in their capes of frozen rain: now hidden, now peeping out of the mist, now shining in a ray of sunlight, now draped in streamers of cloud.

What can be more of a feast for the eye than the reflections of clouds racing across the sides of tall buildings after a quick, sharp rain and a sudden blow from the sea, or the gleam of lights reflected from rain-slicked pavement so black it looks like you are about to fall into the abyss?

Who is immune to the sight of a small child in a yellow slicker and red gumboots jumping into the endless, joyous wonder of new puddles or to the hiss of a squall across the surface of Lost Lagoon, rising to rattle against your raincoat, preferably one of those stiff, Irish green poacher coats of waxed cotton?

At night I can think of nothing more satisfying than the staccato spatter of raindrops driven by a brisk southeaster while I lie snug in my bed, listening to my wife's steady breathing, and behind it, to the wind sighing through cedars in ancient voices from our dreamtime that speak to all of us in the same language, a language everyone understands regardless of the self-imposed illusions of racial, ethnic, linguistic, national, religious or any other difference.

The sound of rain is the sound of life. The touch of rain is the quickening of existence. I love it.

TOFINO'S FRED TIBBS: ECCENTRIC PIONEER SETTLER

4

Excerpted from Tofino and Clayoquot Sound: A History *(2014),*
by Margaret Horsfield and Ian Kennedy

The year 1908 marked the arrival on the west coast of a self-effacing young man, Frederick Gerald Tibbs, destined to become one of Tofino's best-known characters. At first glance not a prepossessing character, Tibbs appeared stocky and rather shy, painfully self-conscious about a facial disfigurement dating back to a childhood injury in England and made worse by various surgeries. Benignly good-natured and cheerfully eccentric, Tibbs first settled on land he pre-empted at Long Bay (Long Beach), the area now occupied by Green Point Campground, a considerable distance from Tofino and from other settlers. Strangely keen on physical exercise, Tibbs caused locals to shake their heads when they heard he took a plunge in the breakers at Long Bay every morning, followed by an energetic run round and round a huge tree stump on the beach. Tibbs wrote voluble, friendly letters to Walter Dawley [owner of the store and hotel on nearby Stubbs/Clayoquot Island], including fussy and precise shopping lists. He ordered such items as "limewater glycerine" for his hair, lemons, mouse-traps, nails, thimbles, a blue sweater, and on one occasion a can of bright

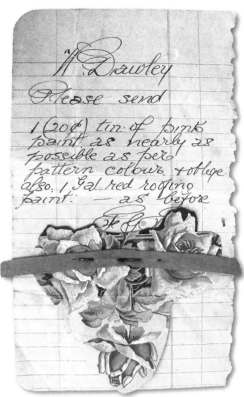

Right: Frederick Gerald Tibbs, pictured here with his cousin Vera Marshall, stands out as one of Tofino's best-known eccentrics. He settled at Long Bay (Long Beach) in 1908, and later moved to Dream Isle off Tofino, where he clear-cut the island and erected a castle-like home.
Image F-03427 courtesy of the Royal BC Museum, BC Archives

Far right: A sample of wallpaper covered with pink roses, sent by Fred Tibbs to storekeeper Walter Dawley in 1909. Writing from his home at Long Bay, Tibbs requested that Dawley obtain matching pink paint.
Image MS-1076, Walter Dawley fonds, box 9, courtesy of the Royal BC Museum, BC Archives

pink paint, enclosing a sample of rose-covered wallpaper providing the hue to be matched. After passing on good wishes to everyone in the "liquid dominion of Clayoquot," as Tibbs called Dawley's establishment, he signed his name in a flourish of calligraphic curlicues. While living at Long Bay, Tibbs gave his return address as "Tidal Wave Ranch." He did no ranching there, but filled his days clearing land and establishing himself in a rough little cabin "built out of driftwood and gas cans and made quite ornamental," according to Mike Hamilton's memoirs, and featuring—if the paint did arrive as ordered—a rosy pink interior.

Early in 1910, Tibbs left Tidal Wave Ranch and took a job on remote Triangle Island off the northern tip of Vancouver Island, which he described as "this mountain top, surrounded by ocean." Tibbs assisted there with the construction of a new lighthouse, sending to Dawley for tennis shoes and a "good deep-toned mouth harp" to be shipped up on the supply vessel *Leebro*. He saved enough money for a trip to England, but by November 1911 he was back at his "ranch," in his spare time busying himself as president of the Clayoquot Conservative Association. The following year Tibbs took a job at the Kennedy Lake salmon hatchery and found himself increasingly drawn to Tofino. A small, 2 ½-acre island in the harbour caught his fancy, so he sold his property at Long Bay and bought the island, which he christened Dream Isle, painting the name in huge white letters on the rocks. Here, Tibbs began to pursue his dreams, with the village of Tofino watching in complete astonishment.

In the first of many unexpected moves, Tibbs set about clear-cutting the entire island, blasting out stumps whenever he could. He had a fondness for using large amounts of dynamite; loud explosions from Dream Isle became commonplace. Ignoring [fellow settler] Jacob Arnet's kindly suggestion that he leave at least some trees

for wind protection, Tibbs left only one tree in the centre of the island, an enormous spruce that he topped at 100 feet. Over time, he removed every limb, leaving a tall, standing spar. Up this he built a sturdy ladder, almost a small scaffold, mounting all the way, step by step, to the top, where he constructed a narrow platform. According to local legend, he would climb to the platform every morning with his cornet and serenade Tofino with lively tunes, in particular "Come to the Cookhouse Door, Boys." Having first lived in a tent on the island, Tibbs gradually built his dream home, a wooden castle, three storeys high, complete with a crenellated tower and battlements. Painted red, white and blue and held to the rocks with steel guywires, the castle eventually housed a piano and a phonograph, with a garden alongside featuring trellised roses, a loveseat and a sunken well. Inside, the walls were "beautifully ornamented by artistic designs in plaster work," according to George Nicholson, who managed Dawley's hotel at Clayoquot during the 1920s. Tibbs lived on the ground floor; the upper levels remained unfinished and accessible only by ladder. In the years leading up to World War One, Tibbs had just begun all this work; he continued doggedly on, year after year, with each new development establishing him ever more firmly as one of Tofino's leading eccentrics.

Although few could compete with Tibbs's highly visible idiosyncrasies, from the earliest days of settlement the west coast consistently attracted its fair share of oddballs: independent, stubborn individuals determined to go their own way, brooking no interference. Solitary, a little—sometimes very—peculiar, these men (and they were always single men) tended to disappear up the inlets or into the bush, finding remote places to live undisturbed, coming to town only when it suited them.

World War One changed everything. One by one, men enlisted and went off to

A view of Tofino in 1913, with the recently completed St. Columba Anglican Church on the left and the dock and lifeboat station on the right.

Bert Drader photo: Ken Gibson Collection, Tofino

Below: In the foreground is Arnet Island, also known as Tibbs, Dream or Castle Island, after Fred Tibbs cut down all the trees but one to build his "castle" and tower.
Image A-05272 courtesy of the Royal BC Museum, BC Archives

Right: Tibbs's dream home was a wooden castle, three storeys high, with a crenellated tower and battlements. Painted red, white and blue, it was held to the rocks with steel guywires.
Image F-03428 courtesy of the Royal BC Museum, BC Archives

Bottom: Vancouver photographer Frank Leonard took this photo of Stubbs/Clayoquot Island in the 1920s. The saltery is at the end of the dock, and Walter Dawley's store, with its square, white front, stands on the far right. The Clayoquot Hotel, rebuilt after the fire of 1921, is the dark building to the left of the store. The beach in the foreground is where the body of Fred Tibbs washed up.
Frank Leonard photo, Vancouver Public Library 16677

fight. Tibbs was among them, joining up with the Canadian Forestry Corps. However, before he headed off to serve, he sounded one final blast on his cornet from his treetop platform, saying goodbye to his island domain. He told no one he was going, simply boarded up the windows of his wooden castle and left. On one window, up in the tower, he painted a picture of a beautiful princess; some say she looked like Olive Garrard. No one knew at the time, but Tibbs harboured secret romantic attachments, not only to Olive but also to Alma Arnet. Some thought he also fancied Winnie Dixson. "Oh, he tried all of us, all the different girls," Winnie later commented. "I didn't have much interest…I had about 300 chickens."

Neither Alma nor Olive had any idea what lay ahead. Tibbs had made his will before setting off to war, leaving the island "and everything thereon, excepting the house and ten feet of land on either side of the house site," to Alma Arnet, "because she is the nicest girl I know." He left the house and contents, except for his gramophone, to Olive Garrard, "because it was built for her." If Olive married, the house should go to Alma "if she is still single." Returning intact from the war in 1919, Tibbs resettled on his island and resumed his land-clearing, his gardening and his risky experiments with explosives. On New Year's Eve in 1919, he tried to explode dynamite from his tree platform, to "blow the old year to the four winds," but the explosion did not go off with the bang he had hoped, the dynamite being frozen.

In his wooden castle, Tibbs entertained visitors who came to listen to his gramophone and drink cocoa, and he often went to Tofino to collect mail and to "have some music, as there are two or three damsels here who play very nicely." He attended community events and dances—though he never danced—and he also took up a new job. Rowing his skiff around the harbour, he tended the navigation lights, coal-oil lanterns mounted on tripods on wooden floats. Every second day when the lanterns required refilling, Tibbs would tie up to the floats and clamber on to fuel the lights.

In early July 1921, Francis Garrard noted that Tibbs had been blasting rock on his island; "he had got badly powdered and had been quite ill from the effects." Immediately after this, on July 4, the Clayoquot Hotel went up in flames. Along with every other available man, Tibbs rushed over to Stubbs Island to assist in fighting the fire. The following day he went out to tend the lights, but after landing on one of the floats, his skiff drifted away. He dived in to swim after the boat. Not realizing what had occurred, a Tla-o-qui-aht man who saw the empty skiff towed the boat to Opitsat. Tibbs turned and made for the nearest land, on Stubbs Island. Perhaps overexertion, combined with the effects of the dynamite powder, had weakened him, for although he was usually a powerful swimmer, the effort proved too much. "He made the spit alright," Bill Sharp recalled. "He crawled up on the sand and lay there." A Japanese fisherman alerted the authorities; the telegram sent from the Clayoquot police to their superiors in Victoria read "Frederick Gerald Tibbs found exhausted on beach at Clayoquot by Jap fisherman early this morning." Tibbs could not be revived. "When the Doctor arrived…," wrote Francis Garrard, "Tibbs was already dead…it was a very sad affair." The gravestone for Frederick Gerald Tibbs stands in the old Tofino cemetery, on Morpheus Island.

Following Tibbs's death, the Garrard and Arnet families reached an agreement

Fred Tibbs limbed his one remaining tall spruce, and then built a ladder up it, which he ascended regularly to a narrow platform where he played his cornet.
Image F-03431 courtesy of the Royal BC Museum, BC Archives

Tibbs Island as it looks today. In 2015 it was listed for sale for $698,000.
Donna Fraser photo

about his unusual will. Olive Garrard relinquished her share of the inheritance, his castle home, to the Arnets, and Dream Isle became Arnet Island. A group of men went over to the island shortly after Tibbs's death to cut down the 100-foot-high "tree rig," deeming it unsafe, and as time passed the clear-cut island slowly greened over. A few others attempted to live on the island, renting out Tibbs's castle, but the place became associated with bad luck and sudden death. According to Anthony Guppy, after several unfortunate fatalities and mishaps there, the "strange little castle remained unoccupied for a long time…People began to believe it was haunted. It became a sort of game for young people to go over there, get inside, and make the most hair-raising ghostly noises." The stories of Tibbs lingered and grew; by the late 1920s, "Fred Tibbs had already acquired the gloss of a legendary figure," according to Guppy. The year after Tibbs died, Alma Arnet married; Olive Garrard also married in 1923. Had Tibbs lived a bit longer, perhaps he would have reconsidered his will. He certainly would have enjoyed the livelier social scene that began to emerge in Tofino in the ensuing years.

WHAT THE SEA PERHAPS HEARD

by Rachel Rose

Killer whales hunt a blue whale calf
and eat his tongue. As he bleeds to death,

blood seeps without a sound into my body.
Gulls come, screaming their belly-greed,

small fish unstitch flesh with needle teeth.
The mother blue has more grief

in her massive body
than anything else I have held.

No one has seen what I see: how great white
sharks copulate, fitting together in secret method.

When the octopus siphons me inside her,
and I unfurl her delicate legs with warm currents,

she blushes for me alone. I hold the tight curl
of the seahorse's tail as he pivots,

protecting his basketful of life.
Observe the spaghettini arms of starfish

reaching for drifting food. Hear their little song:
the stomach, the stomach! Dear urchins, sweet limpets,

all feast in me. In the heat of my armpit
waves curl their black seaweed, stones groan

as they are ground to sand. I rock them.
In my cold brain I am rational,

I do not weep to feel the polar bears
scrape my frozen cheeks.

From Song and Spectacle *(2012), by Rachel Rose*

COUGAR HUNT

Excerpted from Tales from Hidden Basin *(1996), by Dick Hammond*

Cougars have always held a fascination for the people of the Coast—Native or European. Whenever hunters gather, tales of the secretive cats, of their strange mix of daring and cowardice, of rashness and cunning, are sure to be told.

There are no cougars on Nelson Island, but to brothers Cliff and Hal, they were the most interesting of all animals—even more interesting than the great bear, the grizzly. For just about everyone who hunted had seen one of those, but some men had hunted all of their lives and not seen one of the big cats.

Cliff and Hal's greatest ambition was to go on a cougar hunt with the Old Indian, an event he had hinted might be in the future. But when they heard the familiar *Puff—Puff—* of Charlie's old engine one November morning, they weren't thinking of cougars; they were just glad he was there for a visit. Charlie's visits to the farm were welcomed by everyone. His kindness and sense of humour endeared him to their sisters and their mother. His knowledge—which he was always willing to share—was valued by Jack, their father, who liked the old man and was impressed by his practical wisdom. And the boys could never get enough of his stories of hunting and fishing and of the old times. For his part, Charlie relished the good food and appreciative audience.

Alistair Anderson illustration

But certain chores had to be finished, so by the time they got to the float the boat was tied up, and their father and Charlie had been talking for some while.

"Charlie, hey Charlie!" The grin on the face of the old man disappeared. He said severely, "Lazy boys. Boys no good. Not come down to meet Old Indian. Probably sleeping."

"We weren't sleeping. We were working. Ma wouldn't let us go 'til we'd finished."

"Yes. That's right, Charlie. You know we'd have been here if we could!"

'Well-ll, maybe Old Indian believe you. He not very smart. Try to make hunters out of farm boys."

"Farm boys! We're not farm boys. Just because we live on a farm..."

They were almost speechless at the insult. Charlie grunted, "Hmph. Real hunters eat'm fishy duck, like it."

"I like fishy duck, Charlie. It's good," said Cliff.

"Me too," lied his younger brother manfully.

Their father spoke. "Charlie thought you might want to go on a cougar hunt with him." His eyes twinkled. "I said I didn't think you would be interested, but that he could ask you himself."

He watched with amusement their frantic attempts to correct this second monstrous misapprehension.

"Well, perhaps I was mistaken. If you're going to go, you'd better hurry and get your things. The tide's dropping."

There wasn't much to get. Coats, hats, hunting shoes. Gun.

As they turned to go, Charlie said, "No gun. Old Indian have gun. One gun enough."

"Aw-w, Charlie..."

"No gun," firmly. No gun it was.

It all happened so fast. One moment doing chores, the next gliding over the smooth surface of Hidden Basin, with the *Puff—Puff—* of the boat's engine echoing from the rocky shore.

Charlie, the Old Indian.
Alistair Anderson illustration

"Where's the cougar, Charlie?" "Where're we going, Charlie?" "How long will we be gone?"

The old man ignored them, his attention on the tricky business of guiding his boat past the rock in the rapids leading out of Hidden Basin. That done, he condescended to notice his passengers. He looked them over, stern-faced.

"Noisy boys. Worse than seagulls. Like crows with owl. Cougar hear, he run away, never come back."

"Aw-w, Charlie. You know we don't make any noise when we're hunting."

He relented somewhat. "Maybe so. Maybe could be worse. We see how quiet boys be when tired, hands cold, shoes full of snow." His voice lost its bantering tone. "Cougar go after old lady's chickens in Pender Harbour. Old lady's dog bark. Cougar go into hills. Dog follow, not come back. Old lady call police. Cougar hounds all away somewhere. Police remember Old Indian, say, 'Get cougar.' Old Indian say, 'Sure.' New snow, easy track cougar. Come get boys."

There was no wind. The boat slipped easily along, making about four miles an hour—the speed that Charlie found most fuel-efficient. It seemed that he wasn't in any hurry. At the rate they were going, it would take about three hours to get to Pender Harbour. The land slid by, looking like a picture postcard of Christmas with the still, reflecting water and the dusting of snow on the trees, which became thicker as they rounded the point and turned north. Time passed quickly as the old man—stimulated as ever by an appreciative audience—told them stories of hunting and the old times. All too soon they arrived at the dock.

As the old boat had no reverse, docking could be an occasion of some excitement. You had the choice of making a one-eighty turn to kill momentum, which took a good deal of water, or stopping the engine, gliding up to the dock and leaping out to "snub" the line on whatever was convenient. As Charlie's lines were almost as old as his boat, they tended to snap under tension, giving added drama to already tense proceedings. This time, having deck hands, Charlie chose the second method. The ropes held, the boys knowing enough to let them slip a bit to ease the strain.

Safely docked, Charlie donned his wool jacket. Sanctified by many hunts, the wool retained traces of every odour with which it had ever been in contact. Then he took his old gun from its corner. Smelling heavily of the ratfish oil he kept it soaked with, it was loaded, hammer cocked, ready for any emergency—such as a potential dinner presenting itself within range. The boys were horrified. They had been taught, with great firmness, that one never kept a loaded gun around, much less one that was ready to fire!

Cliff said hesitantly, "Ah, Charlie, do you always keep your gun like that?"

"Like what?"

"You know, with a shell in the chamber, and cocked."

"Sure. Why not? Who going to pull trigger? Come around point, see seal, click of hammer maybe make dive. Boys know nothing."

They subsided. This would take some thinking about.

Years later, Father would say, "You know, it's a funny thing, but I found out as I got older that people who really use guns, and have lived with them all their lives, are the most careless with them. You see someone doing all the right things, checking the chamber, safety on, that sort of thing, chances are he's a weekend hunter. I don't say it's right, mind you, but that's the way it is."

As they started off, Hal—always the practical one—asked, "How about food, Charlie?"

The old man grinned. "Oh," he said enigmatically, "I think we find plenty of food for hungry boys."

He hung a rolled-up blanket over his shoulder by a strap, but it was obviously just a blanket.

They walked briskly along the shore on the trail that led to the old lady's house. There was about an inch of snow on the ground, but though there were many foot-prints, there was no other sign of life. A dog barked somewhere, and there was a faint smell of woodsmoke. They passed several houses, seemingly deserted, and came to a cottage with a red-shingled roof. Smoke drifted from the chimney. The snow in the yard and around was heavily trampled.

"Sh-sh," whispered Charlie. "This house of old lady. No spook-um."

He led the way to the back of the house where the chicken pen was. There were many tracks in the snow: dogs, people, chickens. Charlie pointed to a track like a large dog's.

"No claws. Cougar."

The boys were immensely thrilled. Their first cougar track! Charlie walked toward the chicken pen. The chickens, made nervous by the cat's visit, cackled and clucked at the strangers.

Immediately a door opened. There was the old lady, an impressive-looking gun grasped firmly in her hands, the muzzle pointing more or less in Charlie's direction. She peered at them as they stood frozen.

Lowering the gun, she said, "Well, it's about time! I don't know what you men do; it takes you so long to do anything. It's been a whole day almost that my Hopsy has been lost, but does anyone care? They do not! What are you doing there scaring my chickens? Why aren't you out rescuing my Hopsy?"

With his inscrutable look firmly in place, Charlie weathered the wordstorm. When it finally subsided a bit, he said with great dignity, "Old Indian come many miles to help find little dog. Travel over water, over land. Never stop. Now we are here, not worry. Old Indian find dog." He finished gravely, "We go now."

"Well, I should hope so. My poor Hopsy out in the woods all alone. I don't know why someone couldn't have done something before this..."

Her voice faded as Charlie hastily led the way around the corner and up the trail. The words became indistinct, but her voice could still be heard until they went around a rock outcrop. When it could be heard no more, Charlie sighed. "Cougar fool to come here. Old lady talk 'm to death, sure."

As they went up the trail, he pointed to the marks in the snow.

"Cougar come up here. Dog come after. Dog go 'yap—yap—yap.' Cougar not like noise. He not afraid of dog, not go very fast. Head for high ground soon."

They went on another 100 yards or so. The boys studied the tracks with great care, scarcely able to believe that they were actually following the trail of a cougar. Charlie walked steadily on, not bothering to look at the trail at all, or so it seemed.

The right-hand side of the trail became steeper until the bank was almost vertical for the first fifteen feet or so. Charlie said, "Boys, watch. Cougar's trail go away soon." Sure enough, in a few more paces there were only dog tracks going back and forth and running around in circles. Then the single track of a running dog led up the trail.

"What happened, Charlie? Where'd he go?"

"I'll bet he jumped away off down there in the brush," guessed Cliff.

The old man shook his head sadly. "Boys use mouth. Not use eyes. Even dog not use mouth until he have something to talk about."

The embarrassed brothers kept silent and began to study the trail. In a moment they found, half obscured by dog tracks, two deep parallel gouges in the ground, with well-defined claw marks facing the steep bank. They looked up. There was a ledge about three times their height, but there were no marks in the light cover of snow on the bank.

"You mean it jumped up there and didn't touch the bank? Ah-h Charlie, you're joking. Nothing could jump that high!"

The old man shrugged. "Boys so smart, maybe teach Old Indian how track cougar? Maybe first go up bank, look for cougar tracks, eh?"

They looked up at the steep slippery bank. Hal said doubtfully, "If we try to go up there, we'll get all wet and muddy and make a lot of noise. Why can't we just follow the dog tracks? The dog knows where the cougar went, I'll bet."

Charlie grinned. "Maybe some hope for boys yet. Okay, we follow after dog."

The dog tracks led only a little farther up the trail, then disappeared into the brush as the bank became lower. Charlie turned to the right, back along the way they had come.

"But Charlie, the tracks go that way!"

"Boys, come, maybe learn something."

So they stumbled along the slippery broken rock with its coating of wet snow. Strangely enough, it didn't seem to be as slippery to the old man, although he wore boots much like theirs. Soon they were at the ledge above the marks on the trail. Charlie pointed, and there, plainly to be seen in the snow, was the mark where the big cat had lain. It had crouched there above the trail, watching the dog.

Charlie said, "What cougar thinking about? Why not jump on dog? Maybe too close to house. Maybe just not hungry enough!"

The boys looked at each other. They'd had visions of finding the lost dog and bringing it back to the old lady. But suddenly the woods didn't seem quite so friendly, nor the prospect of a happy ending so certain.

They were both wishing right then that they had the nice comforting heft of a gun in their hands. Hal was sure Old Charlie knew just what they were thinking. Why else would he have been grinning like that?

Back they went to follow the dog and cougar tracks. It was hard going. The trail headed almost straight up the hill. The ground was rough and covered with thickets of salal and salmonberry brush.

They had turned north around the shoulder of the hill, and the snow was now about four inches deep. They were soon sweating under their wool coats. Snow found its way down their necks, up their sleeves and into their boots. They were forced to make the most heroic efforts to keep from gasping or panting, for Old Charlie was strolling along as if he was on a good level trail, his breath coming and going silently, his footsteps almost as silent. This was a humiliating experience for two boys who prided themselves on their woodcraft! They began to watch how the old man walked. He never seemed to be looking at the ground just ahead of him, but he never slipped. Always his step took advantage of some foothold, a rock or a root, a stem or a branch, or a bit of log. They began to study the ground ahead, to plan their steps.

Several times the tracks showed that the cougar had leaped to a high place and watched as the dog came trotting busily along his trail. Suddenly, Charlie put up his hand in the signal to stop. He spoke very quietly.

"I think we find dog very soon. Maybe cougar too. Boys, stay here, make no noise."

He looked at his gun, slid the lever enough to see the shell in the chamber. Though the barrel showed rust, the action worked smoothly and quietly. He took off his wool mittens and put them in his coat pocket. Then he moved off. They thought he had moved silently before; now he was like drifting smoke. It seemed impossible to the boys that a human could make so little sound, even in snow.

About 100 feet ahead, a good-sized fir tree had blown down many years before. Though almost prone, it still lived. The top was against a rock bluff, the middle some twenty feet from the ground. Charlie went up to the root of it, where he stood still for a long time. The boys were in an agony of excitement. Finally he moved, just a shadow in the falling snow.

He was gone only a few minutes, but the boys had never known minutes to last so long. He reappeared and beckoned for them to come. He stood patiently as they slipped and scrambled up to him, all caution forgotten.

"Did you see the cougar, Charlie? Do you think he's around here? Maybe it's watching us! What did you see? Why'd you make us stay back?"

The old man raised his hands in mock horror.

"Boys not need guns. Old Indian right about that. Bad as old lady, find cougar, talk 'm to death!"

They subsided, waiting for him to tell them in his own time.

"Well," he said matter-of-factly, "anyhow, we find old lady's dog. Old lady's dog find cougar."

He pointed to the tracks. Those of the cougar had disappeared.

Alert this time, they looked at the fallen tree. Not near the root, but well up off the ground. Cliff pointed. The snow was disturbed. Charlie nodded approvingly, led them farther on. He said, "Dog find cougar; cougar find dinner."

There was blood on the trampled snow, and drag marks leading to a dark shape already whitened with new-fallen snow. It was the dog, partly eaten.

"We camp here," said Charlie.

The boys looked around them. In the excitement of the hunt, they hadn't paid much attention to anything else, even discomfort. Now reality came back to them. It was late in the afternoon, perhaps four o'clock. Already the shadows under the trees were growing dark. Everything was covered with wet snow. It hung on the branches and clung to the trunks of the trees. The whole woods were wet. The boys were soaking wet, their wool Mackinaws heavy with water. These famous coats were supposed to protect the wearer in all-day rain. Indeed, they were very good. The raindrops caught in the dense wool and trickled down to drip off the lower edge. The wet wool kept its wearer warm and absorbed sweat. However, the brothers' coats were old, thin hand-me-downs, and their shirts—also wool—were soaked. This didn't matter while movement kept them warm, but as soon as they stopped moving, they felt the damp. There is an old Irish saying about wool that goes, "No matter how cold and wet you get, you're always warm and dry." It has some truth to it, inasmuch as you will probably never, in our coastal conditions, die of exposure while dressed all in wool. But you can get very cold and uncomfortable.

And uncomfortable the boys were. Their wool pants were sodden, their boots full of partly melted snow. They had eaten nothing since breakfast, but if Charlie had any food, it was well hidden. They had no tarp and no blankets. Charlie had the tightly rolled blanket on his shoulder strap but it was small and very wet. Wet snowflakes were coming down quite fast now, and there was no shelter in sight that seemed the least bit adequate. They looked at each other.

"Well," said Cliff, "now we'll see how a real Indian Woodsman builds his camp."

"I hope," said Hal, "that we'll see how a real Indian Woodsman finds dinner!"

Meanwhile, Charlie had been ambling about the line of broken bluff against which the tree had fallen. Now he called to them.

"Boys, come."

They scrambled up to where he was standing in the partial shelter of a slanting rock face. He was scuffing the snow away from an area about two feet square.

"We build fire here. Come," he ordered.

He led the way back to the fallen tree where, taking the little hatchet that he always carried from his belt, he walked along until he found some dry ribs of fir bark to his liking. Splitting off some of the cork-like bark, he handed the pieces to Cliff and indicated the direction of the fire-to-be with his thumb. Finding a pitch-soaked place by a knot, he gouged out a handful, which he gave to Hal. He then walked back to the root where there were some bushes of leafless huckleberry, cut several bunches and gave them to the waiting boy. Again, he indicated the camping place with his thumb.

The boys delivered the loads, and seeing Charlie walking away, rushed to join him. They didn't want to miss a thing.

Hal could stand it no longer. "Charlie, what are we going to eat? Why didn't you tell us to bring some food?" (They thought this hardly fair, for he had told them at the boat not to worry about food.)

"Well, never mind. Old Indian know there be food here."

Charlie led them over to where the dead dog lay, now just another white mound in the snow. He took out his big clasp knife, reached down and, seizing the dog's hind leg, rolled it over. Its entrails flopped about messily. The cougar had eaten the soft underparts.

"Cat lazy, eat soft bits, leave good meat for boys." Expertly, he cut away the hind leg he was holding.

Hal felt his stomach flop over and try to slip up to his throat. He looked at what was left of the dog.

"Charlie," he stammered, "we're not going to eat that dog, are we? Not really? Dogs are pets. We don't eat our pets!"

The old man looked at him, his face showing no expression at all.

"Boys, listen. Dog NOT HERE. Dog go away someplace. Indians tell lot of stories, but they not know where dog go. White men say they know, but they lying. They not know. But Old Indian know one thing. Dog not here. What is here is dog MEAT. That good to eat. Okay?"

Back at the rocks, Charlie put down two pieces of bark with a bit of pitch between them. He fished a tin of matches out of a pocket, extracted one and put the tin back in his pocket. He struck the match on his thumbnail and applied it to the pitch, which blazed up quickly. Then he carefully placed a few more bits of bark on the little fire. In a few minutes, he had a small, hot, almost smokeless fire going.

Cliff asked, "Do you want us to get some armloads of bark, Charlie?"

The old man laughed. "Just like a white man. Build big fire, stand away back, carry wood all night. Indian make small fire, stay close."

With a few quick knife strokes, he skinned the leg, sliced the meat and cut out the bone. Handing them each a slice, he then took the bunches of huckleberry and cut off three of the biggest stems. Taking a third slice, he shoved the end of the stick through it and held it over the fire.

"Boys, eat," he said.

In a moment there were three dog steaks sizzling in front of them. It didn't smell all that bad. In fact, the smell of roasting meat made Hal's mouth water.

At length, Charlie said, "Enough cooking. Too much cooking, all good gone from meat." He sniffed his meat appreciatively. "Dog meat, good. Make boys strong. Not get very often."

He handed them each a bunch of the huckleberry stems, and taking one for himself, put a bunch of tips in his mouth and stripped off the dormant buds with his teeth. "Boys, do same," he commanded. "Buds good for you; all meat, no good. Next year's leaves good for you. Taste good too."

Hal contemplated his piece of charred dog steak. He looked at his brother. Cliff had just taken a large bite and was chewing strongly, swallowing the mouthful as his brother watched. Cliff wasn't fussy about food. He would eat just about anything, usually with great enthusiasm. But Hal had always been very critical about what he ate, and he was very doubtful if dog meat came under the right heading.

He thought, "Well, if Cliff can do it, I suppose I can." So he took a bite of dog.

"I knew I was in trouble as soon as I took the first bite. As soon as it touched my tongue, it reminded me of wet dog. I made myself chew on it, but the more I chewed, the bigger it seemed to get until my mouth was completely full of this lump that tasted like wet dog."

He decided to swallow it whole, but distinctly heard his stomach say, "You send that down here and I'm sending it right back up again."

He slipped it out of his mouth into his hand, and flung it under his arm onto the snow behind him. He looked over at Charlie. He was watching with a wicked little grin on his face. Hal's mouth still tasted like wet dog. He took a handful of the huckleberry tips and suddenly there was a taste that reminded him of spring and fresh berries.

Cliff threw away a bit of gristle.

"Aren't you going to eat your piece, Hal? Can I have it?"

Wordlessly, Hal handed the piece of meat to his brother. His supper consisted of huckleberry tips. Nothing else.

It was now dark. Small as it was, the fire of bark gave out quite a bit of heat, which the sloping rock face reflected back at them. Their wet clothes were steaming a bit, and the boys realized that they weren't nearly as uncomfortable as they had expected to be. Charlie picked up his blanket from beside the fire and unrolled it. It turned out to be three small wool blankets about five feet square. He handed one to each of them and folded the other around his shoulders. Then he began to talk. He told them stories of the days when there were no white men, of tribal wars and sudden raids, of warriors and hunters, gods and demons.

Hal later said, "I sat there on a rock, soaking wet to the skin with an empty stomach and wet feet, and dozed off into a sleep as sound as if I was in my own dry bed at home."

Hal woke up once about midnight. Charlie was carefully putting a small piece of bark on the fire. Cliff was lying on his side, curled up toward the warmth. He was covered with about half an inch of snow. It was warm and comfortable under the blanket. He went back to sleep.

He woke to a gentle pressure on his arm. Embers glowed where the fire had been, and there was just the faintest trace of light in the morning sky. Cliff was rubbing his eyes sleepily.

Charlie spoke, his voice just audible. "Boys, stay. Be quiet. No move, no talk, no breathc." With this somewhat impractical admonition, he stalked off as silently as any ghost, carrying his rifle, ready for action.

The minutes dragged endlessly. They huddled there in damp clothes on rocks that seemed to have grown much harder overnight with wet snow on and about them. They were cold, stiff and hungry but daren't whisper so much as a word to each other about it. Just as they could begin to see around them in the growing light, they heard footsteps in the snow as Charlie crunched up to them, making much more noise than usual. He was talking to himself, using guttural words they'd never heard before. He leaned his gun against a rock and, not saying anything to the boys, picked up the rest of the pitch and put it on the still-warm ashes. When it began to smoke, he blew on it and it burst into flames. The air became filled with the smell of burning pitch. He put dry bark on the pitch, and in a few minutes he had another cheerful, smokeless fire. Reaching into his coat, he pulled out the other leg of the dog and with a few deft moves had it skinned, deboned and sliced.

"Eat," he growled.

Cliff was never one to be slow to speak. Even though Charlie's manner gave him little encouragement, he dared to ask, "What happened, Charlie?"

The old man looked at them from where he squatted by the fire. For a while, they thought he wasn't going to answer. His face appeared as if carved out of a piece of hard, dark wood. Finally, he growled, "Old Indian getting too old. Bad as foolish boys. Forget to throw out shell when last shoot gun. Try to shoot cougar with empty shell!"

With the meat about half cooked, he kicked the fire apart and began to eat, Cliff following his lead. Hal hadn't even pretended to want any. Charlie picked up his gun.

"Okay. Boys ready? Had nice rest, good breakfast. Should be able to walk fast."

He watched sardonically as they scrambled to roll their blankets with muscles half paralyzed by cold and soreness. They were ready quickly, but he started just soon enough to make them scramble to catch up. Running uphill in the snow did have the very salutary effect of getting their muscles warmed up and ready for work.

And work it was to keep up with the old man. He cut diagonally up the hill, apparently with a definite goal in mind. He didn't speak, and the boys couldn't, needing all their breath to keep up. After travelling for almost an hour, Charlie stopped. The boys threw themselves down on the snow, their wet clothes steaming from the exertion. After a few minutes' rest they got up and went to where Charlie was standing, his back toward them.

He was looking down a steep, narrow draw. They could see about 100 yards down it through scattered old-growth fir trees. There were a few small clumps of salal, but the ground was mostly clear.

"Why are we stopping here, Charlie?" asked Cliff.

Charlie looked at them. His face was relaxed, and when he spoke his voice was mild.

"This, our last chance. This draw has deer trail that lead up hills to cedar swamp. Deer winter there. Eat cedar branches to keep belly full. Cedar, no good food. Deer get weak, easy to catch. Cougar know this. Old Indian think he head for there by easiest trail. This trail. He not here yet. We wait."

He hunched by a fallen tree where he could see down the draw with only his head showing, and rested his rifle on the log.

"Boys, find place to sit," he ordered. "Can look down trail but only with one eye," he chuckled. "Now we see what kind of hunters boys make!" His voice became stern. "No move, no make noise. Breathe slowly through mouth. If itch, no scratch. If cramp, no move. If nose run, let drip, no sniff. Blink eyes quietly! If cat come up trail, then turn and run away, Old Indian go home with two skins instead of one!"

He puffed out a cloud of breath, which drifted slowly off to their right and up the trail. He pointed to it. "Wind right. Now we wait."

They waited. Remembering it as a grown man, Hal said, "I never thought just sitting could be such misery. Cliff and I had done this sort of thing before, watching deer, but we didn't have Old Charlie watching us then! I had got myself into what I thought was a comfortable position, but pretty soon my 'comfortable position' seemed like the worst sort of torture. I knew I had to relax, but I itched, especially my back and arms. If you can scratch when you want to, you never even think of it, but when you can't... and we were wearing wet wool! My nose started running, but I daren't move a hair to stop it. I could see Cliff's face out of the corner of my eye. He looked as a man might, sitting on an anthill. That made me feel a little better!"

He was so wrapped up in his misery, he almost missed seeing the cougar. Suddenly it was just there, about twenty feet from where he should have first seen it. It was all he had imagined one to be, and more. It belonged there in the woods more than anything else he had ever seen, and he had a feeling that they didn't. He had never felt that way before. He wondered why Charlie didn't shoot, then he figured he had the gun

Alistair Anderson illustration

pointed at a certain spot and wasn't going to move it. All of a sudden Charlie made a quiet sound, something like a low whistle. The cougar stopped in its tracks, looking up toward them. Charlie fired, and the cougar turned and leaped, all in one movement. It soared through the air, all grace and wildness. It hit the trail about twenty-five feet down, but it was dead when it landed, and it hit all limp and crumpled. Charlie had shot it right through the heart. It was a good shot, about eighty yards, and downhill. The boys hadn't thought that either he or his old gun had it in them!

Before the echo of the shot had come back, Charlie was up and trotting down the hill. Cliff and Hal followed, but Hal's legs were so cramped he thought he was going to go down the hill head first. Cliff was staggering as badly as he was. Charlie was by the cougar before they were more than halfway there, but they soon limbered up and ran down to him. He was kneeling by it, having first made sure it was dead. He stood up. His left hand was cupped, and the boys saw that it was full of blood. He stepped over to them, dipped two fingers of his other hand in the blood and drew them across Cliff's forehead, then down both cheeks in a sort of pattern. Then he did the same thing to Hal. As he did it, he said something in the strange language he had used that morning.

Then Charlie put his hand up to his mouth and licked the blood out of it. All of it. Hal felt a bit squeamish, but somehow he felt it was right.

Charlie said, "Old Indian forget exact words, but good enough. Spirit of cougar satisfied. Boys not be full hunters, but got good beginning. Old Indian think might be hope for them yet!" He pulled out his knife, went over and squatted beside the cougar. He looked back at them.

He said, "Now, boys, build fire. Old Indian skin cat while still warm." He grinned. "Small fire," he said.

They got pitchy bark from a fir tree, split some wood from a cedar windfall with the hatchet. Then they found a flat spot, brushed away the snow and carefully built a fire between three rocks as they had seen Charlie do. A small one.

Hal said, "I don't think we should use cedar. You know how it sparks and crackles."

"I think you're right. Charlie wouldn't like that, would he?"

So they went back and got more fir bark. Charlie called, "Bring hatchet." He took it and cracked the thighbone after slicing the meat around it. They looked with awe at the huge jumping muscle of the hind legs.

Cliff said, "I wish I had muscles like that." Charlie looked at him, his face impassive.

"Boys' legs make pretty good meat just like they are." He cackled at his own joke. Charlie was in a fine mood. He had guessed correctly. He had made a fine shot. The bounty for the cougar plus the hide would bring a fair bit of money. And they had fresh meat!

These were much bigger steaks than the ones from the dog. They toasted them on forked sticks of hemlock, peeled so the bark wouldn't give the meat a bitter taste. Hal had no qualms about this meat. It was dark and wild tasting, but at the first bite his stomach informed him, "Yes, you can send some of that down, and the sooner the better."

While they were eating, Charlie picked up a handful of the split cedar and threw it on the fire. "Cedar make nice crackle," he remarked.

The boys regarded him silently. The only thing you could predict about Old Charlie was that he would be unpredictable!

After they had eaten, he chopped off the other haunch. "Too good to leave."

He sliced a hole between the bones of the lower leg and shoved a stick through for a carrying handle. Then he rolled up the hide, tying it in such a way that the legs formed carrying straps. Tossing it to Cliff, he said, "You carry hide." He tossed the rest of the meat from the haunch they had cut to Hal. Then he put the stick with the untouched one on his shoulder and started off down the draw.

When they had gone a little way, Hal remarked to his brother, "It seems kind of a shame to leave all the rest of that meat to go to waste."

Charlie heard. "Meat not go to waste. Listen."

They listened. A raven croaked not far away. Another answered from the flat below. "Nothing go to waste in the woods."

They went a bit farther. A raven called almost over their heads.

"Raven say thanks. Maybe even send good luck."

The grey sky began to send down a fine mist of rain, and though it wasn't enough to make them really wet, it made the snow more slippery. But the way back seemed short, as the way back always does. They reached the trail in less time than they would have thought possible, and soon enough, there was the house of the old woman. Charlie went to the door and knocked. Her face peered out of the window suspiciously. Then it disappeared and the door opened. She was talking as it opened.

"Well, you're back. About time, too. Where is my Hopsy? Did you find him? You've been gone long enough!"

Charlie backed off a few steps.

"Ah-h-h—" he said, then stopped and looked desperately around at Cliff and Hal. They looked back at him silently.

Suddenly Hal was inspired. Perhaps it was the adventure stories he had read. He spoke out boldly.

"Ma'am," he began, "we found your Hopsy but we were too late to save him. He died fighting that savage cougar. He put up an awful fight but it was too big for him. Mr. Charlie buried him and put a cross on his grave. He carved 'Good Dog' on it. He thought you would like that."

Cliff and Charlie were looking at him with awe. He almost began to believe it himself, it sounded so good. He continued, warmed by their appreciation, his voice solemn. "Mr. Charlie swore he would get that cougar to revenge poor Hopsy. We tracked it all that night. In the morning it climbed a tree and Mr. Charlie shot it, and there is the skin!" He pointed to Cliff's shoulder. The old woman was actually speechless. There were tears in her eyes. Finally she spoke to Charlie.

"I knew he was dead. I could feel it. But it was so good of you to do what you did, I'm going to give you a special reward."

She turned and went into the house. Charlie's eyes glittered brightly in his impassive face. He hadn't expected this! In a moment she was back, carrying an envelope in her hand.

Cliff whispered, "I wonder how much she's going to give him."

She pulled out a square of cardboard, handed it to Charlie. "This is a picture of my Hopsy. You may have it to keep."

The two boys looked at Charlie's face. Then they looked at each other. It was too much for them. They ran across the yard, down the trail and on around the bend. There they stopped. They had to—they couldn't run for laughing.

Charlie came around the corner, walking with great dignity. He looked with disapproval at the boys. Cliff was lying on the wet ground, out of breath from laughter. Hal was trying unsuccessfully to remove the grin from his own face.

Charlie said sternly, "Foolish boys. Boys know nothing." He shook his head sadly. "Poor boys. No one teach them sense. Only Old Indian, and he think maybe too big a job for him!"

He took the picture out of his pocket, handling it with great care.

"Indian would know that this is great thing. Old Indian hang picture in cabin of boat. Spirit of dog be glad, bring good luck. Even foolish boys know that good luck is best thing you can have!"

He headed down the trail. The cougar hunt was over.

WHAT NOT TO WEAR TO A NUDE POTLUCK

Excerpted from Adventures in Solitude: What Not to Wear to a Nude Potluck and Other Stories from Desolation Sound *(2010), by Grant Lawrence.*

Beginning in the 1970s, CBC radio personality Grant Lawrence spent his summers at the family cabin in Desolation Sound (north of Vancouver) after his father purchased a block of land for subdividing. —Ed.

"Pot" would in fact be the keyword to Aldo's potluck invitation. Much to their consternation, my parents were figuring out that besides apples and oysters, there were a few other crops that could be successfully harvested in Desolation Sound. With its rare coastal microclimate of warm, wet air and long, hot summers, Desolation Sound is perfect for growing bountiful bushels of marijuana.

Aldo's potluck was a five-minute boat ride away in the next bay. As our motorboat rounded the rocky finger that separated our bays, we heard the potluck before we saw it. The caterwaul of a party in full swing danced across the open water like radio waves. As we drew closer, my innocent young eyes widened upon seeing a scene of total hedonism.

Intertwined brown bodies lay outstretched all over the sun-drenched shoreline, smoking, drinking, laughing, singing, making out and making love. Seemingly wild, long-haired children ran among the cavorting adults, leaping off the rocks into the green ocean water. The aesthetic that united the party was a revealing one: every single man, woman and child was totally and utterly nude. It was like the moment Charlton Heston discovers the humans at the oasis in *Planet of the Apes*. Just add a cranked-up Deep Purple cassette and matching purple bong smoke that hung low across the bay: "Smoke on the Water," just like the stereo blasted. This outrageous scene was more than enough for Dad to start vigorously turning the boat around, but Mom wouldn't let him, reasoning that:

a) she was bringing banana bread;

b) we were going to have to meet the rest of our neighbours eventually;

c) how would it look if the big, bad developer and his family suddenly swung their boat around in full view of the entire party and left without even saying hello?

We tied our skiff to a makeshift barge of boats, a barely floating, pell-mell parking lot of rafts, canoes, kayaks and rowboats in various states of sunken disrepair. We had to climb through several of them before we could make our way up the gangplank to shore.

Throughout my childhood, whenever I was extremely uncomfortable or frightened, I developed a strange nervous reaction: my teeth would chatter like I was locked in

Keith Milne illustration

a freezer. Walking up that gangplank on that hot summer night into a foreign, naked scene of hippie strangers, my teeth sounded like a death rattle. My little sister cowered behind me, pulling on the back of my E.T. turtleneck. We were greeted by a beaming Aldo and his festive, long, white beard, flowing down over his bulging brown belly, both of which almost covered his dangling penis. Almost. He gripped a half-full bottle of label-less red wine in one hand and waved in the other a giant doobie, which he transferred to his lips when he extended his leathery, brown hand in welcome. My sister and I stared in shock, eyes like Keane Kids in pale, expressionless faces. My teeth continued to chatter uncontrollably.

Everyone at the party warmly welcomed us with extremely uncomfortable hugs, introducing us all around. Pungent pot clouds filled the air like a skunky London fog. Elaborate bongs gurgled and hissed, threatening to stain Mom's pink pedal-pushers. Mom later said she had never maintained such steadfast eye contact in her life and took extra caution when reaching out to shake hands with the guys. When Aldo sat down on a stump and spread his legs like Santa in a sauna, she strategically placed the pan of banana bread directly on his lap. Painfully, my sister and I were torn away from our parents' side when two gregarious, naked kids bounded up to us and insisted that we try their rope swing. They pranced barefoot down the rocks with the effortless agility of nimble forest creatures while we gingerly followed as if blindfolded. At the edge of a cliff overlooking the water was a lineup of more naked brown children of various ages, all shrieking happily while taking turns on a thick, bristly rope swing that was looped around a branch of a giant fir tree that grew out over the water. They'd place a foot in a loop at the bottom, grab the rope with their hands, swing out over the ocean and let go just at the right moment to plunge into the warm, green water below.

My sister and I were expected to follow suit. My teeth had stopped chattering long enough to politely refuse, but these friendly naked children with names like Sunpatch and Birdsong urged us on, insisting that we remove our clothes and join in the fun. (Similar pressure in far more adult situations was being put on our parents back in the heat of the bash.) For whatever bizarre societal reason, being the only clothed individuals at a nudist party at the edge of the wilderness felt as uncomfortable as if one were to be suddenly dropped naked onto a downtown sidewalk. And there would be no "Grin and bear it"—literally—for the Lawrence family on this night. The closest thing we got to public nudity was in our bathing suits once or twice a summer on a Vancouver beach, and even then I would never dare take my shirt off.

I struck a deal with the Lost Boys. Neither my sister nor I would remove our clothes, but I would try the rope swing. A pair of naked, deeply tanned identical twin boys with matching shocks of shaggy black hair held the rope for me. I pushed my glasses up from the end of my nose and nervously placed my shaking Keds sneaker inside the loop. I took hold of the rope. Its fraying fibres bit into my silky city palms. With a simultaneous shove from the twins I was suddenly airborne, hanging on for my young life, all my tiny muscles contracted, my body wrapped around the rope in a kung fu grip.

As I arced out over the ocean, the setting rays of the sun spilled across the surface, turning it to gold, illuminating the shoreline rocks with an illustrious shimmer. I felt something deep within let go and give in. Panic turned to acceptance, then calmness, then serenity as I hung over the glimmering ocean, frozen in space. Time stood still and all sound ceased. As if in a dream I gazed back toward the cliff edge at my sister and the naked children. They were calling to me . . . waving, yelling something and making hand gestures. The moment of serenity evaporated as quickly as it began. Real life, sound and motion roared like a train from a tunnel. I heard the words "Jump! Now! Jump! Let go of the rope!"

I didn't jump, and I didn't let go. I held on. Momentum swung me back toward the ledge filled with children like a nerd pendulum. I heard the words "No!! No!!" as they began to scatter. I slammed into the crowd, knocking kids off the ledge, sending them plunging into the water like lemmings. My runners' toe grips scraped the rock ledge but couldn't hang on.

The rope took me swinging out over the water again. I shut my eyes and hung on so tight the fibres cut into my palms. This time, when momentum swung me back toward the cliff, since I had cleared it of children, I slammed face first into a wall of granite. My glasses clattered to the ledge. Blind and stunned, I dropped to my hands and knees and searched until my fingers found them, bent but not broken.

My sister was pushed out of harm's way thanks to a very kind, older, fully developed naked girl, who also helped me with my bleeding nose, her perky brown breasts at my direct eye level. While the rest of the kids pulled themselves out of the water below, the kind girl suggested we head back to the main party and find our parents. Both my sister and I readily agreed and followed her round brown bum back to the party.

Christy Nyiri illustration

We spent another ninety excruciating minutes at the party. Since the only pot my parents touched sat on our stove simmering Kraft Dinner on Friday nights, they weren't blending in any better than Heather and I were. After the umpteenth uncircumcised male member bounced past my sister's eye level, she eventually slipped into something akin to a catatonic shock, desperate to escape back into the 1880s' world of heavily clothed bonnet-to-boot characters of *Little House on the Prairie*. I pushed my bent glasses up my nose to get a better look at the bronzed, pregnant hippie ladies, spread out on the rocks like melted candles.

Mom eventually signalled our exit . . . "Aldo! Thank you so much for having us!" in a volume shrill enough to frighten birds into flight. "We'd better get the kids home now, but this has been an absolutely fabulous party!" On our mostly silent boat ride home, Dad muttered that the party had been an unpleasant cross between *Helter Skelter*, *Apocalypse Now* and a *National Geographic* special on orangutans. I have had a deep, personal aversion to potlucks ever since.

7 JAPANESE FISHERS AND WORLD WAR TWO
Losing Licences, Vessels and Livelihoods

Excerpted from Spirit of the Nikkei Fleet: BC's Japanese Canadian Fishermen *(2009), by Masako Fukawa with Stanley Fukawa and the Nikkei Fishermen's History Book Committee*

The year 1941 was the beginning of a nightmare for Japanese Canadian fishermen.
Canada. Dept. of National Defence/Library and Archives Canada/PA-134097

I was visiting my friend. It was Sunday noontime. They had a radio going and we heard, "Japan attacked Pearl Harbor." We couldn't believe it, you know. "Ah, that's a hoax," we'd say. They kept repeating and repeating all the time...we couldn't believe it. My friend and I were saying, "It can't be." ...Then that night a truckload of soldiers came. —Takeshi Uyeyama

Nikkei [Japanese Canadian] fishermen's knowledge and familiarity with coastal waters made them the chief target of rumours and suspicion of fifth-column activities, and as a result they were the first to feel the impact of Japan's bombing of Pearl Harbor.

In 1941 all of them were either Canadian-born or naturalized Canadians, but although not a single one was detained by the RCMP or the military, they were accused of having within their number Japanese naval officers in disguise. The first act of the federal government under the *War*

Measures Act was to impound the Nikkei fishing fleet and suspend the licences of the Nikkei fishermen. Ironically, in 1938 when Hitler invaded Europe, the Canadian government had ordered all vessels to be marked with NW numbers on top of the cabin and on each side of the boat. This now made it easy for aircraft to identify the vessels belonging to Nikkei fishermen.

At dawn on December 8, 1941, the Royal Canadian Navy proceeded from port to port disabling beached vessels. The few boats that were still out on the wintry seas were ordered by radio to head immediately for one of the nearest of thirteen official fishing ports on the coast. There the vessels were searched for weapons and maps and immobilized. Some 2,090 licences issued to 1,265 Nikkei fishermen—including those held by thirty-seven World War One veterans—were cancelled, and 1,137 vessels owned and operated by them were impounded.

A soldier raises the Union Jack on a confiscated boat. *Canada. Dept. of National Defence/Library and Archives Canada PA-170513*

Meanwhile, Japanese Canadian fishermen up and down the coast offered their assistance and declared their loyalty to Canada. In Steveston, the dantai [the 1897 *Regulations of the Fraser River Fishermen's Association*] volunteered their boats for coastal defence. The Northern British Columbia Resident Fishermen's Association, a Japanese Canadian group in Prince Rupert, followed suit on December 11. They "unanimously affirmed their loyalty as Canadian citizens and offered themselves for any service which Canada may desire of us." On January 10, 1942, *The Province* reported that even during the period when their boats were being stripped, rounded up and impounded, "young men in Steveston voiced their allegiances and services to Canada." The *New Canadian* reported on January 12, 1942, that a mass meeting of Canadian-born Japanese residents in Steveston passed a resolution without a dissenting voice and directed Hiroshi Nishi, president of the Japanese Canadian Citizens League, to send a telegram to the Standing Committee on Oriental Affairs in British Columbia stating their confidence in the Canadian government and the RCMP and that "we earnestly desire to contribute our utmost to Canada's war effort and thereby offer our services in any capacity the government may decide." On January 14, 1942, the headline of the *Marpole-Richmond Review* read "200 Steveston Japs Offer Services for War Effort." Just days before the bombing of Pearl Harbor, the Upper Fraser Japanese

Above: Tatsuo Oura
and his granddaughter,
Christine, in 2004.
Stan Fukawa photo

Top: Koji Takahashi's *Mary
H* was confiscated and
sold, and Takahashi was
relocated to sugar beet
farms in Manitoba.
Courtesy of Ken Takahashi

Fishermen's Association had donated 3.8 tons of canned chum salmon for distribution in Britain. Yet within twenty-four hours of the bombing, Japanese Canadians were being rounded up and their boats impounded.

Within a week of the seizure of their boats, all Nikkei fishermen were ordered to take them to New Westminster. Those on the west coast of Vancouver Island in Tofino, Ucluelet and Clayoquot were the first to leave. On December 15 their trollers and packers departed for New Westminster, each with a soldier on board. In that flotilla was Yoshio "Johnny" Madokoro (1913–2000) on his troller, the *Crown*. He had been enjoying the good life in Tofino as one of the executives of the Tofino Trollers' Co-op, whose members had prospered over the previous two decades by delivering their catches to the fresh markets of Vancouver and Seattle. The boats belonging to his brother, Hiroshi "Thomas" Madokoro, and his father, Kamezo Madokoro, were also in the flotilla. The soldier on Johnny's troller was a prairie boy and was seasick throughout the voyage. They found many of the soldiers to be "decent enough" and were bewildered as to how "individual *hakujin* (Caucasian) Canadians could be so decent, and yet" the newspapers and radio repeatedly said that "Japanese Canadians were all traitors." The Madokoros reached New Westminster without incident.

Tatsuo Oura was born in Steveston and trolled for the Ucluelet Japanese Fishermen's Co-op. Years later, he still remembered the knock on his door and the shock of opening it to an RCMP officer. The officer accompanied him to his boat, the *TO*, searched it for firearms and removed everything that might possibly be used as a "weapon." Oura argued with him about the removal of the iron bar he found there because it was needed to crank-start his engine. The officer, new to the sea, had no idea what Oura was talking about. In frustration, Oura hid the iron bar under his shirt because without it his boat would have no power and could not be controlled.

The flotilla consisted of sixty or more boats under guard of the navy vessel HMCS *Givenchy*. The weather was foul, as it often is in December, and they were caught in a storm and had to wait it out in Bamfield without food, warm clothing or any means of keeping warm. Their every step was watched with a rifle pointed at them. Oura says, "Thankfully, Kenneth Miller who had worked as an engineer on a Japanese packer boat in Ucluelet heard of our plight and he and another fisherman, Thompson, brought supplies to Bamfield for us." The flotilla waited there three days before the storm subsided.

The usual day-and-a-half trip from Ucluelet to Steveston took five days. All the boats except one reached Steveston, and on December 23 the *Givenchy* started the search for Tsunetaro Oye and his boat; they located him the following evening on the United States side of the border. The US Coast Guard handed over a mortally injured Oye to Canadian officials, who brought him by car to the Vancouver General Hospital where Kanzo and Larry Maekawa, as former and active officials of the Ucluelet Japanese Fishermen's Co-operative, visited him. He was completely covered with bandages and, though conscious, was unable to speak. He answered queries with gestures, confirming he had been beaten and his throat slashed by his captors in the United States. He subsequently died and was cremated without his bandages being removed.

Harold Kimoto, who left from Clayoquot with a sailor on board his ship, found that except for one sailor who stole a fisherman's wallet, the navy men were nice enough individuals. However, when they reached New Westminster, "a whole gang came on board and they took everything that was left on the boat. They took batteries, everything. I didn't care because we were leaving the boat anyway, but gee whiz." Others reported similar lootings. Tommy Kimoto said, "Those navy guys stole everything. They even stole anchor chains." Another said, "You could go into New Westminster and hear that compasses were selling for two dollars. It used to be a joke. Buy a Japanese compass cheap. Or a spotlight anywhere, cheap. Batteries. Hard to get. You could buy them anywhere. These navy guys were looting our boats of everything they could tear off and selling it for beer. I guess it is natural. I've seen it happen in other places. But the navy was supposed to be the protectors of our property."

On December 14, Masao Nakagawa and Isamu Kayama were cutting wood for the winter at Port Essington when the police arrived and ordered them to take their boats to the Inverness Cannery. Thinking that this was as far as they had to go, Nakagawa on his father's boat, Kayama on his own boat and Jitsuo Uyede on the *J.U.* started out prepared only for a short trip. They were given no time to inform their families or to take on provisions, and having stripped their boats for the winter, they had no food, warm clothes or fuel for their stoves on board. At the Inverness Cannery they were ordered to Tuck Inlet near Prince Rupert, where they waited for two days until sixty gillnetters had been assembled. They were not allowed to go ashore. When they learned they were going to New Westminster and that the navy was confiscating their boats, they were sick to their stomachs.

Just one hour before they left the inlet on the 16th, Minoru "Min" Sakamoto and Juichi Matsushita, who were young boys at the time, were given permission to obtain provisions. They returned with bread, canned goods, sugar and tea from the Yamanaka store in Prince Rupert and three sacks of coal for the fifteen boats with stoves. The food lasted them for two days. They left that morning at 8:30 with two Canadian Navy

Fisherman's Reserve vessels, the *Leelo* and the *Kuitan*, towing the gillnetters in two long lines, the boats stretching for about three-quarters of a mile. They were joined by the corvette HMCS *Macdonald* and the tugboat *Stanpoint*. The fishermen had no idea that the journey ahead of them would take fifteen long days and that their lives would be in danger all the way as they fought wind, fog and ice floes.

As soon as they left the harbour, they ran into trouble. A strong westerly wind blew all day and the waves became so high they seemed to come from the sky. At about 2 am they sought shelter and anchored near Lowe Inlet. On December 18 the flotilla ran into heavy seas again at the mouth of Milbanke Sound that made navigating a nightmare, and twice the *Stanpoint*'s tow line broke. The corvette crew spent three hours repairing the damage. Meanwhile, six boats had drifted loose and the sea became so rough that they had to seek shelter in a nearby channel. At this point the *Leelo* proceeded to Bella Bella to obtain gasoline for the twenty boats with engines still in running order.

At midnight the rest of the flotilla reached Bella Bella, managed to purchase groceries and left again in the dead of night. None of the skippers had suitable clothing and, cold and wet, they huddled for warmth in their cabins. As they had slept little since they left home and they had no food left, there were now tired and hungry men at the wheel, bracing against the waves that hit their bows. They ran all night through log-strewn waters, and as only a few boats had lanterns on board, they began colliding in the dark as the rough seas lifted them and brought them down with a terrible thud that shook their bones. Now and then a propeller would spin helplessly in mid-air.

Boats were often mishandled during confiscation.
Province *photo, Vancouver Public Library, VPL 1352*

Near Namu a fisherman from North Pacific Cannery, having closed his cabin too tight to ward off the cold, was overcome by gas fumes and his boat was observed running in circles. Another boat took her in tow. The sea became rougher. Many of the men became seasick.

Although wind data is not available for 1941, Jim Attridge, a former meteorologist who has researched the weather for this period, says that based on the known temperatures and rainfall at that time, the weather must have been similar to the conditions that existed in December 2004, when virtually all weather stations in coastal BC reported above-average temperatures and copious amounts of rain. The data from Solander Island off the northern tip of Vancouver Island shows that on December 15, 2004, the average daily wind speed was 37 miles per hour (mph) gusting to 66; 37 mph would produce "near gale" conditions with mounting thirteen-foot waves and foam blowing streaks downwind. By the time the wind speed reached 56 mph, there would be waves of nearly thirty feet, a heavy sea roll, a generally white surface, and visibility would be impaired. Wind gusts of 66 mph produce waves as high as thirty-six feet, and this is classified as a "violent storm." It was just such a storm that Masao Nakagawa and Isamu Kayama experienced during their "terror-filled" trip down the coast to Steveston, and Roy Ito recorded and wrote about it for the *New Canadian*. Although all Japanese-language newspapers had been shut down immediately after war was declared, the *New Canadian* was still allowed to publish but it was heavily censored. When the censor killed this story, Ito saved it to recount in *Stories of My People*, published in 1994.

The day that the flotilla stayed in Takush Harbour was spent playing cards while the temperature dropped lower and lower. Some of the fishermen broke up their cabins for fuel while others boiled water in tobacco cans and hugged them for warmth. Christmas was a day they would never forget. Seven fishermen pooled their resources and bought the only meat they could find in Alert Bay—one chicken. Combined with a little cabbage boiled in salt water, it became their Christmas dinner. They left Alert Bay that night, and sometime during the night one of the boats from Prince Rupert submerged until only the cabin appeared above water.

They reached Steveston on December 28, and as some of the fishermen had left home with no money, they had to borrow from friends and relatives in Steveston for the return fare. "We spent New Year's Day in the same clothes we wore when we were cutting wood fifteen days before our long voyage south," Masao Nakagawa said. "We went home to Essington wondering what the future had in store for us. Losing our boats meant our livelihoods were gone. Why was it necessary to impound our boats? Why was it necessary to take them to Steveston? We wondered how this could happen to Canadian citizens." His father, Sasuke, had been born in Shiga-ken and was working on the Skeena when he volunteered to fight for Canada in World War One. He served in France with the 10th Battalion and was wounded. Now he, too, had been declared "an enemy alien."

In Nanaimo, the Mizuyabu family was living a relatively tranquil life when all Japanese fishermen were ordered to stay in port. Yukiharu Mizuyabu remembers that:

soldiers equipped with bayonets on their rifles stood along the waterfront road to ensure that the Japanese Canadians abided by the curfew imposed upon them. A few weeks later my father and the other fishermen were ordered onto their boats and escorted by the Canadian navy to the mouth of the Fraser River where the boats were impounded. They were forced to return to Nanaimo by ferry. Without their boats, all Japanese Canadian fishermen were suddenly deprived of their only source of income, but the callous politicians made no provisions for families affected by these actions.

Many fishermen would relive the traumatic events of the confiscation until they died. Amy Doi says that her father, Ihachi Hamaoka, "tells with shame his story of being forced to lead the fleet of Japanese fishboats [from Powell River] through a dangerous pass that the fisheries people would not dare navigate in order to take them to be impounded." He was incarcerated in Hastings Park until he was sponsored by Mr. Oishi, a farmer, enabling the family to be relocated to Kamloops. "Our family has been here ever since. My mother refused to go back to the coast and fishing after the evacuation order was lifted."

Nikkei fishermen of the inner coast, including the Fraser, were similarly ordered to return to port. Their vessels were searched by naval personnel for firearms, and they were told to remove their valuables and personal effects. Their boats were then immobilized, tied together and towed to the Annieville Slough, where vital engine parts and certain navigating instruments were removed.

Yoshio "Joe" Teranishi, twenty-eight years old, was putting the finishing touches on the roof of the new house belonging to his uncle, Mo-yan (Mosaburo Teraguchi), in Steveston when he heard from his cousin that war had started. They were given instructions to run their boat to Annieville and tie it up. He cannot recall how he got back home

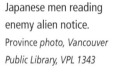

Japanese men reading enemy alien notice.
Province photo, Vancouver Public Library, VPL 1343

without the boat. He observed that there was no watchman at Annieville, and some of the boats were sinking. After witnessing this scene, he sold his own boat for $400, $200 less than its real value, and he never returned to Annieville. "I heard it was awful."

Tatsuro "Buck" Suzuki described the incomprehensible actions of the government and his own feelings to Barry Broadfoot, who published them in *Years of Sorrow, Years of Shame* in 1977. Suzuki had been the secretary of the Upper Fraser Japanese Fishermen's Association when he received a call to report to naval headquarters at nine the next morning. The commander told him quite frankly, "Mr. Suzuki, we were caught with our pants down," and then he ordered all fishing vessels to be turned over to the authorities immediately. Suzuki told Broadfoot, "Don't think that the authorities weren't waiting for us when Pearl Harbor came. Within two hours things began to happen. Two hours. To this day I don't know what they thought about those fishing boats. They were our living. They were small boats, made of wood. We had no radar, no radio, no echo sounder. Why, we could go into Vancouver any time and buy British Admiralty charts of every single mile of the coast." Suzuki tried to convince the authorities that the Japanese fishermen were not spies, that "we were just ordinary fishermen…[but] as far back as the late 1890s they had determined that one day they would kick the damn Japs off the river. There was one common statement you could hear along the river: There's only one damn good Jap and that's a dead Jap."

In *Wild Daisies in the Sand,* Tom Sando (Tamio Kuwabara) wrote:

On the chilly morning of Saturday, December 6, 1941, my father, younger brother Shig and I, Tamio Kuwabara aged nineteen, traveled across the choppy waters of the Georgia Strait on our small fishing boat Hokui No. 1. *We tied our boat down in Steveston Harbour…We had a bright outlook and big plans. We were going to buy a larger boat that would permit*

Confiscated Japanese Canadian fishing vessels held at the Annieville Dike, 1941–42.

Canada. Dept. of National Defence/Library and Archives Canada/PA-037467 us to fish all year round. Of course, we would be spending the salmon season, the months of July and August, in Skeena River, but we would return to fish the BC coast for halibut, cod and shark for the remainder of the year...Our bright future was shattered the following morning when we heard the shocking news on the radio—Japanese planes had bombed Pearl Harbor...Ten days later we received a notice from the RCMP to remove our fishing boat to an impound yard near New Westminster. We tied down our small fishing boat upstream on the Fraser River. It was heartbreaking to see our beloved boat left behind.

In 1948, Shiromatsu Koyama's *Hawthorne II* sold for $195.50.

Courtesy of Faye Ishii

Harry Yonekura recalls his final farewell to his boat as it was being towed to the Annieville Slough in New Westminster.

Standing beside me to witness this travesty was Unosuke Sakamoto, president of the Fishermen's Association, and Yoshio Kanda, a district representative of the association. The three of us decided to complain to the commandant at the Garry Point Naval Base. Reluctantly, the commandant admitted that he had placed inexperienced men in charge of towing our fishing vessels. He also told us that he had been placed in charge of impounding all 1,137 boats and his deadline for this mission was December 27, 1941. It was now December 14. This meant that he had only thirteen days left to deliver the remaining boats. There were about 450 to 500 fishing boats to impound in Steveston alone! Tentatively, Mr. Sakamoto suggested that the Japanese Canadian fishermen be allowed to sail their own boats to the Annieville Dike. The offer was readily accepted. There was just one hitch in the plan—how would we get back to Steveston? The commandant did not hesitate to offer us passage back to New Westminster on a naval ferry, from where we pooled our resources and paid for transportation back to Steveston.

I guess we all needed one last voyage on our own boats before bidding them farewell, possibly forever. I will never forget the overwhelming sadness and sense of disbelief I felt at the Annieville Dike as I patted my boat and tied it up securely one last time. Then I quietly said goodbye and got up, resolving to put aside my emotions and accept the situation. My country was at war and I had to do whatever was necessary to prove my loyalty.

The scene at the Annieville Slough was chaotic. Ann Sunahara wrote that vessels arrived at the rate of 125 a day to facilities that were totally inadequate to handle the numbers, and they were moored some fourteen abreast without regard to their respective size or relative draft at low tide. Some 980 boats remained idle there for six weeks, some swinging at anchor while others were damaged and lying waterlogged on the banks of the Fraser at

JAPANESE FISHING VESSELS DISPOSAL COMMITTEE

RELEASE AND DISCHARGE

FISHING VESSEL: "Hawthorne II"   CLAIM No.: 522-828

REG. or LIC. No.: Victoria 1438   Owner at Time of Impounding: Shiro KOYAMA, #09929, File 1507

NAVAL No.: VE 045-A

CLAIM PAYABLE TO: Present Owner: Abandoned Vessel

Shiro KOYAMA, #09929

This vessel was damaged while in the custody of the Royal Canadian Navy, and was declared a total loss by the surveyors for Naval Service and Japanese Fishing Vessels Disposal Committee.

The owner has agreed to accept $200.00 in full settlement of his claim for the loss of his vessel, which is considered fair value by the surveyors aforementioned. The sum of $195.50, being $200.00, less expense charges of $4.50 is approved by the undersigned and accepted as adequate compensation.

In consideration of the payment of the sum of   ONE HUNDRED AND NINETY-FOUR.

DOLLARS AND FIFTY CENTS --------------------------- ($ 195.50)

(of lawful money of Canada) (the receipt of which is hereby acknowledged). we, the undersigned. being the owners and/or mortgagees, shipyard repairers and all others having any interest, claim or demand against the said motor vessel registered at the Port of Victoria, B. C. Official or License No. 1438   DO HEREBY RELEASE and forever discharge His Majesty the King, as represented by Royal Canadian Naval Service or any patrol or auxiliary service, acting through or under the authority of Royal Canadian Naval Service, and all boards, commissions or departments of His Majesty's Canadian Government and of from claims which we may now have or which hereafter may arise and which now could or at any time hereafter be made in consequence of damage sustained or any alleged damage sustained, to the above-named motor vessel while in custody of His Majesty's Royal Canadian Naval Service or any auxiliary patrols, commissions, boards or departments hereinbefore named.

AND FURTHER, we covenant that we are the owners and/or mortgagees, shipyard repairers and all others having any interest, claim or demand against the said vessel and are the only parties of persons having any interest, claim, lien, demand or charge over the above-named motor vessel, and should any claim hereafter be made by or through any parties whatsoever, we hereby agree to indemnify and save harmless His Majesty the King as represented by any of the naval services, boards, patrols, departments, or commissions hereinbefore referred to.

AND FURTHER, that this discharge and release enures to the benefit of and is binding upon all the parties hereto, their respective heirs, executors, administrators, assigns, successors and representatives.

DATED at Montreal, British Columbia, this   3rd   day of   January   1948.

low tide and awash at high tide, their engines sludged with silt. Equipment and gear were stolen despite an armed naval patrol, and by the time the boats were re-moored six to eight weeks later, 162 had sunk. It was heartbreaking for fishermen to witness their beloved boats being so ill-treated and it was beyond their comprehension why they had been confiscated.

These events were all the more devastating to the Nikkei fishermen since, after enduring half a century of racist government policies, their lives had started to improve. The fishing in 1941 had been good on the Fraser, and 1942 promised to be even better because it was the year of the big Adams River sockeye run. At the same time, the war in Europe had increased the demand not just for canned sockeye but also for pink, coho and even chum salmon. The fishermen's new confidence was reflected in the fact that they had been spending heavily in improving their equipment and gear so that they now owned some of the best vessels in the industry.

The Nikkei fishermen had fully co-operated with the navy because to do otherwise would have been considered unpatriotic. But they also thought that the issue of national security would soon be resolved and that their boats would be returned to them in time to have them back in operation for the fishing season. "We still had our nets and gear in our net lofts, so a lot of Japanese fishermen thought it was just a temporary thing and when it was straightened out they'd get their boats back and we'd be fishing by spring. After all, they still had their nets."

The value of the 1,137 impounded boats and their equipment was between $2 million and $3 million. The table below shows the vessels impounded, by gear type.

Gear Type	Number of Boats Confiscated	Number of Japanese Canadian Owners	Number of Boats Released to Non-Japanese Owners*
Gillnet	860	715	145
Troller	120	115	5
Seine	68	67	1
Packer	147	138	9
Cod, other	142	102	40
Total	1,337	1,137	200

*A number of vessels belonging to non-Japanese were rounded up by mistake and impounded. They were subsequently returned to their owners.

With the removal of 1,265 fishermen from active participation in West Coast fisheries, the government of Canada faced a production crisis just when an uninterrupted food supply was necessary for the war effort. The government's response was to issue Order-in-Council PC 251 to return the Japanese vessels to active fishing in the hands of fishermen "other than Japanese origin" by charter, lease or sale. This was followed by PC 288 that ordered the establishment of the Japanese Fishing Vessels Disposal Committee (JFVDC).

To overcome the belief still held by some Nikkei that they would be getting back

NOTICE OF SALE

The Custodian of Enemy Property offers the following boats for sale:

Fishing Boats

"S. I."	No.	6603	Vancouver
"Bumper Catch"	No.	152918	Vancouver
"B. Y."	No.	3363	New Westminster
"Departure Bay III"	No.	154949	Vancouver
"Departure Bay V"	No.	155241	Vancouver
"Gardner M"	No.	154669	Vancouver
"Garry Point No. 4"	No.	154971	New Westminster
"Gigilo"	No.	154554	Vancouver
"Holly L"	No.	152459	New Westminster
"I. M. P."	No.	973	Vancouver
"Izumi No. 3"	No.	153369	Vancouver
"Izumi No. 8"	No.	170430	Vancouver
"Kamtchatka"	No.	153169	Vancouver
"Merle C"	No.	154384	Vancouver
"Otter Bay"	No.	155110	Vancouver
"Yip No. 2"	No.	154972	New Westminster
"K. K."	No.	3368	New Westminster
"Kimio"	No.	6598	Vancouver
"K. N."	No.	3364	New Westminster
"Lion's Gate"	No.	1359	Vancouver
"Mizuho"	No.	134292	New Westminster
"Point Yoho"	No.	154539	Vancouver
"Three Queens"	No.	155094	Vancouver
"Kanamoto"	No.	141788	New Westminster
"Newcastle 4"	No.	138688	Vancouver
"George Bay"	No.	154349	Vancouver
"Rose City"	No.	138305	Vancouver
"Jessie Island No. 9"	No.	155231	Vancouver
"Kitaka"	No.	138608	Vancouver
"Moresby 2"	No.	150875	New Westminster
"R. K."	No.	2776	Vancouver
"Worthman T"	No.	152919	Vancouver
"Y. O. 3"	No.	2779	Vancouver
"Y. O. 5"	No.	2780	Vancouver
"Y. O. 6"	No.	2781	Vancouver
"Fragrance"	No.	6602	Vancouver
Gas Fishing Boat	No.	3362	New Westminster
"Y. O."	No.	2777	Vancouver
"Y. O. X. 2"	No.	2778	Vancouver
"Newcastle 8"	No.	150252	Vancouver

Other Boats

"Blue Fox"	No.	154927	Vancouver
"Louise"	No.	2907	New Westminster

All offers must be in writing, for individual boats, and accompanied by a certified cheque for 10% of the offer.

Offers for fishing boats, if accepted, will be those from bona fide fishermen or Fishing Companies who are entitled to own vessels of Canadian Registry.

The highest or any offer not necessarily accepted.

Arrangements to examine the boats may be made with the undersigned. All offers should be addressed to the undersigned and will be accepted up to 12 o'clock noon the ninth day of March, 1942.

G. W. McPherson,
Authorized Deputy of the Secretary of State and/or Custodian,
1404 Royal Bank Building
Vancouver, B.C.

FRANK A. CLAPP COLLECTION

After the vessels were confiscated, they were leased or sold to fishermen "other than Japanese origin."
Courtesy of Frank A. Clapp, The Province, February 21, 1942

into fishing, district representatives were appointed to obtain signatures authorizing the sale of their boats. The Nikkei fishermen had no option but to sign over their boats because their families were being separated and dispersed with no means of support, but it was not until January 25, 1942, that any hope they had of fishing the 1942 season was finally dashed. In *Steveston Recollected*, Unosuke Sakamoto described the procedure adopted by the JFVDC:

Each district chairman was responsible for getting signatures on the procuration forms, and since all the Japanese knew they had to leave the Coast, they signed them. The Government then advertised for buyers. They listed all the boats—so much for this, so much for that—and white men and Indians chose the boats they liked. At first it was all right. The Government asked us to set prices so they would know the actual value of the boats. Then they let us know the offered price and we notified the owners in the places they had been sent to. I would write to them telling them the price and asking them what they wanted to do. They all knew they had to sell their boats cheap, so they sold them—with tears. But by the end if someone wanted a boat which we priced at $1,000 and if that person didn't have that much money he would say, 'I have only $500, but I want this boat so sell it to me.' The Government would then make the bill of sale on its own authority. A lot of boats were sold this way. Nothing could be done about it because we were all under the War Measures Act.

The release of over 1,000 boats created a glut in the market in which buyers could more or less dictate their prices. *The Province* reported on March 17, 1942, that "the commission has full power to force Japanese owners to sell. Any white Canadian who cannot reach a settlement with a Japanese owner has merely to write to the commission offering to buy and naming a price. The commission will do the rest. If the offer is judged fair, the Japanese owner will have to sell."

HARRIET'S GRAVLAX WITH MUSTARD SAUCE

Excerpted from Seasonings: Flavours of the Southern Gulf Islands *(2012),*
by Andrea and David Spalding

The run of spring salmon is eagerly awaited on the West Coast. Springs—also known as chinook salmon—make their way to our waters as early as March. A favourite West Coast way to serve this salmon is in the form of gravlax, and it is found on many restaurant menus. However, it is rarely prepared at home, except by British Columbians of Scandinavian descent who have grown up familiar with the process.

We hope that this recipe will demystify gravlax so this moist and succulent dish is available to everyone. The recipe is very easy, but it takes time—three days—so plan ahead. Don't panic, though, as for most of the time the salmon sits in the fridge and you ignore it! Gravlax is "cooked" in brine and the juices it generates. Served in very thin slices, gravlax is delicious as a dinner appetizer. It can also be served at breakfast, with a poached egg, buttered toast and a topping of Mustard Sauce.

Our Pender Island friend Harriet Stribley, originally from Sweden, gave Andrea this recipe many years ago. As is the way of recipes, adaptations crept in. Now we don't know what Harriet's original recipe was, but this one is an easy, terrific way to impress guests with a West Coast staple food.

Makes 10 servings

Gravlax

1 spring salmon fillet, approximately
   2.2 lb (1 kg)
⅓ cup (80 mL) aquavit*
Sprigs fresh dill (lots—Harriet said you
   cannot have too much!)

4 Tbsp (60 mL) sea salt
4 Tbsp (60 mL) sugar
2 Tbsp (30 mL) lemon zest
1 Tbsp (15 mL) freshly ground pepper

*A Scandinavian liquor available in liquor and wine stores.

Three days before you plan to serve the gravlax, rinse salmon fillet in cold water. Pat dry and carefully remove bones. Score skin side in four places, and freeze fillet, laid flat, for at least 24 hours (freezing will reduce the risk of illness caused by parasites).

The next day, defrost fillet. Pour aquavit into a glass or ceramic baking dish large enough to accommodate the fillet. Place some dill sprigs in the dish and lay the fillet, skin-side up, on top. Cover and marinate in the refrigerator for at least 6 hours, basting the top side with the juices every couple of hours.

Turn fillet skin-side down and sprinkle the remaining ingredients evenly on top. Baste with the juices. Cover tightly and marinate another 24 hours in the refrigerator. (This "cold cooks" the fish.)

On the third day, drain the fish and lay it skin-side down on a serving platter. Slice as thinly as possible through the flesh at an angle, down toward the skin. Start slicing from the tail end, letting the knife curve away at the skin so you don't cut through it.

Mustard Sauce

4 Tbsp (60 mL) Dijon mustard
4 Tbsp (60 mL) sweet mustard
4 Tbsp (60 mL) sugar
4 Tbsp (60 mL) vinegar
2 Tbsp (30 mL) aquavit

2 Tbsp (30 mL) lemon juice
½ cup (125 mL) olive oil
2 Tbsp (30 mL) chopped fresh dill
Salt and pepper

Place all sauce ingredients in a blender and process to combine.

Assembly

Chopped fresh dill
Twists of lemon

Garnish the gravlax slices with chopped fresh dill, drizzle with the sauce and top with twists of lemon.

FRENCHY AND SIMPSON

Excerpted from Fishing with John *(1992), by Edith Iglauer*

We awoke in the morning to rain brushing against the windows. Right after breakfast, John started the Gardner diesel and we ran back down Cousins Inlet to a marine crossroads; this time, we took the left-hand waterway, the much wider Dean Channel. Our goal, three hours away, was a pocket-sized opening called Eucott Bay. It was 1973 and the United Fishermen and Allied Workers' Union was on strike, but John had obtained written permission from the strike committee before we left Namu to food-fish for ourselves while we were travelling. It was almost noon, and I was preparing a salmon chowder with one of two small cohos John had caught, along with one fair-sized spring salmon, fishing briefly on one line on the way to Ocean Falls. He looked in the red stewpot on the stove. "We'll take some of this to two old fellows who live in a floathouse at Eucott," he said.

Almost immediately afterwards, he slowed down and turned left into a small bay hiding among the trees and stopped a few feet inside. At the far end, I could see what appeared to be marsh grass and a sandy beach. Beyond, through a V in the low hills covered with green firs, I glimpsed snowy mountains blending with a mass of white clouds floating across a bright-blue summer sky. It had stopped raining.

John anchored, and pulled down a chart. We were in fourteen fathoms, but directly in front of us it was only three. He said, "We'll have to wait for high tide to call on Frenchy and Simp*son*, because right now it's low tide and their dock is resting in mud." He pronounced the latter name with emphasis on the *son* to give it a French twist. "They live in a floathouse, an old abandoned fish camp that's been pulled up on the grass. It's just out of our sight now, beyond those three pilings over there." Farther ahead of us, perhaps 200 yards away, where the chart showed a depth of half a fathom, was a small unpainted frame house on floats with a ramp to the beach. "A retired fisherman lives there, when he's around," John said, "but he doesn't like visitors much. Don't mention him to the old men when we visit them. They aren't speaking."

"Who else lives in this bay?" I asked.

"That's all," John said. "All winter long, just the three of them are here, except for an occasional visitor from Ocean Falls or when the United Church boat, the *Thomas Crosby,* stops in to check up on them."

"There are only the three of them in this bay and this man and the two others don't speak?"

"That's right."

"Why?"

John shrugged. "It could be anything, but I think it was a political disagreement. It doesn't matter; they may not even know themselves. These guys living in isolated spots like this tend to get paranoid."

In the afternoon, John put the dinghy over the side and said, "It's high tide, so we can go over to see Frenchy and Simpson." He poured some of the salmon chowder into a container and put it in the dinghy along with a bag of apples and oranges, the custard pie, a six-pack of beer and the bottle of Scotch he had bought at Ocean Falls. At the last minute, he went below and got the spring he had caught on the way, and brought that along, too.

I took off my Stanfield's, put on my red turtleneck sweater and got into the dinghy with John, who was resplendent in his Norwegian cardigan. He started rowing us across the bay toward the three pilings. There we entered a channel in the flat, grassy

Taking a break from picket duty during the fishermen's strike, the author and John travel from Bella Bella to food-fish and to visit Frenchy and Simpson.

Harbour Publishing Archives

marsh. At the far end, half hidden among the trees, was a low, flat-roofed, oblong wooden building with a covered porch. It was dark red, with white trim on the eaves, the frames and the mouldings around the six panes of glass in each of its small square windows. The building, a foot or so off the ground, was on a scow that was on skids; and in the grass behind were an indeterminate assortment of half-ruined, unpainted small shacks. We came slowly to the rough plank dock in front of the scow as a slight, somewhat bent little man rounded a corner of the porch, hurrying toward us. He was wearing the usual dark wool fish pants, held up with suspenders; and a yellow, red and black plaid wool shirt wide open at the neck, with a broad expanse of dingy-grey underwear showing underneath a medal on a chain. A wide-brimmed felt hat was pulled down to his large, long ears, and his welcoming smile revealed toothless gums below a hooked nose. He had a small, deeply lined face, with a day's growth of beard. I climbed out of the dinghy to the dock on my knees, and when I stood up I was looking straight into his bright, dark eyes; we were the same height—five-two. He bowed low and removed his hat, revealing a bald head encircled by white hair.

"Hello, John, we see you come in today, and now you bring your lady to see old Frenchy and Simpson, yes?" he said, speaking with a pronounced French accent. He turned to me. "My name is really Leo Jacques, and sometimes they call me Jack, but people know me as Frenchy. My friend's name is Albert Simpson. You want to see Mr. Simpson, John?"

"We came to see you both, Frenchy," John said, as he straightened up from tying the dinghy to a rotting plank. He handed me the custard pie and chowder, and gave the spring salmon to Frenchy, then picked up the bag with the beer and whiskey that he had set out on the dock, tucking it under one arm and holding the bag of fruit with his other hand. He looked fondly at Frenchy. "You look very well—better than the last time I saw you. You were having trouble with your stomach."

The author and John on the stern of the *Morekelp*.
Harbour Publishing Archives

"Boy, I wish I had a stomach like that old man Simpson," Frenchy exclaimed. "Oh, well, I am *certainly* okay and I do a lot of praying for Simpson. He's my friend." He started walking ahead of us, then stopped and said to me, "That old man, he looks like Churchill. I'm eighty-four this month, but that man Simpson is eighty-eight." He held up the spring. "I'm sure glad to get fish. We haven't had any for long time."

The dock teetered drunkenly when we walked across it, and the plank connecting to the grassy shore quivered when I stepped on it. We passed rows of neatly piled firewood, uniformly cut alder, on the way up the path, and crossed the rotting porch. Frenchy opened a door, and we went into the house. It was so dark inside that it took my eyes a minute or two to get adjusted. We were in what must once have been a store, with a counter and shelves behind it just past the entrance. There was a calendar on the wall with a picture of a Japanese girl in a white kimono, and above it a green pennant that said, "Alaska, 1969." Farther along the wall was a magazine cover with a picture of de Gaulle, and above that a set of antlers was mounted on a board. An oil lamp hung from the ceiling, and several dark socks were draped along the sill of a dusty window.

"Come on, old man, see what company I brought you!" Frenchy shouted. I looked down the narrow, rectangular room in the direction he was shouting and saw a large, elderly gentleman wearing an old-fashioned brown fedora. He had a round moon of a face and looked absolutely like Winston Churchill. He was sitting up rigidly erect, smoking a cigarette in a holder held upright between two fingers, thin, stuck straight out. He was dressed in a blue-and-white-checked flannel shirt and grey pants, and his feet, which were swollen, were encased in bedroom slippers. A crutch was hooked to one arm of his chair.

Frenchy drew up two chairs, then darted over to Simpson, leaned over him and pulled up the open fly on his pants with the tender gesture one would reserve for a child. We sat down facing the big man, who was staring at me. Frenchy seated himself on a bed against the wall and mopped his brow. "I get so nair-vous and excited," he said apologetically. "Just with people I like. The others I don't give a damn about. I pay no attention." Simpson, meanwhile, had finished his cigarette and was fumbling to pick another out of the package he held, but he dropped the package on the floor. Frenchy jumped to pick it up, took out a cigarette, lit it and handed it to him, saying to me, "This old man fell off a roof t'irty years ago and landed on his hands, so he broke them, and they aren't much use. He can't walk, neither. Since he had his stroke, he's partly—partly—" Frenchy paused, searching for the word.

"Paralyzed?" John suggested.

"Right you are, sir. That's the word for it." Simpson spoke for the first time, slowly, in clipped, precise English. His voice was unexpectedly deep and clear. "I have been living in this bay with Frenchy for fifty years, since we met and teamed up together." He turned his head toward me, paused to move his hand slowly to his mouth and puffed on his cigarette. "I am of Scotch background, from Nova Scotia. We were a family of eight, and most of my family is around Boston now. I have a sister who writes often, and another sister who left a hundred thousand dollars to her church."

"The money we have, we decide to leave it to hospital," Frenchy announced.

"What hospital?" John asked.

"Oh well, whatever hospital we decide to die in," Simpson replied. "We split everything fifty-fifty. Frenchy's a smart man. He's a Frenchman, but he's honest."

"That Simpson, he's not a very good trapper, he's no good at all," Frenchy said. "He has trouble even catching a mouse!"

Simpson removed his cigarette between stiff fingers and gave a deep easy laugh, revealing gums as toothless as Frenchy's. "Yes, I could learn a lot from Frenchy," he said.

"Have you been back to Nova Scotia often?" I asked.

"I never wished to go home again," he replied. "I worked first in Alberta, but I wanted to fish, so I came to BC and went trolling. Frenchy is from Trois-Rivières, in Quebec. We used to troll together, but he's had traplines as well, trapping marten and, later, mink. He made five hundred dollars one month."

Simpson stopped talking, and Frenchy jumped up again. "Do you want a bottle of beer?" he shouted at Simpson, and Simpson nodded. Frenchy opened a bottle from the six-pack that John had put on the counter, and handed it to him. Simpson raised it clumsily between his two hands to his mouth, took a healthy swig and managed to set it down on a table beside him. Frenchy offered us some, but John shook his head, so Frenchy poured us each a mug of coffee from a pot on a kerosene-drum stove under the window.

"I never went back to Quebec, neither," Frenchy volunteered. "My father was a doctor, and my mother died when I'm two year old, and he had a nurse take care of us children. My older brother had a big farm, but I left home very young and crossed the country. I never went to school. I got shot in the First World War." He opened his shirt. "See that hole?" He leaned over so we could get a good view of a small round scar. "The bullet went out back. And I got slit with a bayonet right across here." He ran his finger across his neck, then pulled back his shirt collar to show us that scar, too. "Only four or five come back, but, by jeez, this crazy Frenchman, he come back! I got a bunch of medals, but they sank in my boat."

"Show them the document that was presented to you with your King George medal," Simpson said.

Frenchy went to a drawer and took out a folded sheet of faded paper, which he handed to me. "Old King George and the Queen came to see me when I was pretty near dead in University Hospital, London," he said.

I opened the paper. "Read it out loud," John said.

Below the Royal Crest in red at the top, and the words "Buckingham Palace, 1918," I read, "'The Queen and I wish you Godspeed, a safe return to the happiness and joy of home life, with an early restoration to health. A grateful Mother Country thanks you for faithful services.'" It was signed "George R.I."

Frenchy nodded proudly while I read. He pulled a card out of his shirt pocket and handed it to me. It was a holy card, with a picture of the head of Jesus wearing a crown of thorns, above a prayer in French, printed in green ink. "I had this in my breast pocket when I got shot," Frenchy said. "I kept it from 1918, and I been all over the world with it on them freighters I used to go on—especially on the Great Lakes." He patted it and put it carefully back in his pocket.

"I had half my army pay going to my sister, a very lovely woman, and when I came home I find she give two hundred dollars I send to help her priest to say prayers for me," Frenchy went on. "So I never send her more, and when I leave, I tell her, 'You won't hear from me, because you worry too much.' I never been back to see her—not since 1919—and I never wrote, neither. Not to my own sister."

It started to rain. Two or three raindrops hit my shoulder, so I slid my chair an inch or two back from a leak in the roof. Frenchy leaped up and put a tin can on the floor to catch the drips, and from then on, the patter of rain on the roof was accompanied by a musical *ping*. Frenchy sighed. "Someone brought this old fish camp here on a scow and left it all to rot. When we move in, she look like hell. I pull her up here and push some cedars under her when the tide is in. I patch the roof real good, but I guess I have to do it again. Last winter, John, we live real nice. Someone from Canadian Fish Company tow a fish camp with a store here, and we look after it, so we got to live on it until spring. Especially because it have an oil stove, it is much more comfortable than this old wreck. I have a lot of work carrying five-gallon drums of oil inside for the stove, but it's good all the same to wake up in a nice warm house, and we had very little snow." He laughed. "By golly, I sure never want to go back to Quebec. Too cold!"

A sudden crash. Simpson, lifting his cigarette to his mouth, had knocked over his beer bottle. Frenchy scrambled after it as it rolled away, and he muttered, "We have more trouble from morning to night." Without warning, he burst into song. "Ho! Ho! Ho!" Then he sang it in a faster rhythm—"Ho-ho-ho!"—smiling at Simpson. "We get some good laughs," he said.

John Daly catches up with correspondence at an out-of-the-way bay near Namu.
Harbour Publishing Archives

"Yes, we do," said Simpson, with a deep chuckle. "We'll have the Seventh-Day Adventists in here soon and have a gospel night." We were all laughing now; Simpson's heavy body was shaking with mirth. "The United Church boat, the *Thomas Crosby IV,* stops in here every three weeks to see us," he said finally, taking out a blue bandanna and wiping his forehead. "I know that boat," John said, still smiling. "It's a big steel one, eighty feet long, that goes anywhere in any kind of weather."

Frenchy went on singing little "Ho-hos" to himself as he skipped back to the bed where he had been sitting. He picked up a handsome patchwork quilt and a yellow-and-blue crocheted blanket there and brought them over for me to see. "We asked the *Thomas Crosby* to bring us sleeping bags," he said. "The one they gave us for Simpson was too small, so the United Church at Prince Rupert sent us these and I put them on this old man's bed instead."

"We had quilts like that in Nova Scotia," Simpson interjected. "Mother used to make them."

Frenchy ran to an alcove behind me, which was evidently his bunk, and came back with an armful of quilts, announcing, "I got two or t'ree more quilts that the Church brought us, and the five girls who crocheted blanket come to see us. One of them church girls give me a kimono, but I don't say not'ing." The quilts were handmade and beautiful.

Frenchy removed his old fedora, scratched his head and put the hat on again, but Simpson never removed his for any reason. In fact, I never saw Simpson without a hat. (Later, when I asked John if he had ever seen Simpson without a hat, he said, "No, and nobody else I know has, either.")

Frenchy said, "We hire a guy to bring our groceries every four weeks—wintertime, too. He's a paperworker from the Falls, a Prussian with a nice boat that takes an hour and a half to go twenty-eight mile to the Falls. He do everything for us." He chuckled. "When I used to go to Ocean Falls, I used to go to the Happy House, right around the bend at what we call Pecker Point. The alders have *cert*ainly grown over that Happy House fast since it closed."

Simpson was frowning, shaking his head at Frenchy, who suddenly stopped talking.

Looking amused, John picked up the conversation. "That German you hire must have a powerful boat. It took us three hours to get here with my seventy-two-horse-power, five-cylinder Gardner," he said.

Simpson leaned back in his chair, cackling. "Oh, I know that one. It's a good one."

"I used to have nice boat, troller, for seventeen years," Frenchy said. "The *Albatross,* built at Sointula, on Malcolm Island. In 1936, I get twenty-four cents a pound for springs and six cents a pound for coho in Namu—forty cents for a whole coho. A lot of people were living in this bay then, in small shacks in winter, mostly loggers and fishermen, but there was a woman here who sold baths. She had bathtubs in little huts, and you could take a bath for two bits or a dollar—whatever you thought it was worth. She would lend a towel to you for ten cents, or sell it to you for twenty-five; the only thing, she was such a bad cook. I know because I used to chop her wood to have a cup of tea and whatever she gave me to eat."

"What happened to the *Albatross*?" I asked.

"I sink it, I t'ink in '43, maybe '44," Frenchy said. "The manifold and exhaust and fumes, they put me to sleep and *bingo!* she went on the rocks. I get out in a rowboat, and someone from Bella Coola in a gillnetter came along and picked me up. No insurance, so I lost the whole works. I bought another boat the next year, and someone walked on it and stole eight hundred dollars." He shrugged. "Fishing from daybreak to night was too long, anyway. I got dizzy from the exhaust and from looking up at those lines."

He got out four glasses and poured us each a Scotch, handed them to us and said, "There are some nice big ducks around and we don't even shot one. We like to see them around. We used to make homebrew and then t'row away the corn, and when ducks came around they'd get drunk and go round and round like this." He lay down on the floor on his side and flapped his arms, hopped up and sat down again on the bed, still talking. "They was fat and in good shape, and once in a while a hawk or owl came around and got one. We used to have lots of owls at night, but no more now."

"Every night, they used to howl 'Hoo! Hoo!'" Simpson said. "Another thing, we used to have a lot of Japanese here from the Falls. There was this old fellow who was

The author with Frenchy beside his motorboat at Eucott Bay, near Bella Coola.
Harbour Publishing Archives

eighty-four, a gillnetter, who used to hang around here in the winter. He wasn't a bad fellow, either. Better than that fellow that's over there now."

Frenchy leaned over and said to me in a low voice, "I don't mind, but him and Mr. Simpson don't get along well."

My eye had been attracted by a white ceramic angel with a gold halo on the shelf behind Simpson's impressive head, and when my glance shifted to binoculars hanging from a hook on the wall next to it, Frenchy said loudly, "From here, Mr. Simpson can see a bear way up at the head of the bay without glasses. He's got to do somet'ing, that guy. I shot two black bears last year. There used to be a lot of deer, too. They would come in evening at low water and drink, but I don't see none now. I fish for Simpson, but I wait until there is more than one fish in the water and then I don't make too much noise. Seals and otters come right up to your boat if they t'ink you have fish. They walk on the bottom, those otters—I see the tracks—and they say when seals come like that, fish are coming in. Seals walk one-and-a-half mile to this lake above here, and then another mile to another lake. We saw twenty wolves in one bunch, too; they come down for fish. They howled right alongside here, right around our door."

Simpson signalled for more Scotch. Frenchy poured some into his glass. "Thank you, sir," Simpson said. He held the glass up between both hands and drank, put it down and said, "We had the best cat in the country, and the wolves got him. Oh, he was a wonderful fellow."

"When anyone came, he just sat by Simpson and growled!" Frenchy said.

"Oh, the wolf caught him right at the door—I know he did," Simpson said mournfully.

"That black-and-white cat, Ta-puss, would sleep up on the pillow against Simpson's head and would snore," Frenchy said. "Simpson would wake up and say, 'Quit your snoring,' and push that cat to the wall. One night, he was sleeping right beside Mr. Simpson, snoring, and Mr. Simpson tried to push him off once too often and Ta-puss bit him in the hand." Frenchy began to laugh, rocking back and forth. He laughed so hard he had to wipe his eyes with his sleeve.

Simpson wiped his eyes, too, and said, "Ta-puss would push on the doorknob and then push the door open."

"Old Ta-puss, I wouldn't take fifty dollars for him," Frenchy said.

"I wouldn't take a *hundred* for him," Simpson said, shaking his large head solemnly from side to side. "Oh, I wish we had him now. He would never catch the mice in here. He would just sit and look at them walking back and forth in front of him."

The light coming in through the windows was fading, and the room had become even more shadowy. John rose to go. "Tomorrow, we're going to Nascall Bay. We'll stop in on our way back from there," he said to Simpson, who was looking downcast.

Frenchy walked back to the dock with us. It was now totally dark, and we rowed home in a driving rainstorm. Without my Stanfield's on, I was thoroughly chilled. It was so cold when we got back to the boat that John turned up the stove while we shivered, taking off our wet clothes. We ate supper surrounded by the smell of soggy clothes drying out on a clothesline that crisscrossed the cabin from wall to wall.

We were in bed long before ten o'clock, when the strike news came on. Nothing had been settled. John said gloomily, "It may be another week before the strike is over, but anyway it gave us a good chance to come here. I always stop and see those wonderful old fellows once a summer, even if it means losing a day's fishing. I sure admire Frenchy. It's not easy for a man his age to do all that cooking, and he washes their clothes, too, by hand. Frenchy tells me he has to lift Simpson sometimes; I don't see how he does it, Simpson is almost twice his size. No, no, Simpson is not an easy man to take care of. He liked you, by the way. If he hadn't, he would have sat there like a sphinx, not saying a word."

John moved the *Morekelp* to a different position during the night, because of the wind, and just before we left the next morning, we looked out the window toward Frenchy and Simpson's place. With the tide out, we could see a neat grey speedboat tied up at the small dock that I hadn't noticed before because of the tall grass around it. John said, "It's Frenchy's and it's sixteen feet, with a little cabin and a gas engine. If their floathouse burned up, he could put Simpson on that boat."

10 CANADA DAY AT YUQUOT

Excerpted from Off the Map: Western Travels on Roads Less Taken *(2001),*
by Stephen Hume

As an antidote to the tired assumptions that always seem to colonize our Canada Day weekends, I decide that for the first one of the new millennium I'll take my ten-year-old daughter, Heledd, to Yuquot to visit the place where modern history first collided with the West Coast's ancient and mysterious past. We first drive 165 miles north from Victoria to Campbell River, then another 55 miles through the rugged mountains west of Campbell River to Gold River, where Margarita James, director of cultural and heritage resources for the Mowachaht/Muchalaht First Nations, dispatches us for another hour by boat, dodging deadheads and crashing through glossy swells.

A centre of commerce during the fur trade, Friendly Cove, or Yuquot, now has only one resident family.
Elsie Hulsizer photo

Yuquot is where the compelling Mowachaht Chief Maquinna confronted the European superpowers of his day just over two hundred years ago. A place of stunning beauty, it straddles a narrow isthmus connecting several rocky outcrops to Nootka Island. Think of two crescent moons lying back to back. That's both the shape and the luminous colour of the two great canoe beaches, one opening to sheltered waters, the other facing the booming green combers of the outer coast. The old village site is one of those places that resonates with energy from the moment you step ashore and notice the strange, perfectly oval pebbles that are polished as smooth as glass beads and left in heaps by the tireless sea.

It's a difficult feeling to describe, an eerie combination of history and some less tangible spiritual presence. But perhaps this feeling is merely the burden carried in by the visitor who has taken time to read about the mysterious, mystical whalers' shrine that was located on an island in a sacred lake. It was here, long before Europeans had even arrived in the New World, that Mowachaht inhabitants of E'as and Tsaxis, two ancient villages farther north on the wild, hurricane-lashed western fringe of Vancouver Island, first began hunting and harpooning gray and humpback whales, later bringing their knowledge to Yuquot. Whatever I might have felt from the weight of this history, my carefree daughter is soon wading through the sun-bronzed grass that nods over the ruins of a settlement from this culture that was already ancient when the Greeks went to sack Troy. The surf booms and seethes up the shingle, the breeze makes cat's-paws on the rippling meadow, nectar-laden bees fumble at the Indian paintbrush and blue camas and the air is rich with the sweet scent of clover. Some things never change.

We stop to chat with Ray Williams and his wife Teresa, the last continuous occupants of the site, largely abandoned in 1967 when the federal government moved the inhabitants to Gold River. "The chiefs asked us to move, too, but we said no," Ray tells us. "We stayed. We're the caretakers of Maquinna's lands. That move, that was a

Yuquot, or Friendly Cove, on Nootka Island, as painted by Thomas Bamford in 1897.
Image PDP00705 courtesy of the Royal BC Museum, BC Archives

mistake—a really big mistake. The government moved our people right next to that pulp mill in Gold River. It was an awful place, babies were getting sick." Ray gestures to where his talented son Sanford is at work carving a new totem pole and directs us to where we might look at some ancient poles, now down, moss-covered and already rotting back into the earth as they were meant to do. "This place is our people's spiritual centre," Ray says.

I follow my daughter along the beach and into the trees. Below us glimmers Jewitt Lake, named for John Jewitt, captive of Maquinna for two years after the rest of the crew of the ship *Boston* had been killed by Mowachaht warriors in 1803. It surrounds the island where the whaling chiefs had the shrine that is also known as their Washing House, certainly the most important monument in the West Coast aboriginal whaling culture. The shrine, a spectral structure of carved wooden figures and human skulls, was the focal point of the long and arduous rituals of purification and preparation that had to be undertaken by the chiefly lineages, which, like the kings of Europe with their royal deer and Indian rajas with their tigers, reserved to themselves alone the right to hunt whales. Although the Whalers' Shrine is considered one of the most significant artifacts from that interface between the physical and supernatural worlds inhabited by both mythic and shamanic figures on the pre-contact West Coast of Canada, its power is defined as much by the absence of reference points as by anything else.

Collected by George Hunt at the instigation of anthropologist Franz Boas in 1905, the shrine was dismantled and removed to the American Museum of Natural History, where it resides to this day. Yet even stories about it obtained from First Nations informants are scattered and scarce, as though even those who knew what it signified were reluctant to talk about its origins and the way the rites practised here shaped the society around them. One thing is clear: Like a dark body that's discerned by astronomers through its influence on the space surrounding it, the gravity exerted by the Whalers' Shrine upon the spiritual cosmos of the Nuu-chah-nulth who lived at Yuquot made it a pretty skookum place.

Yet there's another residual power here that affects newcomers, too. This is where, in 1778, Captain James Cook became the first European to set foot on the Northwest Coast. These days it's popular among the politically correct to sniff at the accomplishments of men like Cook, but his voyages of exploration in small wooden ships on an uncharted sea so vast it could drown all the Earth's continents is more akin to journeying to the moon than our technological hubris likes to acknowledge. Cook, in fact, was greeted with enthusiasm by Maquinna, who quickly seized the political opportunity to make himself a crucial power-broker and established Yuquot as a key base in the commercial fur trade that followed. During a visit eight years later, one Mr. Strange, a passenger aboard a visiting sailing ship, gave Yuquot its English name: Friendly Cove. It proved a good name.

Britain and Spain were at the brink of war over rival claims to the Northwest Coast when the Spanish established a fort here in 1791. Maquinna invited Captain George Vancouver and Captain Juan Francisco de la Bodega y Quadra to a formal dinner, helping defuse the tension while a solution was worked out between the two great European powers. In 1795, when Spain peacefully withdrew, the British commissioner presented Maquinna with the Union Jack that had been raised when London's claims prevailed.

Today, Friendly Cove is a national historic site and these great events are commemorated with a cairn and various plaques—not one of which, my daughter observes, makes any mention of either Maquinna or the Mowachaht people who had been there for 4,300 years. But that soon changes. Up at the white glare of the abandoned church with its stained glass windows depicting the historic events that entangled these three nations forever, we find the pews pushed aside, the smell of fresh paint and a bustle of activity amid the rainbow splinters of light that spill across the age-darkened floorboards. Robin Inglis, director of the North Vancouver Museum, and Bob Eberle, a theatre professor at the University of British Columbia, are frantically preparing for a remarkable event—the arrival of three crates aboard the coastal freighter *Uchuck III*. They contain a gift to the Mowachaht and Muchalaht from the Spanish government. It's a collection of high-quality artistic reproductions of the charts and drawings of Yuquot and its original inhabitants made by Tomás de Suría and José Cardero, members of Quadra's crew more than two hundred years ago. "These are the images you see in all the textbooks," Robin says. "What an interesting thing for the Mowachaht to have this collection of images from the moment of first contact." Robin and Bob are helping to set up a summer-long exhibition at the site in preparation for a celebration when the Mowachaht of Gold River will hold a reunion at Yuquot. Visitors were invited to join them for a salmon feast, traditional songs and dances while the Spanish were to formally present their gift.

Stained glass windows donated to the church at Yuquot in 1954 portray the meeting of Captains George Vancouver and Bodega y Quadra in 1792.
Elsie Hulsizer photos

In the meantime, an extra set of muscles is welcome and I am pressed into service helping load the heavy crates aboard an all-terrain vehicle and then keeping them in place behind the driver as we bounce our way back up the overgrown plank road from the wharf to the church through the salmonberry canes, blackberry brambles and salal. At the church, a young woman comes down to help unload. Marsha Maquinna, daughter of the present chief, reaches in and lifts out a picture. It is Suría's imposing portrait of her own ancestor, the great chief Maquinna himself. And as my daughter observes, on this coast, you can't stuff much more Canada into a Canada Day than that.

11 THE SCHOONER *BEATRICE* AND THE GREAT PELAGIC SEAL HUNT

Excerpted from Westcoasters: Boats that Built BC *(2001), by Tom Henry*

And since our women must walk Gay
And Money buys their gear,
The Sealing boats must go that way
And filch at hazard year by year.
—Rudyard Kipling

After a day's hunt, sealers skinned their catch.
Image B-00619 courtesy of the Royal BC Museum, BC Archives

If, as is often alleged, life was slower in the old days, then how did so much get done? In the time it takes a modern urban planner to conceptualize a shopping mall, pioneers built, lived in and abandoned whole towns. Plodding horses, hand-wrung laundry and the slow slap of sail on a windless day may be the ascendant images of the late nineteenth century, but when they saw opportunity, the province's colonists moved at rip speed.

This ability to turn chance to account was especially well developed in the marine industry of the late nineteenth century. Shipbuilders had two great advantages over their modern counterparts (three, if you count gumption). One was easy money. A man wanting to build a ship simply marched into the smoky, red-velvet lounge of Vancouver's Alexandra Hotel, where the wealthy seamen marshalled, and made a pitch. If his idea was sound, he walked away with the cash in his pocket. The other great benefit was lack of regulation. Shipyards were more a matter of attitude than zoning, and certainly unfettered by environmental rules. A shipwright staked out an area above the high-tide line, purchased or pinched a few logs and set to work.

It was this ability to wed capital and enterprise that helped BC seafarers cash in on the great pelagic seal hunt. Sealing was to the 1890s what the gold rush was to the 1860s—a free-for-all pitting men against the elements in pursuit of fortune. The hunt set country against country, made and ruined many men and established Victoria as a major Pacific port. Like the gold rush, it was a pivot in history, anchoring BC in the Dominion of Canada at a time when America was contemplating annexing the West Coast from Washington to Alaska.

Between 1885, when the Canadian sealing industry was launched, and 1911, when Canada withdrew from the seal hunt, no fewer than 125 sealing vessels were built in BC, many in makeshift and obscure yards. These ships were alike: strong, sturdy, simple. Sail-powered, they were between sixty and eighty feet long. They were also beamy, which made them good craft in the rough waters of the Bering Sea where the bulk of the seals were taken. Sailors on the best of these craft, it was said, could wear carpet slippers on deck and never get them wet.

The *Beatrice* in its early days as a sealing schooner. Workers appear to be scraping the hull.
D. Hartley collection

One of these ships was the *Beatrice*. By any measure a remarkable vessel, the *Beatrice* laboured at so many tasks that its registry reads like a mongrel's genealogy: sealer, towboat, fish packer, marine research platform. It was also lucky, outlasting several generations of the seamen who trod its plank decks. Like a centenarian peasant who attributes her longevity to a daily stint cutting cordwood, the *Beatrice* survived on work, work, work.

The Canadian sealing industry was a decade old when the *Beatrice* was launched, from James Doherty's False Creek Shipyard in April 1891. The harvest centred around the migratory habits of *Callorhinus ursinus,* or the northern fur seal, whose undercoat of short soft fur was prized by furriers and costumers. Roaming over the North Pacific in search of food, the animals gathered by the hundreds of thousands each summer at the breeding grounds around the Pribilof Islands in the Bering Sea.

Until the breeding grounds were pinpointed, sealing was a chancy harvest, limited by the sealers' ability to find and keep up with the swift-moving herds. Then in 1885,

Beamy and deep of draft, the *Beatrice* was designed to be stable in all but the worst weather.

D. Hartley collection

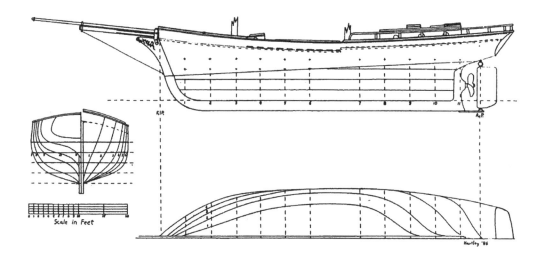

Victoria was home port for the great pelagic sealing fleet.

Image D-05993 courtesy of the Royal BC Museum, BC Archives

two vessels, the *Favorite,* from Sooke, and the *Mary Ellen,* from Victoria, returned from the Bering Sea with 4,382 skins, worth an astounding $35,000. The industry exploded; by 1892, 122 schooners with three thousand men were taking part in the pelagic seal hunt. The ships ranged throughout the North Pacific, scouring the waters off the Aleutians and down the Siberian coast to Japan.

The *Beatrice* made a number of runs to the sealing grounds—all were more remarkable for accident or intrigue than for harvest. The first trip was under the registry of Charles G. Doering, a Vancouver brewer and rose gardener par excellence, and his bearded, barrel-chested father-in-law, Hans Helgesen, whose long and varied career matched that of the *Beatrice*. Doering bought the ship to make money; Helgesen was in it, as a son later said, to "have one last fling at the sea."

Helgesen was born in a small town west of Christiania, now Oslo, Norway. His father was a farmer and shipbuilder. He had first gone to sea in 1847, at age eighteen. He joined a sailing ship and worked his way via Cape Horn to the American west coast. In San Francisco he caught word of the California gold rush and jumped ship, walking ashore on a pier made out of cookstoves. He panned for gold in California, then came north on the *Brother Jonathan*. In Victoria he built a scow and made his way to Hope. For several summers he panned gold on the Fraser River, camping and keeping company with a polyglot collection of adventurers. On one of the expeditions a companion of Helgesen's shot a caribou—which is, according to one story, how the Cariboo region got its name.

Gold gave way to farming and an unsuccessful attempt at a sedentary life. In 1862 Helgesen bought a fertile section of ground on a south-facing hill in Metchosin, on southern Vancouver Island. Several years later he left to go prospecting in Nevada, followed by a stint cod fishing in the Queen Charlotte Islands. Cod fishing gave way to provincial politics, which gave way to mining in British Guiana. Between stops at Metchosin to father seven children, he had a mini-career as a fisheries overseer on the Skeena River and revisited a lost gold lode in the Cariboo.

Helgesen was sixty-two when he and Doering purchased the *Beatrice*. He knew local waters and had hoped to captain the vessel. But he lacked proper papers. Reluctantly, he hired a Captain Bjaerre, a Danish deep-sea sailor with papers but no local knowledge. Under Bjaerre's command (and Helgesen's watchful eye), the *Beatrice* departed Victoria and headed south until it intercepted the seal herd off California. Then it turned and followed the herd north.

Seamen have long known that a ship owner and a captain make a volatile combination. Authority is vested in one by proprietorship, in the other by tradition. The two mix like guns and religion. Aboard the *Beatrice,* Helgesen had a number of complaints about the way Bjaerre was handling his ship. He thought it was carrying too much sail, and was sometimes near capsizing. He said as much to Bjaerre, but Bjaerre insisted he knew what he was doing. He didn't.

Two hundred nautical miles off the Queen Charlotte Islands the *Beatrice* hit a severe storm. While the little schooner plowed into the heavy seas, Bjaerre ordered the fore and aft staysails set. The wheel was lashed to keep the seas just off the bow. Then he and the crew went below to ride out the storm huddled around the tiny woodstove. Helgesen, too, was below deck. His philosopher's brow furrowed in thought, he watched the flickering oil lamp and listened to the ship's groaning timbers. As usual, he did not like the situation. Only this time he was convinced Bjaerre's boldness—Helgesen would have called it foolishness—was going to end in calamity. The captain had too much sail forward. The risk was that the schooner would pay off—turn broadside to the weather. Once broadside, all it needed was a large wave to send it somersaulting.

The farther the *Beatrice* rode into the storm, the more Helgesen fretted. Finally he donned his heavy oilskins and clambered onto the deck. The only other person there, according to Helgesen's account, was the cabin boy, Joe Devine, who was clearing food scraps. The two were clinging to the rails, watching the sails, when Helgesen spotted a wall of water looming on the windward side. It was what seamen call a rogue wave—a freak of wind and current. Helgesen only had time to bellow and take cover.

Top left: Sealers aboard a vessel in the Smoky Sea. The hard masculine life appealed to author Jack London, but even he found the slaughter excessive. *Image B-000617 courtesy of the Royal BC Museum, BC Archives*

Top right: In the rush of the hunt, slaughtered seals were often heaped on the deck of a sealing ship until there was time to skin and salt the pelts. *Image F-05169 courtesy of the Royal BC Museum, BC Archives*

A gust turned the schooner broadside, the wave hit and everything was sent spiralling. Devine was launched into the sea. Helgesen, clutching a belaying pin, was dragged underwater as the ship capsized. Below decks, the crew were sent tumbling down onto the galley ceiling. (The ceiling sported their marks for years.)

How long the *Beatrice* stayed under no one knows—for later all felt it was days. But slowly, freighted by wet sail in water, it righted. As the rigging emerged it scooped the flailing Devine and hoisted him aloft. Stunned, the lad was left straddling a backstay. Like the rest of the crew, he was thankful to be alive. From that point on, Bjaerre and Helgesen appear to have had a more harmonious relationship.

Out on the sealing grounds, the *Beatrice* operated much like any other sealing vessel. At the cry "Boats Out!" the sealers clambered over the side of the ship and into specially designed craft they called shells. It took three men to handle a shell: a steersman or gaffer, a rower and the hunter. Some Native hunters used shells, but most preferred canoes. Canoes carried two, the hunter and a paddler. The paddler was often the wife of the hunter. Once overboard, the canoes and shells fanned from the mother ship. The search for seals often took sealers fifteen nautical miles away, until the *Beatrice*'s masts were sticks on the horizon. Each boat was provisioned with a keg of water, hardtack, bully beef and, if the ship's cook was up early enough, prune pie, which was a staple of the sealing fleet. Only the captain and the cabin boy remained on the schooner.

Sealers divided their quarry into three categories: travellers, seals that raced through the water, jumping from wave to wave; moochers, lollygagging seals that raised their heads now and then to look around; and sleepers, seals that lay on their backs snoozing. Sleepers made up the bulk of seals taken. Hunters had to approach silently, so as not to waken the animal. When the craft was close enough, the hunter raised the spear, took aim and sank the metal tip deep into the seal's blubbery side. It was then the gaffer's job to gaff the seal and haul it to the boat. If the gaffer missed, the seal sank. Some hunters shot bullets into the water to force seals under. After several panicked dives, the mammals were too exhausted to evade the spear. When guns were prohibited in the harvest, hunters attached a rope to the weapon's stock. If a patrol boat approached, the gun was lowered over the side.

The first seals caught each day were left whole, for ballast. Any other seals were skinned on sight, the hunter taking care to leave plenty of blubber to insulate the hide from the burning effect of salt, which separated layers of pelts in the hold of the sealing ship. For the first fifty sealskins taken, the hunter received two dollars per head; for the next fifty, three dollars; after a hundred skins the hunter received four dollars apiece.

The money had to be good because the job was hazardous. The North Pacific is not a good place to be in a small boat. Among the many dangers hunters faced, the greatest was fog. Great banks of impregnable white mist rolled over the Bering Sea with such frequency the area was known as the Smoky Sea. Within moments a crew with a clear view of the mother ship would be lost. The greatest aid in overcoming the difficulties of navigating in fog was the intuitive sense of the hunters, some of whom accurately guided their tiny boats through thick fog for several hours to arrive at the side of their ship. The mother ships, too, attempted to help crews home. After the small boats pulled away in the morning, the captain would take the ship downwind, so the shells and canoes were likely to blow to it rather than away from it. If visibility was poor at the end of the day, the schooner fired guns, and the cabin boy was sent aloft to light an oily rag at the masthead.

Back on the ship, unskinned seals were stripped and their hides salted and stowed. It was a grim sight, even by the standards of the day. Author Jack London, who in 1893 travelled for seven months on the sealing schooner *Sophia Sutherland,* described the scene in his book *Sea Wolf:* "It was wanton slaughter…No man ate of the seal meat or the oil. After a good day's killing I have seen our decks covered with hides and bodies, slippery with fat and blood, the scuppers running red; masts, ropes and rails splattered with the sanguinary colour; and the men, like butchers plying their trade, naked and red of arm and hand, hard at work with ripping and flensing knives, removing the skins from the pretty sea creatures they had killed." For London, the horrors of the skinning were compounded by the fact that the entire enterprise was done in the name of fashion, so that the skins "might later adorn the fair shoulders of the women in cities."

On August 20, 1895, the *Beatrice,* under Captain Louis Olsen (and new owners), was working near the Pribilof Islands when it was boarded by American revenue officers from the cutter *Rush.* The *Rush* was one of several American and British gunships in the area, enforcing the terms of an 1893 accord brokered by an arbitration tribunal in Paris that attempted to regulate the harvest. The sealing nations had agreed that all vessels must keep official logs of the harvest and must present the logs for inspection.

In truth, however, the boarding was part of a systematic harassment of sealing ships by American officials. In 1886 the US, afraid of losing a virtual monopoly on sealing, attempted to ban all foreign harvesting, claiming, ludicrously, that since the seals were born on American lands, they were domestic animals. The Russians, who formerly owned Alaska and had tried the same manoeuvre, reminded the Americans of the illegality of their position, and the Americans grudgingly changed their policy—but only technically. In the hold of the *Beatrice,* American officers discovered a number of sealskins not entered in the official log. The ship was seized and, following the protocol set up by the arbitration tribunal in Paris, handed over to a British patrol vessel. It was sailed to Victoria where the skins were sold. The Crown then brought charges against the ship's owners. As punishment for not maintaining an accurate log, the Crown asked the courts to order the ship sold. The owners and the captain were outraged. In court, lawyers for the defence testified that the captain had kept perfect records. The mix-up occurred, they said, because it was a temporary log; when the captain had a moment he would have transferred this information into the official log. He had recorded all the information required, but not in the right place.

The judge hearing the case was unimpressed with the Crown's arguments. He declared the arrest of the *Beatrice* to be unlawful. Furthermore, the judge said that the *Beatrice* was in pursuit of profit and might reasonably have expected further profit. The Crown was ordered to pay $3,163.50 in damages.

Predictably, the judgment made the *Beatrice* a marked ship on the sealing grounds. The following season, on August 5, 1896, an American patrol boat seized it again, this time for killing seals in a prohibited area. Once more the vessel was transferred to Her Majesty's Service and sailed to Victoria. In court, the captain's defence was that overcast skies made it impossible to properly determine his position. He said that a strong current must have nudged the *Beatrice* into the no-hunting zone. The judge pointed out that it was seized six nautical miles within the prohibited area, the logbook contained scratches and crossed-out areas that suggested hasty alteration, and the master's testimony in court was at odds with his own records. The defence collapsed and the owners were required to pay a fine of several hundred dollars.

By 1911 it was clear that the seal population was seriously depleted. Where it had numbered in the millions in the 1870s, it was now estimated to be only 150,000. Japan, Canada (represented by Britain), Russia and the United States signed the International Pelagic Sealing Treaty. This treaty ruled that the Bering Sea was to be closed to all pelagic (open ocean) hunting of seals for the next fifteen years. The aboriginal inhabitants of the area were permitted to hunt using traditional methods, i.e., with spear and canoe. Americans could take a limited number of seals on the Pribilof Islands, and the Russians on Robbens Island. In return for keeping its ships from the sealing grounds, Canada was to be given 15 per cent of the catch.

Thus, with the signing of the treaty in July 1911, thousands of men lost their livelihood. Valuable schooners became floating liabilities. Some, like the *Borealis,* were converted into halibut schooners. Others became rumrunners. Many rotted. However, even before the treaty was signed, the *Beatrice* had retired from the sealing industry. It was rescued from the boneyard when the Butchart family set it to work as a lighter in Saanich Inlet. In 1908 it was bought by Captain Albert Berquist of Sidney, on Vancouver Island. Berquist rebuilt boats for a hobby and a living. He was helped by his sister, a fantastically strong woman who could push a shipwright's plane as well as any man. The two cut down the *Beatrice*'s masts, built a deckhouse and installed a 200-horse-power oil-burning steam engine. Thus began the *Beatrice*'s career as a tug. In 1962, Harold Clay bought the *Beatrice*. The ship had been gutted by fire while laid up at the North Vancouver ferry dock in 1958. At the time the fire appeared disastrous, destroying the wheelhouse and much of the deck. In the long term, though, the blaze may have done for the old ship what fires do to grassland—reinvigorated it. Clay rebuilt the wheelhouse and refitted the ship with a diesel engine. He changed the name to the *Arrawac Freighter* and used it to carry everything from frozen strawberries to diesel engines upcoast.

Keen to use the *Arrawac Freighter*'s ample hold, Joe Moyles bought the ship in 1972 and set it to packing sea urchins and clams on Vancouver Island's west coast.

In 1981, the *Arrawac Freighter* was bought by Doug Hartley, who renamed it *Beatrice* and used it for gentler purposes, including training oceanographers from Royal Roads Military College.

The *Beatrice*'s semi-retirement ended in the early 1990s, when it was sold to David Francis, a former sea urchin diver who returned it to service packing sea urchins. Francis skippered the *Beatrice* on every trip, except the last. In April 1993, the *Beatrice* snapped its reverse gearshift and put into Prince Rupert for repairs. Francis, whose wife was ill, flew home. When the shipyard called early to say the ship was ready, Francis told his engineer to take it across to the Queen Charlottes to fetch a load of sea urchins. On the way back the ship was caught in a gale. When the engine made an unusual sound the engineer went to investigate. The engine room was thigh deep in water. A hull plank had opened, and water was coming in so fast two pumps could not keep up. Attempts were made to take the *Beatrice* under tow to Masset, but by the time the ship reached the dock the stern was awash. The vessel was secured with heavy lines and the crew left. But it was too heavy. The hawsers snapped and the *Beatrice* rolled into the current, where it was swept away. Later, using a sounder, Francis scanned Masset Inlet for the hull but came up empty. Because there wasn't a ticketed master on board when the *Beatrice* ran into trouble, there was no insurance. Thus ended the legacy of one of the oldest vessels on the coast.

The *Beatrice*, renamed the *Arrawac Freighter*, moored at Victoria in 1969.
Vancouver Maritime Museum

OOLICHAN GREASE

by Howard White

Oolichan grease gold, you hear about it
how the Tsimshian empire held
the whole coast to ransom for it
brought the poor stick Indians begging
from the interior, beating paths
between the mountains you could
follow in the dark, by nose
the "grease trails" that let the
white man in, later on—
a beautiful woman professor told me about it
paler than butter she said,
but like butter without salt
and not at all repugnant to
the European palate
used as a condiment
but I ask you, are empires
sustained by condiments?
It was their oil, for the flame
in the flesh and more
                    I found it finally
in Bella Bella 1976 price $48/gal.
and it smelled like the cracks
between the deck planks of an old fish barge
if you can imagine spreading that
on your bread—quite enough to hurl
the European palate toward the nearest
toilet bowl which is how far
Indian is from White how far
learning is from knowing how
far we are from this ragged place
we've taken from them, for that,
the smell of fish left in the sun
and let go bad, that is the old
smell of the coast, known, as scent
is the final intimacy known of lifelong mates

take that barge plank, let it toss
ten years on the tide, knock on every rock
from Flattery to Yakutat, bake another
ten in the sun, take it rounded like
an Inuit ivory and grey as bone
crack it open and sniff the darker core
and you will know
what Vancouver knew ducking through
his first Nootka door pole, the essence
the odour of their living here
and however far you are from loving that
is how far you are
                    from arriving

Processing oolichan on the Nass River,
ca. 1884.

*Image C-07433 courtesy of the Royal BC
Museum, BC Archives*

From Writing in the Rain *(1990), by Howard White*

NAMING ROCKS THE HARD WAY

12

Excerpted from The Encyclopedia of Raincoast Place Names:
A Complete Reference to Coastal British Columbia *(2009), by Andrew Scott*

Having a coastal feature named for you is normally a great honour. Having a rock or reef named for you, however, can be somewhat of a disgrace. According to nautical tradition, if you manage to wreck your boat on an uncharted rock, that rock is named for you—or, more commonly, for your vessel. But this really only happens if your boat is quite large or if you are important enough for notoriety to ensue. Usually the rock or reef in question has already been named for some unfortunate earlier wreckee.

The BC coast is littered with rocks that commemorate marine mishaps and enshrine the shame of certain skippers. At the entrance to Mantrap Inlet in Fitz Hugh Sound is Barracuda Rock, where the survey launch *Barracuda* came to grief. The British merchant steamer *Benmohr* "grazed" Ben Mohr Rock in Trincomali Channel west of Galiano Island, and the *Wellington* did the same to Wellington Rock in Seaforth Channel. The venerable Union steamship *Cutch*, originally built as a pleasure craft for an Indian maharaja, had the dubious honour in 1899 of christening Cutch Rock in Metlakatla Bay near Prince Rupert. The steamship *Danube* crashed into Danube Rock in Skidegate Inlet, and later, renamed the *Salvor*, became a specialist in salvaging wrecks on reefs. The list goes on and on.

Danube Rock in Skidegate Inlet is named for the steamship *Danube*, shown here at Port Essington, ca. 1898.

Image D-01382 courtesy of the Royal BC Museum, BC Archives

Most ships with rocks named for them survive their fraught encounters. They are refloated by rising tides or pulled off by tugs and taken to dry dock for repair. Many go on to give long and eventful service. The 130-foot patrol boat *Armentières*, for instance, spent much of its life on the BC coast. In 1925 it struck unreported Armentières Rock in Pipestem Inlet and sank, but was raised, towed to Victoria and refitted. Forty years later it was still at work, though under a different name.

Other reef-bound vessels are less fortunate and suffer tremendous damage. Consider the uss *Suwanee*, an iron sidewheeler that had been built during the US Civil War for river use, with a shallow draft and front-and-rear rudders. On its way to Alaska in 1868, the warship became firmly grounded on an unmarked rock (known today, of course, as Suwanee Rock) in Shadwell Passage off the north end of Vancouver Island. As the tide dropped, the ship broke in half and was utterly destroyed. The crew survived, and salvage operations retrieved the guns, ammunition and machinery. The wreck has been a popular dive site for years, and artifacts from the *Suwanee* adorn the homes and gardens of several recreational divers.

If you're a ship captain, a far easier method of attaching your name to a dangerous rock or reef is to discover the threat without getting wrecked and then report it to the Coast Guard. Thus we have Marchant Rock in Hecate Strait, spotted in 1869 by master George Marchant while he was ashore enjoying breakfast on dry land. Hewitt Rock in Finlayson Channel and McCulloch Rock in Dixon Entrance received their names after captains James Hewitt and William McCulloch, respectively, located these menaces and described them to naval officials.

It is possible, should you end up on some reef, to avoid having your name, or your

A painting by Edward Bedwell, second master of HMS *Plumper*, shows the ship aground at Discovery Island.

Image A-00238 courtesy of the Royal BC Museum, BC Archives

vessel's name, printed on the charts for fellow mariners to chuckle over until the end of time. Just blame the person who sent you on your journey! The success of this strategy can be seen in the name of a rock in Trincomali Channel. HMS *Plumper* was anchored at Nanaimo in 1859 when its master, Captain George Richards, received an urgent order from Governor James Douglas to return to Victoria. En route, at full speed, the *Plumper* hit a rock where there weren't supposed to be any. Damage was negligible, fortunately. Richards and his officers felt that it was Douglas who had ordered the voyage, and Douglas, not them, who should forever be associated with the site of the accident. They named the hazard Governor Rock.

13

DRAMA AT
MISSION POINT

Excerpted from That Went By Fast: My First 100 Years *(2014), by Frank White*

Back in Abbotsford it didn't take long to run through the small savings we had left and I was back feeling the pinch to get some money coming in. I decided to go drop in on Charlie Philp. I'd worked for him before and knew he was always mixed up in some side action in the woods. When I walked into his office, he was on the phone listening to quite a tale of woe by the sound of it. "That bad, eh? That's tough. Well, I wish there was something I could do..." Then he looks up at me and it's like a light bulb went on. "Well, just a minute, somebody just walked into my office—let me call you back."

Me, back in the day.
Harbour Publishing Archives

So he sits me down and pours me a drink and treats me like a long-lost friend and eventually he gets around to talking about this pretty decent little camp on Nelson Island sitting on some damn fine timber but the guys just aren't cutting the mustard—they're a couple of moonlighting teachers and they're screwing everything up. Charlie's got some money tied up in the operation and he needs somebody up there who knows how to get logs in the water. This time Charlie is talking about a partnership deal with me right from the start. So we agree I will go up and size things up, get the camp on its feet and decide whether I want to get in any deeper. I found the idea attractive.

The truck-logging boom that had started back on Vedder Mountain in 1939 was still flooding the BC woods with small operators, and a lot of guys I'd worked with were

86

running their own shows and making good dough. Well actually, it turns out most of them were not making good dough, or any dough, but that was not the story they told when you met them in the beverage room of the Rainier Hotel. It looked good to me and I wanted to get in on it.

I'd proved to Charlie I could run a camp, and logging was the one place I could see where a man could still make it if he played his cards right and worked hard. I had all the tools, I knew that—I knew every part of logging, except the business part of selling the logs, but Charlie could help me learn the ropes there. I was wary of Charlie; if there was a dollar to be had, his idea was not to split it with you but to take all of it, but I should be getting to where I could deal with that by now. If this was any kind of a camp, and Charlie assured me it was a great location with plenty of untouched timber, this might just be the opening I'd been looking for.

I had never heard of Nelson Island before and had to get a map to look it up, figuring it would be one of these little islands you could spit across, of which the BC coast has too many to remember. I was quite surprised to find Nelson Island was actually one of the larger islands in the Gulf of Georgia, bigger than Gabriola, Denman or Lasqueti and only a little smaller than Saltspring. It had hardly any people living on it and no villages, only a few gyppo logging camps and a couple small resorts. It was on the mainland side of the gulf, about sixty miles north of Vancouver, kind of blocking the mouth of Jervis Inlet. It had a lot of bays, lagoons, basins and lakes, and Charlie's camp was tucked into a little nook on the south side called Green Bay. The timber was pretty much untouched except for a little handlogging in the early days, but it was nothing like the first growth I'd seen on Vedder Mountain. It was very stunted and scrubby around the edges where it was exposed to the ocean winds, but the interior had some heavy stands that would make for nice logging once you worked your way into it.

The nearest settlement to Green Bay was the fishing village of Pender Harbour, seven miles down Agamemnon Channel, which had several stores, a post office, schools and a hospital. It was too far from Pender Harbour to get the kids to the schools, which would be a problem since my daughter Marilyn was going into Grade 3 and my son Howie would be starting Grade 1 in a year. My wife, Kay, was game as usual—she was always ready to move on to the next thing, especially if it looked like it might finally work into a decent opportunity. She was in top form and ready to do her part, whatever that might be.

There was a steamer service to Pender Harbour, not Union Steamships, the famous pioneer steamboat company that settled the BC coast, which was already cutting back on its routes by this time, but a newer outfit called the Gulf Lines that had three war surplus ships all called the Gulf something—Mariner, Wing and one they'd already lost when it slammed into Dinner Rock off Powell River a few years before, the *Gulf Stream*. The *Gulf Mariner* and the *Gulf Stream* were minesweepers and the *Gulf Wing*, which we would get to know all too well, was a Fairmile, a smaller, wooden class of sub-chaser around 100 feet long and narrow, maybe twenty feet wide. For a while, the war surplus Fairmiles were all over the place but you seldom see one now.

For this first trip Charlie said I wouldn't have to worry about the Gulf Lines because they had a new camp boat I could run from Vancouver up to the camp. As a Fraser

Valley boy, boats were not my thing and I had never run a boat that far before, so this was a bit of a challenge. Still, I'd run boats for short distances here and there and was at home with motors so I thought that was fine. I packed my bag, picked up the usual collection of machinery parts and logging supplies around town, and drove down to Granville Island where Charlie's truck yard was and where this boat was tied up at a place called Clay's Wharf, a grimy False Creek institution that persisted into recent times.

It wasn't hard to spot my command, even among the peeling derelicts that populated Clay's Wharf. It looked like a typical gyppo logging camp boat, a sad-looking thirty-two-foot hulk on its last stop before the boneyard. It was a long, narrow-gutted, low-slung thing with a drooping bow, long passenger cabin with big square windows—several of which had lost their glass—and a V-to-flat bottom with the chines built out to form little sponson-wings toward the stern. This was an unusual feature I later found made handy shock absorbers for knocking against logs, although I'm sure the designer had some higher purpose in mind. There was no name or numbers painted on it, though I learned it had been one of a pair of quite famous sister ships, one called the *White Hawk* and the other the *Black Hawk*. I never did know which one this was, because for reasons I could never imagine somebody had renamed it the *Suez*. I should have expected trouble from a boat named after an Egyptian ditch.

What the *Hawk* boats had been famous for was speed. The *Suez* had originally been powered by an Allison V12 airplane engine that was said to push forty knots, making it the fastest boat in Vancouver Harbour. It was supposedly built to serve as a water taxi for running log scalers back and forth between Vancouver and the big log-sort grounds in Howe Sound, although I met people who insisted that had only been a cover story for its real purpose, which was running booze into Puget Sound during Prohibition. Certainly it had the classic design of a lot of rumrunners—their idea back then was to get speed by making the hull long and narrow so it would cut through the water; they hadn't come up with the idea of the planing hull yet.

The big Allison had long since been replaced by the standard cheap boat power of the day, a six-cylinder Chrysler Crown salvaged from a wrecked car, which drove it at a plodding seven knots. The engine conversion was typically haywire with straight sea-water cooling and a dry manifold that used to get so hot it glowed red, which proved handy for brewing coffee. We even used to fry eggs and make toast on it. There was no motor cover—it ran too hot to be shut up and I wondered how they kept spray from coming in through the missing windows and killing the engine.

I didn't know much about boats at that point but I knew enough to see this was a boat best used in calm water, and I had a little twinge of concern thinking about the kind of long crossing through open water I was about to attempt in it. The marina owner's son, a smartass kid who manned the gas pump, didn't do anything to ease my nerves.

"You're not taking this thing out today, are you?" he chirped. "Where you taking it? Nelson Island? You're nuts. I wouldn't go across the harbour in this floating coffin today. Have you even checked the weather?"

He jabbered away like a squeaky young crow without waiting for answers. As a

Once the pride of Vancouver's water taxi fleet, the MV *Suez* was a typical sad-sack camp boat by the time I took charge of her.

Harbour Publishing Archives

matter of fact, I hadn't thought to check the weather beyond the farmer's forecast, which consisted of a quick glance at the sky, but I wasn't about to give this sawed-off little shit the satisfaction and made like I knew what I was doing. He just shook his head and said, "So long, buddy. It's been nice knowing ya. Any last words for your wife and kids? I'll keep this space open in case you come to your senses and turn around."

This was Harold Clay Jr., a.k.a. Squeak, who in later years would move to Pender Harbour and carry on where he'd left off getting under my skin. He was honestly one of the most annoying individuals I ever had the misfortune to know, and the most annoying thing about him was that he was just about as smart as he thought he was, at least around anything to do with boats.

I wasn't out under the Lions Gate Bridge before I realized there was no way I should be out there in that punky old wreck. There was a pretty good southeaster blowing up and the clouds were black and menacing. I only had a sketch map that Charlie'd pencilled on the back of a letter because the route was supposed to be so simple, but the vista of low grey humps I saw before me now bore no resemblance to the map. There was an unreliable-looking little car compass mounted on the dash that seemed to be working, and checking it against the map I picked out what I thought must be the left side of Bowen Island and the mountains of the Sunshine Coast beyond.

It looked like a thousand miles of ugly cross-seas I had to survive before I got to the next shelter, and I think I would have turned around and gone back if it hadn't meant having to face the taunts of that smartass kid. The old *Suez* was no good in a beam sea—it was no good in a following sea or a head sea either—and all the cargo

I'd packed was soon flying around and falling into the bilge, and spray was pouring into the cockpit, which was open and had no self-bailers. I couldn't let go of the wheel to run back and save anything or check the bilge, which I could tell was getting full by the sloshing sounds. I had to keep plowing grimly ahead until I was past Bowen and coming up on those little islands off Gibsons where I could get some shelter and stow things a little better and bail the bilge.

I'd been pinning my hopes on reaching Gibsons where I could wait out the blow, but it was still early in the day by the time I got there and I hated to quit. I got things nice and shipshape and figured what the hell, I might as well keep going and at least get a little closer to my destination. The trouble with this plan was that I was about to enter what towboaters call "The Stretch," which is the thirty miles of exposed shoreline between Gibsons and Secret Cove where there is no sheltered moorage. I had a vague idea about this from what some towboaters had told me in the pub but I figured I had a good six hours of daylight, which would be plenty of time to get me to Secret Cove or Pender Harbour where there would be good shelter for the night.

I might even make it all the way to Green Bay if things went well. What did vaguely bother me was this was all lee shore, meaning if the motor conked out the wind would blow you up on the beach, but so far the old Chrysler Crown was purring along like a champ so I figured I might as well keep pushing. I've never been good at resisting the temptation to squeeze in an extra mile before dark.

The weather had all been coming at me from the port side, which was the boat's good side—there were no missing windows. What I discovered as I turned up past Gower Point and started along toward Roberts Creek was that the seas were now behind me. The *Suez* had a full stern and a narrow bow which made it hell to handle in a following sea, and not only that, the cabin was completely open at the back and now the spray was funnelling into the boat and hissing where it hit the hot motor. Again I was in the position where I couldn't take my hands off the wheel, the way the boat was wallowing around. That bleak, menacing shore seemed to go on forever. The boat seemed to be dead in the water, even though the motor was grinding away as normal.

I was discovering what a lot of unhappy mariners discovered about The Stretch—it's only thirty miles but in a southeaster with an ebbing tide it can seem like three hundred. The current runs two knots against you on an ebb tide, reducing the old *Suez*'s net speed over bottom to five knots, and less than that once you subtracted all the zigzags it was making in the following sea. I cut in close to the steamer dock at Roberts Creek but there was no safe tie-up there that I could see. There was a bit of a haywire breakwater around the Jackson Brothers booming ground at Wilson Creek but the tide was out and it looked too shallow so I kept chugging. I don't know what gets into a guy that makes you want to keep pushing, keep heading into a worsening situation rather than pulling back when you have the chance. There's something so tempting about sticking to your plan even after it's gone all to hell, the momentum of the trip that is so hard to resist.

The three hours had stretched into four and the afternoon light was draining away. As I came up to a couple of wave-washed rocks called White Islets feeling very lonely and exposed with nothing but open sea before me as far as the eye could see and foaming shore on my starboard side, the motor developed a miss. I dashed back to give it a ten-second check, saw nothing, then dashed back to grab the wheel as the boat began to yaw. The miss got worse. The motor was now running only on four cylinders.

I crawled along the coast in the fading light, desperately checking the map and the shore for a place to get a little shelter where I could throw out an anchor—I did have a rusty little thing with hardly any chain and rotten-looking rope—and like so many a sailor before me, I pinned my hopes on reaching the Trail Islands off Sechelt, where it looked like a guy might get a little shelter. If I'd been doing it now, I would have swung way out and got as far from shore as possible, but the greenhorn's first impulse when he's in trouble is to hug in close to shore, not realizing that is your worst enemy if

you lose power. Too late I saw breakers ahead and realized I was running into some kind of shallows way out in the strait where there should have been deep water. I swung to port and took seas hard on the beam, holding my breath with every sputter and miss of the motor.

I wasn't a praying man, even in a spot like that, so I had to make do with yelling, "Come on you son of a bitch, hang in there, don't quit now..." But quit is exactly what it did. I hit the starter and got it going and it went a few hundred feet then quit again. I birled the starter till it started to run out of battery then went out into the stern. I had almost got clear of the spit, which I learned later was Mission Point, the gravel bar formed by the region's largest watershed, but the tide was pulling me right back into it. I searched around madly in the wallowing boat and found a broken pike pole about six feet long. I was able to hold the boat off for a while but it was a losing battle.

Finally, just as the boat was about to start crunching on the gravel bar, I jumped overboard and stood on the spit trying to hold it off. That worked better than the pole but it took a brutal effort with the boat surging and twisting, as if madly wanting to wreck itself. It was now completely dark. I hadn't passed another boat in hours, though there were house lights twinkling along the shore. I don't know how many hours I stood there in that freezing water. I don't know what I thought I was trying to accomplish. I was just trying to save the punky old wreck of a boat, which Charlie had probably traded for a couple truck tires.

The author jumped overboard and tried to push the boat off the spit.
Kim La Fave illustration

I don't know why a man does things like this. If I'd been thinking straight I would have realized I was risking my health if not my life, risking leaving my wife and kids without a breadwinner—and for what? Just to complete a mission, just to not have to phone Charlie—a man who'd cut your throat in a minute if you stood between him and a buck—and tell him I'd lost his junk heap of a boat. But you don't think in a spot like that, at least I didn't. I was always ready to sacrifice myself for the worst broken-down hunk of equipment in the most hopeless goddamn situation.

I don't think I actually hatched a plan so much as my feet found it. Luckily Mission Point is a gravel bar with few large boulders, or the boat would have been kindling. But as I kept pushing the boat out, the waves kept shoving it upcoast, the tide was coming in now, and the water started to get deeper. I somehow managed to drag my half-dead carcass back in and went back to the pike pole. I was now around the point and going down the windward side of the spit, which wasn't so rough. I'd been noticing some kind of structure farther up the shore, and as I got closer I could make out another big steamer dock like the one at Roberts Creek, jutting out into the water. After another hour or so I had worked the boat around to the dock, where I got it tied off to a piling.

I was just about done for. I didn't know what hypothermia was then but I'm sure I had it to the nth degree. I couldn't feel myself. My feet were like pieces of wood. My skin was dead, like canvas. My brain felt like I'd been on a week-long drunk. I was shaking so bad I couldn't close my hands on a knife to cut bread, so I just grabbed handfuls. I felt different than I had ever felt before. I felt like I'd broken something inside myself. I was used to asking a lot of my body and it had always delivered, but it felt like this time I had just asked too much. I was scared. I wondered if I would be found in the morning dead from exposure.

Then I got my eyes focused on shore and realized there was something there called Davis Bay Inn, or something along those lines. A warm bed. Hot food. I had no idea what time it was but I figured I better make an effort to get ashore because I might not make it through the night otherwise. There was nothing to do but swim for it, which wasn't as bad as it seemed because it's shallow there and my feet hit bottom before I got halfway in. The door to the inn was locked, so I pounded and shouted till I got somebody up. A guy stuck his head out of a window.

"We're closed," he says.

"Look, I'm in bad shape," I stammered, my tongue so thick I could hardly talk. "I just about lost my boat and I need to get warm…"

"We're closed," he says again. "If you want a room, go up to the lodge. They'll take you."

"Where's…the lodge?" I said.

"Top of the hill. Can't miss it." *Slam.*

So I drag my shivering ass up Davis Bay hill, which seemed like Mount Everest, and I get into this little flophouse where they're not too overly thrilled to see me either, but they give me a bed and I eventually stop shaking enough to sleep.

The next day it's sunny and calm. The boat is sitting innocently alongside the wharf, still as a picture. I find a skiff on the beach and paddle out with a piece of driftwood for an oar. It's easy to see why the motor stopped. It's white with dried salt

from the blown spray. Every spark plug is shorted out. It's a wonder it ran as long as it did. I clean up the plugs and wiring real well, knowing I don't have much battery, but it starts right off and purrs like a kitten. For some time, the asshole from the inn has been standing on the shore shouting about his skiff so I grab the stubby pike pole and paddle it in.

"What the hell do you think you're doing?" the guy says. "That dinghy is for inn guests only."

I get up good and close to him and say, "How would you like a punch in the god-damned nose?" I really wanted to give it to him too, and I guess he could tell because he was suddenly a whole bunch more understanding and agreed to row me back out.

It was a beautiful day without a ripple in sight. It was hard to believe this was the same ocean as the day before, and it also made me realize what a damn fool I was to be out on it. All I had to do was listen to Squeak and wait twenty-four hours. I felt good about having survived the ordeal but I had that strange feeling that I had strained something inside that was never going to be 100 per cent right again. It was an odd feeling, one I'd never had before.

Looking back, I can admit something that I wouldn't have admitted then, and that is that I was past my peak. I was thirty-five and at a point where a man's physical abilities start to go into decline. I'd always been sound as a dollar physically but now I started to have a lot of back trouble. Already I'd lost the ability to sleep, and I was tired a lot. I had stiff joints in the morning. And somewhere around then I started to experience the first twinges of phantom pain in my face, a tic that would become more familiar over the years. I still had forty years of working life in me as it turned out, but it worries a young guy when he encounters his first whiff of mortality. It wasn't an auspicious start to this new phase in our lives.

The *Suez* tied up at the Green Bay logging camp.
Harbour Publishing Archives

14 MAXINE MATILPI: CAPSIZED IN SEYMOUR NARROWS

Excerpted from Working the Tides: A Portrait of Canada's West Coast Fishery *(1996), by Vickie Jensen*

I've been fishing for most of my life. My grandfather Henry Speck was a fisherman. My father, Charlie Matilpi Sr., was a fisherman. All my brothers fished. My first husband was a fisherman. He operated the seine boat *The Star of Wonder*.

The accident happened when we were out on James Walkus's boat *Miss Joye*. It was my first season for herring, and it was probably the third week we were out, near the end of November. There were seven adults on the boat: Kenny Lambert and his father, Forest; Bruce Rafuse; Gary McGill; Fred Anderson (my ex); myself and Kenny's wife, Betty, with her six-month-old baby, Jason.

It was rough that morning, and we had travelled all night from Ganges because James wanted us to go to Deepwater Bay. He'd said that the first boat to catch thirty-five tons would get to go home after delivering to Vancouver and would get the week-end off. *Miss Joye* was the first one to catch the tons, but instead of us going home, James pumped the herring from our boat to his boat and travelled south to deliver while we travelled in the opposite direction.

We were supposed to stop in at Campbell River for at least a couple hours for all the

The *Miss Joye* was headed north to Deepwater Bay to seine for herring when disaster struck.

Rick Tanaka photo

crew members to get proper rest, to get groceries and fuel up. Betty and I and the baby were in the galley, and we thought for sure we were going to pull in to Campbell River. But as we got closer we looked out the window and Betty said, "Holy shit! We're going through instead of stopping." The tide was running at its full ebb through Seymour Narrows, but we kept on going.

It seemed like not even five, ten minutes into the Narrows when we hit the first whirlpool. It was ever so slow. We didn't know what we had hit then, but when we came creeping back to position and travelled farther along, we could see it. We had rolled way over, so that if the window had been open, we could have touched water. We just braced ourselves. Betty said, "Oh my God, I hope nothing happens to me." I said, "Betty, don't talk like that." For some reason she felt fear that day, and she was not a person who was easily scared.

Kenny was the captain. As we were going through, he was on the radio trying to talk to James to tell him that we were going through rather than stopping to wait for the tide to slacken off. We were trying to hug the shore. Bruce was on the wheel. It seemed like it took all his effort to control the boat. I remember looking into the pilot house, and Kenny had his legs braced far apart. Normally, a lot of boats will pull back the throttle, shut the engine off and just glide through. But for some reason that morning while Bruce was on the wheel, the throttle wasn't pulled back until we almost were into the second whirlpool. Fred, my ex, had just gone to bed along with the other crew member, Gary. Forest was awake; he was the engineer. We'd had engine problems that night, so he kept getting up to check on it.

That boat was so cranky, so top heavy, that anything could've happened even before we got to Seymour Narrows. Plus we didn't put the net in the hatch to stabilize the boat. Then we hit the second whirlpool. The first one that got thrown was the baby, who was sitting in between us on a table in a cuddle seat. He went flying and hit his forehead on a counter by the sink. Betty and I got thrown, too. She was the one that was closest to the stove. I remember there was a huge pot of boiling water on, plus there was a big kettle that was almost to the boiling point because we were planning to make stew for dinner that day. We were sprawled out on the galley floor, which was at an angle. She kept on saying, "Keep his head out of the water. Push him up." But by the time we got hold of Jason, he was already limp. I knew right then and there he was dead.

You could feel the boat tipping over more and more, then the water started gushing through. It seemed like it came from the pilot house first. I just remember feeling the cold, cold water. Betty was by the stove, and the big pot dumped all over the right side of her body. All she kept on saying was, "Oh my God, oh my God. Keep his head out of the water."

I could hear Kenny trying to talk to James, but the phone was breaking up terribly. By then the throttle got pulled back. When the engine shuts off, a bell rings in the engine room. My ex heard it and came running up in his underwear, saying, "What the hell is going on here?" We were ankle deep in water. Betty picked up the baby, and Kenny came right behind Fred and said, "Every man for himself. Get out of the boat. Get out of the boat. We're going to sink."

Kenny and Betty and the baby went toward the pilot house to get out that way. Fred and I were in the galley, trying to open the galley door, but there was too much water pressure. So we grabbed a frying pan and kept banging the window by the sink, but it just kept bouncing off. By then we were almost standing on the stove. The water was coming up fast, really fast. We were three-quarters upside down by then. By the time it got to our chests, we were completely capsized. I don't know how many times we tried to get out of that window, and we just couldn't. Finally, we just hung on to the lazy Susan with our noses pressed right up against the floor to get any air.

I don't think it took that boat fifteen minutes to completely capsize. Meanwhile, Bruce, Gary and Forest got out of the boat. The net had already started to unwind from the drum. Bruce had a pocketknife on him so he was able to cut himself out of the net. That saved his life.

Forest got free of the boat but was too exhausted to swim back to it. He hung on to this wooden refrigerator box, but the current was too strong. The last they saw him, he was hanging on to this box. When they turned around, he was gone. He never surfaced again.

In the galley, I could feel somebody tugging at my legs. I thought this person who was tugging on me wanted to breathe, so I kinda kicked my feet to let them know there was air up here. But I was too afraid to go under the water. That happened twice, and then the person just quit. I thought it was Betty, maybe, but it was actually my ex. He had dove under and finally kicked the window out after we ran out of air. The window was quarter-inch-thick Plexiglas; he didn't realize that he had cut his foot badly, all the way around. He cut a main artery. When he got up to the surface, the crew members helped him to get to the keel; that's when he realized that he was bleeding. The cold water saved him from bleeding to death.

All three guys were on top of the bottom of the boat by then. Underwater, I found

This photo taken from a Coast Guard rescue helicopter shows the upturned hull of the *Miss Joye,* in which Maxine Matilpi was trapped for two and a half hours.
Courtesy of Maxine Matilpi

my way to the pilot house. The interesting part was when I decided to leave the galley, it seemed like I felt my grandfather's presence, Henry Speck. For some reason I just had to follow this feeling that told me to get to some light. So I dove down and saw this light like a lantern, and I followed it. I came up to the surface, ready to burst, and sure enough, I had at least five feet of air in the pilot house. I stood on the wheel, but water started coming up really fast. That's when I started to panic and screamed, "Please God. Please God. Don't let me die." I thought of my uncle who had drowned years ago and what he must have gone through.

When water got past my nose, I thought, "Now I'm going to die. This boat's going to sink, and they're never going to find me." So I dove down again. Again I followed this feeling that my grandfather was there guiding me. This time I swam toward the engine room. It was pitch black down there. There's a kind of wraparound stairway, and as soon as I got to it I knew exactly where I was. I just collapsed. I had no energy. I couldn't even lift my legs up.

There was some breathing air. I felt around in the pitch black and knew I was in the engine room. I told myself, "You've got to get out of the water or you're going to have hypothermia and go into shock." I felt around some more and realized I could get myself out of the water completely, so I did.

I started to get super cold. A mattress, clothing, blankets and a sleeping bag floated by. I got back into the water and with all my effort lugged the sleeping bag out of the water, wrung it out and put it around me. The funny part was that I had to pee so bad. I don't know why I didn't just pee my pants, but I struggled to get my pants down before I realized how silly that was. I ended up peeing myself and that's what really warmed me. In the meantime, diesel was coming into my nose, my ears. Every time I touched them, they were just slimy. I could taste it in my mouth. It got into my eyes a bit, and every time I blinked they started to sting. All the fumes were making me really sleepy.

Just then, I found this wooden object and started banging away on the hull. I kept banging away, shouting, "I'm alive. I'm alive. I'm down here." Bruce and Kenny heard me and answered, "We're going to come and get you. You just hang in there." But when they didn't show up, I fell asleep. They thought I'd died.

I must have slept twenty minutes at the most. When I woke up again, that's when reality hit. This wasn't a bad dream. I told myself, "You have to get yourself out of here." So I tried. I got to the washroom and made three attempts to get out of the porthole there. Then I went back to where I was before.

When I got back to the engine room, they yelled to me that four divers were coming

Today, Maxine Matilpi and her partner, John Livingston, create Northwest Coast Native art and regalia.
Courtesy of Maxine Matilpi

through and to stay put but try to be kind of visible, to make a ripple to let them know exactly where I was. So I had to leave the engine room and go back into the water by the stairway. A diver found me and told me that the boat was slowly sinking and we would have to get out within a few minutes. He asked me if I'd ever scuba dived. When I said, "No," he explained how we would buddy breathe. I was wrapped around him as we were going up. I didn't realize how deep we were. I think we were about twenty, twenty-one feet under the surface.

The boat was upside down and the hull was still visible. The diver who saved my life gave me a picture of it later. They got me on *Tamanawas*, a boat standing by, and there was a doctor aboard. I was so cold and all I wanted to do was sleep, but he wouldn't let me. Somebody wanted to give me rum or rye and another suggested a hot shower, but the doctor told them either one would give me cardiac arrest. They took off the wet clothing that I had on, put on these huge pants and a shirt, and got ready to hoist me up to a helicopter.

I insisted that the diver who found me come up with me. I hung on for dear life. I remember him telling me not to look down, but I did.

I could hardly believe it, seeing the situation from the air. I had been in the capsized boat for two and a half hours. I had travelled almost the whole of Seymour Narrows going round and round and round. Forest and Betty and the baby were dead.

After the inquest into the accident, I talked to the diver who rescued me. He came up to me and said, "You probably don't recognize me. I'm the one that got you out of the boat." I just gave him a big hug. I got choked up because I wanted to say so many things at once. I thanked him for my life, and he said, "Well, that's my job." I heard that five or six years later he died.

Shortly after the accident, I got pregnant with my son Aubrey and went right back out fishing. But it was with great difficulty, and it was with great pain and fear. Surviving the capsizing has made me appreciate life. I don't take anything for granted. I was lucky to have the two children I've always wanted, and that's what made life go on for me.

Corporal J.C. Lemay was one of three divers awarded a medal for bravery for this rescue effort. Sadly, Corporal Lemay was awarded his posthumously, as he went missing during a training dive and is presumed dead.

SPLIT AND DELIVERED, OR DELIVER AND SPLIT

15

Excerpted from Dogless in Metchosin *(1995), by Tom Henry*

For the woodcutter, there can be no better month than November. The days are cool and, on the end of Vancouver Island, relatively dry. Mornings in the woodlot are marked by the sound of ravens, seagulls, red-tailed hawks. Always there is the gentle patter of leaves falling. If the sun is out, you might even work bareback, as much for the thrill of cheating the season as for any need.

Yesterday, after an afternoon of just such weather, I finished cutting cords number forty-nine and fifty. Then I helped Wayne deliver them to a customer in Colwood. We'd just begun heaving the wood off when the customer—a slight guy in his forties—mentioned it didn't look too dry. "I, um, I ordered dry wood," he said.

He was right, the stuff we were throwing off was a bit mushy. What he didn't understand was that in the topsy-turvy world of firewood, the customer is always wrong.

Wayne paused, mid-toss. "Look, if you don't want the wood, that's fine," he said. "I've got plenty of people who do." He wasn't kidding either. One ad in the paper and we'd got enough orders to keep going for a month. The customer jammed his hands in his pockets. "That's funny," he said. "That's exactly what a woodcutter said last year."

The biggest problem for woodcutters selling unseasoned cords or short cords is to get the wood off the truck and the money in the pocket before the buyer wises up.

Dave Alavoine illustration

And the oldest trick to distracting buyers—men anyway—is to ask them about their woodstove.

John Steinbeck once observed that a whole generation of American men grew up knowing more about the ignition system of a Model T than they did about the clitoris. Same holds true of men today, but substitute airtight woodstove for Model T. The passion longtime wood burners feel for their airtight stoves is surpassed only by their love of bragging about them. How much their Franklin holds, how long it'll burn without restoking, all recounted with a troubadour's affection.

Wood sellers understand this, and if they see a customer eyeing a chintzy load suspiciously, they will make a casual reference about woodstoves. That is usually enough to launch the buyer on a long-winded tangent. Meanwhile, off goes the wood, into the pocket goes the cash.

There's another way woodcutters gouge customers. A real cord should be stacked very tightly, with few air spaces. Just what this means, however, is a matter of interpretation. A woodcutter in Cowichan I worked for used to tell customers that the spaces between the pieces of wood could be large enough for a squirrel to fit through, but not large enough for a cat. That was for good loads. On poorly stacked loads, he'd change the standard to cats and raccoons. Another trick woodcutters use is a variation of the good cop, bad cop routine. Only with wood sellers, it's bad dog, badder dog.

The loaded wood truck backs into a nice surburban driveway. Two toothy dogs bail out. While one heads up the street after the neighbour's corgi, the other starts excavations in the rhododendron patch.

There's your dilemma: see three years of hard gardening ruined, or face five years' frosty relations with the lady up the street who owns the corgi. Either way, the distraction is enough to allow the wood to be heaved off and the woodcutter to collect the money.

Perhaps the best wood-selling scam isn't really a scam at all—unless you consider advertisements that associate drinking beer with fun-loving chicks and muscular dudes a scam.

The idea of sales, as I understand it, is to sell an idea, a concept. Motor homes, missiles, mushy wood, who cares. It's the notion, not the commodity, that needs to be marketed. And this is why so many woodcutters drive boneyard trucks and are missing front teeth. A cord of wood from Walmart? Bah. There's no chance, no adventure in that.

But a cord of wood from a guy named Randy, who returns your call from a pay phone? It's ripe.

The very best wood seller (notice I didn't say woodcutter) I've run into understood the importance of selling the image, not the product. Johnny sold wood in Victoria in the mid-1980s. His motto was: deliver and split, rather than split and delivered. Johnny drove the requisite crappy truck, with requisite dogs, and had the requisite smell. But Johnny went a step farther on the image thing and spray-painted a quote from Virgil on the side of his truck. And he kept a copy of Henry David Thoreau's *Walden* on the dash, cover up.

I sold wood with Johnny now and then, and it was as if people had been hoping all their wood-burning lives to meet such a person.

"You read *Walden*?"

"On your lunchtime? In the rain? On a log? Awwww."

As if *Walden* and dirty Stanfield's made for the ideal woodcutter.

Of course, those customers never wanted to discuss the finer points of *Walden*, which was a good thing, because Johnny knew as much about Thoreau as he did about ignition systems on Model Ts. But that didn't matter: The customer had bought a lousy cord from a real woodcutter. As Johnny himself once said, better that than a real cord from a lousy woodcutter.

But something makes me think customers may never catch on to woodcutters' tricks. Something makes me think that they don't want to. I've been cutting and selling firewood for sixteen years, and more than a few gyppo loads of wet wood have gone to the same customer year after year. "That wood you sold me last year was none too good," they'll say. "Couldn't burn it until February. Hope this is better." "You bet," I say. "Full cord, maybe a little more." This happens year after year. They must figure it's worth the price of a cord to see a woodcutter doing what he does best.

16 BACK TO THE LAND: WHEN HIPPIES CAME TO SOINTULA

Excerpted from Sointula: An Island Utopia *(1995), by Paula Wild*

Meeting the boat from outside was always an important part of Sointula life. In 1958 the Union Steamships were replaced by the *Island Princess*, a vehicle ferry that travelled between Sointula and Kelsey Bay once a day, hoisting cars on and off its deck with a large crane. When the *Island Princess* began unloading strange-looking people in the late 1960s, "meeting the ferry" took on a whole new meaning.

Jenny and Jim Green were operating an art gallery in San Francisco's Haight-Ashbury during the era of "free love" and "flower power" when Jim was drafted. The Greens piled their possessions into a Volkswagen van and made their way north seeking refuge and a safe place to raise their infant daughter. "We got off the ferry in Sointula in the middle of the night and there were lights and people everywhere," Jenny recalled. "It was 1968 and it seemed like half the town had stayed up all night waiting for the boat to come in."

"After we had been in Sointula for a few weeks we went to our first function at the Finnish Organization Hall," Jenny continued. "We opened the door and all this wonderful music came pouring out. At the top of the staircase were a couple of drunks brawling; they fell down the stairs and landed at our feet. It felt like we had stepped back in time into the Wild West."

Sointula residents gawked at the newcomers' funny cars, baggy clothes and beads, and frowned at the long, dirty hair that was prevalent on the men as well as the women. While non-Finns had moved to the island before, they had never arrived in such large numbers and they had never looked so unusual. The Greens and others like them were full-blown hippies, and most of the people in Sointula had never even seen bell-bottoms before. As well as looking odd, the new people acted differently too. They perplexed Co-op clerks by asking for "health food," and it didn't take the Greens long to determine that they were the only vegetarians in the entire fishing village.

The majority of the new people congregated in the outlying areas of Mitchell Bay and Kaleva Road. Some bought old farms; eighty acres with a few buildings, a tractor, a flock of chickens and maybe a cow could be purchased for $7,000. Others camped in plastic lean-tos, teepees or abandoned saunas.

The newcomers stuck to themselves, coming into town every couple of weeks to pick up their mail and shop at the Co-op store where most had their only contact with what they referred to as "real Sointula people." While the early Finns had advertised their utopia in the *Aika*, rumours of a hippie commune rippled down the coast by word of mouth. There was a lot of coming and going, creating the impression that there was a larger countercultural population on the island than there actually was.

As well as offering sanctuary from the United States draft and the lure of cheap land, Canada was also attractive for its socialized medical care. A trip to Sointula to

An old homestead with sauna and boat shed, 1974. Many saunas were located on the beach so only a few steps were required for that refreshing dip in the ocean.
Rick James photo

Above: A traditional Finnish home on Kaleva Road, 1978.
Rick James photo

Above right: Old Tom, the communist logger, lectures a hippie on "the dignity of the working man," 1974. The light bulb over the door indicated whether the variety store was open or closed.
Rick James photo

visit some friends convinced Kit and Stephanie Eakle to have their baby in British Columbia. They moved to Malcolm Island from California in May 1970, and at the end of the summer they were asked to caretake Jane and John McClendon's place. In 1969 the McClendons had bought an old homestead, which they used first as a summer home and later as a permanent residence. Their Kaleva farm was a destination point for a lot of the hippies, many believing that it was the site of an active commune. While that was not true, Jane did let people sleep on the farmhouse floor or in one of the outbuildings.

"People called Jane 'Mom' because she was a little bit older than the rest of us and she fed everyone," Stephanie said. "When Kit and I were caretaking their place, we felt obliged to continue that tradition. People would show up with two pounds of brown rice and ask to stay indefinitely. We were all city people and didn't really know much about living off the land."

The Eakles decided to have their baby at "home," an old sauna at the McClendons' that had been converted into a cabin, rather than at the hospital in Alert Bay. Other pregnant women were invited, Stephanie's parents came from California, and a sister arrived from New York. An ex-Vietnam medic promised to oversee the delivery but showed up two months late. "It was really exciting until complications set in and my parents had to charter a float plane to take me to Alert Bay," Stephanie recalled. "There was no ambulance on the island in those days, and we weren't connected enough with the locals to know anyone with a fishing boat."

In fact, the hippies' connections with the locals were varied. Many of the older generation of Finns were open and friendly. They looked beyond the long hair and strange clothes and saw people who wanted a simple lifestyle, whose dreams echoed their parents' ideals. They observed the newcomers buying the farms that their children had abandoned and watched while they cleared fields of timothy and wild grasses, repaired broken fences and windows and removed the rubble left from rambunctious teenagers dynamiting chimneys.

Willie Olney noted: "The hippie movement gave Sointula a complete freedom of fashion. They wore weird get-ups but they looked so comfortable. Pretty soon it seemed like everyone could wear whatever they wanted. Before the hippies came, women wore nylons all the time. People die in the winter and most of our funerals are outside. Women used to freeze in the wind and rain, but after the hippies were here for a while it was acceptable to wear pants."

While most of the older residents were accepting, their children were suspicious and sometimes hostile. They had worked hard to improve their lives and found it difficult to understand these strangers who turned their backs on the modern conveniences of life. To compound the matter, none of the new people seemed to have jobs, a fact that irritated and puzzled the hard-working Finns. Also, although only a small percentage of the hippies were draft dodgers, the locals believed otherwise. Many of the middle-aged men, more patriotic than pro-Vietnam, viewed the newcomers as cowards who wouldn't fight for their country. And then there were the rumours about drugs and free love.

"We felt frightened when the hippies came," Bonnie Nelson admitted. "We had to start locking our doors; we had heard stories about people going crazy on drugs. It seemed like there were a lot of them and everyone felt that life would change because of them."

"Life did change when the hippies came," Aileen Wooldridge stated. "Up until that time everybody knew each other and most people were related in some way. We were a tight-knit little community and all of a sudden there were all these other people. It couldn't stay the same. There was a lot of resentment because things were changing."

The youth of the island, in the rebellious years of their teens and early twenties, were openly curious about and even attracted to the hippies. Their interest further increased the tension between their parents and the "long hairs," who were held responsible for the drugs that were beginning to appear on the island.

"After we had been in Sointula for a while I screwed up enough courage to go to Granny's Cafe," Jenny reminisced. "I sat there for twenty minutes and was ignored— they wouldn't serve me. For the first time in my life I knew what it was like to be a minority. A few days later, though, I was walking down the street and there was this older Finn man walking toward me. I smiled at him, and his face just opened up in the most beautiful smile. I realized then that some of the problem was my own shyness and insecurity."

Other reactions to the hippies were more aggressive. There was talk of running them out of town. Local logging truck drivers played chicken with hippie vehicles travelling to Mitchell Bay, and a truck that broke down on the logging road was torched.

In the summer of 1971 an old cellar on Kaleva Road, home to an ever-changing group of hippies, was the site of a pre-dawn drug raid. Rumour had it that the RCMP found LSD hidden in the woodpile but chose to let the prime suspect escape. A few weeks later the cellar burned to the ground. No one was living there at the time and, although no charges were ever laid, most hippies believed that the fire was deliberately set by locals.

While members of the counterculture felt that some Malcolm Islanders were not friendly, they did not necessarily expect them to be and were satisfied as long as the hostilities didn't get out of control. Stephanie reflected: "We felt that the town was not

Right: Jimmy "Slim" Erickson (left), of Finnish descent, has coffee at Granny's Cafe with Walter Miller, an expatriate of Windsor, Ontario, and Miller's son Devin, January 1976.
Rick James photo

Below: The Geisreiters liked the look of what was going to be their barn so much that they made it their house instead. Wood for the house was obtained from their property and the beach as well as from the mill at Telegraph Cove. No nails were used in the construction of the house; all the wood was notched and pinioned instead.
Courtesy of the Geisreiter collection

friendly but we weren't either. We were raised in the city and didn't expect people to care about who we were. But the Finns were curious about us and some did want to be friends. I'm sure we alienated some of them with our attitudes."

Not all the newcomers to the island were hippies. There were others, a little older and with children of their own, who longed to return to the basic values of an earlier time. Dick and Bette Geisreiter, residents of Mendocino, California, bought the eighty-five-acre Halminen farm in 1968 and moved to the island two years later. "It was the era when people were going back to the land," Bette said. "We were burned out from working so hard and were looking for a slower lifestyle. All of our relatives thought we had lost our marbles, but really we had found them. The wonderful thing about Sointula was the simplicity; it was another age. When we got off the ferry a lot of people were there, including a woman wearing a big Mexican hat. Years later I found out that Doris Slider had heard that there were people from California on the boat and had worn that hat to make us feel at home."

Like the Tynjalas who moved from North Dakota in 1902, the Geisreiters brought all their

Dick and Bette Geisreiter and their sons, Billie and John, beginning a new life on Malcolm Island, 1970. *Courtesy of the Geisreiter collection*

worldly possessions with them. Their caravan included five cars, a Volkswagen van converted into a chuckwagon, an old telephone van and a one-ton truck filled with tools and windows for the house they were building. Accompanying the couple were their three sons, friends to drive all the vehicles, Zeke the dog, plus thirteen goats with six kids. Bette said, "We picked the best stock to take with us. To get the goats into Canada, Dick had to dip them in a sulphur solution. I guess that sterilized their skin; it sure turned them a nice lime green."

Everyone who moved to the island attempted to live a self-sufficient lifestyle. Most chopped their own firewood, planted large gardens and canned their surplus produce. "At that time getting back to the land was the Mecca we all said we wanted," one person noted. "Living in Mitchell Bay, we didn't have much choice; that's pretty well all there was."

The Geisreiters, however, were serious about their lifestyle change. "One of our goals was to do as little shopping as possible," Bette remembered. "We grew most of our own food and were self-sustaining to 80 per cent. We sold vegetables and cheese to the Co-op. We also had a milk route and sold milk, butter and eggs. We shopped at the Co-op once a week and every couple of months Dick would go to Vancouver and fill the back of the truck with a couple hundred pounds of flour, sugar and other staples."

The Geisreiters and others like them found that hard work and perseverance paid off in more than just personal satisfaction; it earned them the respect and friendship of the islanders. For many, music was the key that opened doors. "We'd go to Lempi and John Blid's for a sauna and then the gang would come over and we'd play music

Will and Heidi Soltau in front of their army-tent home at Pulteney Point, 1972. Their airtight stove was multi-purpose: it provided heat, sterilized baby bottles and served as the kitchen stove.
Courtesy of the Soltau collection

until 2 or 3 in the morning," Dick said. "There was a mandolin, a banjo, an accordion and sometimes a piano. We played at weddings, funerals and anniversaries. It was a fun way to mix with the community."

Although many of the people coming to Malcolm Island were talented, it was soon apparent that backgrounds in Chinese studies, economics and floral design were not particularly useful in their new home. Just as the early tailors and poets struggled to fell trees and operate a sawmill, so the newcomers had to adapt their urban skills to a rural environment. They met the challenge with a combination of hope and confidence, and even those without any practical experience never doubted that they could build a house and live off the land.

The Soltaus moved to Sointula in 1971 after an abortive attempt to go back to the land in Kansas. They were looking for "a hippie haven, an untapped wilderness, where the government was giving away free (Crown) land." With the Eakles they bought fifty-four acres near the lighthouse at Pulteney Point, and in 1972 moved there with their two-year-old daughter and one-month-old son. Home was an army tent with an airtight heater.

"It seemed like an adventure at the time," Heidi said. "I had blind faith in Will's ability to build a house—he had studied architecture and built some chairs."

"I wasn't really prepared to go back to the land," Will admitted. "I'd always lived in the suburbs. I had some drafting experience, a couple of books and a little generator to run a few power tools. A lot of the house was built with a chainsaw."

The two families attempted to limit their purchases to staples like oil and salt. They caught fish, baked bread, raised chickens and goats and always ate their evening meal together. Even after they had built separate homes, dinners remained a communal effort. Roughing it in the 1970s wasn't much easier than it had been at the turn of the century. Heidi's Pulteney Point memories revolve around

Members of the Treesing tree-planting co-operative at work in the snow at Frederick Arm, November 1975. Standing left to right: Simon Dick, Janey Lord, Stewart Marshall, Kathy Gibler, Edda Field, Barb Imlach, Ralph Harris, Mike Field, Anthea Cameron. Sitting: Sid Williams and Robbie Boyes. Treesing was formed in 1974 to provide jobs for newcomers to Malcolm Island, particularly women.
Rick James photo

Granny Jarvis, the wife of gillnet drum inventor Laurie Jarvis, was born in the Klondike during the height of the gold rush. Here she is taking a closer look at Rob Wynne (left) and Doug, two recent arrivals to the island, 1974.
Rick James photo

wet firewood and crying while she milked the goats because her hands had cramped with the cold. She cooked meals and sterilized baby bottles on the airtight stove and remembers the day the goats broke into the tent and took one bite out of each potato.

Sooner or later the newcomers' dream of living off the land gave way to the reality of having to earn a living. Some found employment on government-funded Local Initiatives Programs making street signs, cleaning seniors' yards and landscaping the hall hill (where they were frequently accused of smoking marijuana behind the hall), but the real money was to be made in the logging and fishing industries. Scrambling through the bush and over windfalls, the philosophy graduate learned to set chokers while the weaver mastered the intricacies of mending a seine net. A side benefit to the on-the-job training were the horror stories about accidents and death, widow-makers and snapped beach lines. Jobs for men were plentiful but there wasn't much in the way of work for women.

Jane McClendon moved to the island permanently in 1972. "Unless you were part of a family with a fishboat, women usually didn't get fishing jobs. So around 1974 I started a tree-planting co-op." An island dump fire that got out of control was Jane's first planting contract. She could only find five experienced planters so she and a few others trained forty more. A core group of twenty newcomers bought shares of $50 and formed the tree-planting co-op Treesing. Half of the membership had to be women and all members had to be Malcolm Island residents. Contracts were run on a co-operative basis; on many jobs the crew lived and ate together, often camping in tents and lean-tos.

At first positions on the board of directors were filled by women, but one by one they found other jobs and the nature of the co-op began to change. As more co-op members moved on to other things it became necessary to hire people from off-island. Originally a true co-op with no paid management, a new, all-male board of directors decided that they should be compensated for their responsibilities. On the verge of becoming a business rather than a co-op, Treesing dissolved in 1988.

Before they became involved with Treesing, Kathy Gibler and Anthea Cameron established their own work-protection plan. One summer they decided to apply for fishing jobs but on their way to the dock realized that they would be lucky if there was a job for one woman, let alone two. They agreed that whoever got the job would split her income with the other.

"Anthea got the job," Kathy said. "Later that week I got a job fertilizing trees for a forestry crew. We ran around with big flour sifters on our backs, which spit out stuff that looked like coarse salt. Anthea and I both worked for three days. At the end of that time she gave me $300 and I gave her $75. We kept that up for over a year. We weren't living in the same house but it seemed like a good plan."

In another communal effort, newcomers to the island joined a Vancouver-based food co-op called Movable Feast. An order book was passed around and volunteers compiled a master list pooling everyone's bulk orders. "Someone would take a truck down to Vancouver, work in the co-op warehouse for a few days, then bring the order up-island," Ralph Harris remembered. "A lot of our basics were provided for that way. The Sointula Co-op didn't carry things that we wanted, like wheat germ, nutritional yeast and soya sauce."

As well as working and purchasing items co-operatively, most of the newcomers became close friends. Sharlene and Roger Sommer and their three children moved to Sointula from Sacramento, California, in June 1970. "Roger was an accountant and I was a housewife who stayed home and looked after the kids," Sharlene explained. "When I first saw the hippies in Sointula I was scared of them, but eventually I became friends with them because most of them were American. Our first Thanksgiving in Sointula I was in tears because I had never been away from my family. All the Americans felt that way to some extent, so we all baked bread and killed our own turkeys or chickens and got together for a big meal. I realized then that family isn't necessarily blood."

Davie and Les Lanqvist keep an eye on the fish tally as the seine boat *The Millionaires* is unloaded at Sointula's Norpac barge, July 1977. Many newcomers to the island broke into the fishing industry on *The Millionaires*.
Rick James photo

But even those who weren't classed as hippies ran into problems with the locals. The first incident occurred in 1968 when a Finn demanded more money from a Californian who had bought his farm. The two men were arguing in the kitchen when one of them grabbed a rifle. There was a struggle, the gun went off and the Finn was shot. Not having a telephone or a car, the American ran to a neighbour's for help and ended up driving the injured man into town on his tractor. In the interim the Finn bled to death. This incident upset the newcomers more than the longtime residents. As an American living on the island at the time, Jenny Green felt that "people looked at us a bit after that, but we didn't really feel like they held it against us as a group until a different American closed the logging road. That really created a lot of hard feelings, more so than the shooting.

Danni Tribe using a modern, aluminum gillnet drum on the north shore of Malcolm Island, 1987.
Paula Wild photo

"When Roger and Sharlene bought their farm it included an access road linking Sointula to the small community and log dump at Mitchell Bay. Everyone used this road, including the local logging company, which paid a nominal fee to do so. When the lease expired, Roger increased the fee, hoping that the loggers would find another route. The logging company balked, negotiations broke down and Roger barricaded the road. A lot of yelling took place, there were threats of physical violence and rocks were thrown at the Sommers' house. Once when Roger went to Mitchell Bay to visit friends the road was blocked so he couldn't get home. When, in spite of the harassment, Roger refused to change his mind, the 'dump' road was extended to become the new link between Mitchell Bay and Sointula."

By the mid-1970s the Finns' hard edges of suspicion and protectiveness had been worn thin by familiarity. Arriving in Sointula via Port McNeill, Vancouver and Detroit, Mary Murphy said: "The people in Sointula were more friendly than any place else I had ever lived. In the city everyone distrusts everyone else, but here people offer you rides and are curious about what you are doing. I was pregnant, and everyone seemed interested in my health and the baby. I got the feeling that the locals approved of us because we had a garden and were starting a family.

"There was a difference after I worked in the Co-op store," Mary continued. "Here you need to show that you are a hard worker to be accepted. Work is more than just a job, it's almost a community activity."

Over the years most of the hippies traded their long hair for more conventional styles and became involved in the routines that owning a home and raising a family bring. An interest and concern about what was happening found them attending community meetings and volunteering for committees. Although there are still some vestiges of "them" and "us," for the most part the newcomers have been accepted. As one Finn said, "They've become such a part of the island that I can't imagine it without them. Besides, they're not really hippies anymore."

17 EIGHT-DAY WILSON

Excerpted from Whistle Punks & Widow-Makers: Tales of the BC Woods *(2000),*
by Robert Swanson

Since time immemorial loggers have been famous short stakers. At the building of King Solomon's temple the loggers in the forest of Lebanon are said to have quit at the slightest provocation, jumped on their asses and journeyed into the nearest town to go on a wingdinger. This trait in loggers has been evident right down to recent times. During the Roaring Twenties, "Seattle Red" was reputed to have worked for seventy-nine logging companies in the state of Washington in one year.

In the BC woods the character who seems to have been the Short Staker Cup Holder was a logger known as "Eight-Day Wilson." His Christian name at the present writing seems to be unknown. Even Bill Black told me that "Old Eight-Day" just happened, and even though Black hired him out for twenty years, his card read "Wilson, Eight-Day: Country of birth—unknown."

Eight-Day Wilson roamed the big clearing back in the days when they cut the stumps above the swell—ten or twelve feet high—and left the big blue butts to rot in the woods. Those were the days when a logger carried his own roll of blankets and hit town wearing caulked boots, stagged-off pants and a Mackinaw shirt.

He got the name of Eight-Day for obvious reasons—he was a fair-weather, eight-day staker. After eight days on the job in any camp he would usually bunch her and head back to town. He was known to hire to a camp and after sampling the grub and washing his socks, beat it back to the bright lights and go on a tear.

A favourite stunt of Eight-Day's was to hire to a camp as hooktender and lie in camp the first day to sober up. After getting a mug-up from the cook in the middle of the morning he would saunter up the skid road and poke around a little. Being a boomer he was sure to know most of the boys in camp from the PF man down to the whistle punk, from whom he would get the lowdown on what the new outfit had to offer in the way of a logging show. If the ground was rough or he didn't like the donkey puncher he would wander back to camp, roll his blankets and head back to town.

One time at Loughborough Inlet, where Jack Phelps was pushing camp, Eight-Day pulled the pin because a green whistle punk sat in his place at the table—that was excuse enough for even a homeguard to tell the ink slinger to write-her-out, but it didn't take much of an excuse for Old Eight-Day. Once when a flunky handed him old hotcakes he bunched her right then and there.

At Cowichan Lake his favourite stunt boomeranged on him. Eight-Day Wilson had

Eight-Day Wilson worked the camps in the days when the stumps were cut above the swell—ten or twelve feet high. This crew, in the Queen Charlotte Islands (now Haida Gwaii), was felling spruce for airplane construction in World War One.
University of British Columbia, Rare Books and Special Collections, British Columbia Historical Postcard and Photograph Albums Collection, BC 1456/62-32

The kitchen of the 120-man Powell River Company camp at Kingcome Inlet, 1915. At one camp, cold hotcakes were reason enough for Eight-Day to quit.
University of British Columbia, Rare Books and Special Collections, MacMillan Bloedel Limited fonds, BC 1930/276-1

Bunkhouses like this one did not encourage loggers to stay put for long periods of time.
Museum at Campbell River 13312

hired out for Matt Hemmingsen and had completed the customary eight days. He needed an excuse to quit, so he resorted to the infallible test: throw a caulked boot up in the air. If it stayed up, he stayed in camp for another eight days. The trick had never been known to fail. He even had his duffel bag packed in readiness when he threw up the caulked boot and it went through the stove-pipe hole in the bunkhouse and stayed up. To save face Wilson had to stay another eight days, but he went on a record bender when he hit the bright lights with a sixteen-day stake.

Eight-Day Wilson was the last of the great short stakers. His kind are dying out and loggers are gradually losing the wanderlust from their nature and beginning to settle down. Eight-Day Wilson, ace short staker, embarked on his farewell journey to the camps of the Holy Ghost some years ago. He said goodbye to the bright lights and then walked off the end of the Ballantyne Pier in Vancouver, BC.

THE RECLAIMED

by Peter Trower

Overwhelmed homesteads
lie crushed to the dirt
by adamant snows
their waterlogged boards
mummybrown huddles
engendering moss,
arrogant blackberries
scratch through their ribs.

Tottering fenceposts
like battledrunk troops
groggy with rot
advance into nowhere
stagnating sockets
of bucketless wells
breed in their dimness
an airforce of gnats.

Sometimes a chimney
revealed like a trick
rears redbricked
from a scrimshaw of creepers
winds of conjecture
retrace a room
on the unhindered air
the echoes of fire.

Stricken to phantoms
the feeders of dreams
lost among stars
the sparks of their laughter
all the high hopes
the gadfly illusions
whimper from bedsprings
and rustgutted stoves.

Wordless the epitaph
decades have wrought
vanishing paths
weedthrottled forgotten;
impotent schemes
abandoned endeavours
quick in her seasons
the earth will reclaim them.

Bus Griffiths illustration

From Bush Poems *(1978), by Peter Trower and Bus Griffiths*

18

MORTS

Excerpted from Writing in the Rain *(1990), by Howard White*

Up in our neck of the woods these days, fish farming is the thing. It's the big action and the big argument. Basically the people who're making a buck from it like it, and everybody else thinks it stinks. Well, everybody agrees it stinks, but the argument sticks on the point of whether or not a little stink and mess might be put up with in the name of a few paying jobs. The jobs are kind of crummy and the pay is poor, but this strip of rock and Christmas trees has been kissing goodbye to jobs for so long there is a whole generation that's never known steady work. Big healthy guys in their mid-twenties still living at home, still driving 1973 Trans Ams. Anything that promises to get their wasting carcasses off the living room sofa and out of the house for a few hours a day has to look pretty good to their families.

But that doesn't apply to me. My sons are still playing peanut hockey. I sit a lot myself, but in front of a computer, not on the sofa. I do better tickling the keyboard of an IBM than I ever did pulling levers on a D8, much as my old construction buddies find it hard to believe anybody actually gets paid for this kind of thing. And not having to work outside anymore frees me to think kind thoughts about it. I have actually convinced myself that I liked physical work and miss it, and from time to time this leads me to dabble in it. I keep a hand in a small sand-and-gravel outfit with two other guys and put in the odd shift over the weekend trying to prove I'm as good a man as I ever was.

You might think I run a certain risk by doing this, and you're right.

It was September 1988. Around here it had been a wonderful month—very sunny and dry. The boys over at the Water Board were issuing handbills banning all sprinkling—even days or odd, before 7 pm or after. They were going up every day to the reservoir with their yardstick and measuring the fall and calculating how many more days of dry spell we could stand before water stopped coming out of all the taps in Pender Harbour. The kids were still swimming in the salt chuck.

This had an implication for the fish farmers. With all the pollen and leaves and dust and other end-of-summer goodies blowing around and stewing up in the warm water, the plankton thought the good times were here again and launched on a record-smashing population bloom. Any time one of these clouds of happy plankton drifted down on a fish farm, the fish choked in the pens. A hundred thousand six-pound salmon died at once, costing someone a million dollars. At first the farmers surreptitiously chucked their "morts" (mortalities) over the side, but when the volume got into the hundreds of pounds, then into the tons, this illegal activity became too obvious. They began burying the morts in limed pits ashore like they were supposed to, but in no time at all every scrap of dirt on the rocky shore became stuffed with dead salmon. Fish tails were sticking out from under every rock and leaf. So the farmers began loading the mushy carcasses into one-ton totes and hauling the totes to the garbage dump, two to a pickup truck. But the morts kept coming, and soon the farmers were out of totes and out of pickups.

This was when I got the call. They didn't call me to compute. They called to hire our truck, a twelve-yard Dodge in fair shape for its age.

I don't get many calls about the truck. I am on the phone all day about books, but I don't place much store in that. Getting a call as a truck operator was something special. The regular hauling jobs that came up—clearing lots for new retirement mansions, cleaning ditches for the Department of Highways—were passed around among the serious sand-and-gravel operators with never a nod of recognition in our direction. My sand-and-gravel partners, when they were around, kept the truck going on projects they always seemed to stir up on their own, but when they were away and I was holding the fort as I was now, the truck sat embarrassingly idle. I felt I was letting our side down, but the construction bunch just didn't want to talk to me. I suppose when any outsider stopping by Blueband Diesel mentioned the possibility of getting our truck on a job, some greasy fellow might say, "I think he's too busy writin' books, ain't he?" There would be sarcastic laughs, and that would be as far as it went.

You better believe I was tickled to be called about the truck. "Say, you got some kind of a truck, dontcha?" the gruff voice demanded.

"Yessir, that we do."

"Well, how would you like to have it up here in the morning?"

I was in the last stages of getting away a contract publishing job worth fifty thousand dollars, and even if they took the truck for a whole day, it couldn't be worth more than two hundred dollars. I was also sick. My padded leather chair was shiny with sweat and my heart was pounding and my mind kept evaporating and blowing out the window. It had gone on too long to be anything usual, and later in the month I would finally drag myself off to the doctor's and discover my metabolic system was going

Alexandra Burda illustration

mad under the influence of an overactive thyroid, but at this point I was assuming it was all just something that came with turning forty-two. I could barely hold my pen. At the slightest exertion I would collapse in my chair, panting and shaking.

"Wh—what is it you want hauled?"

"Ha-ha. Whaddya think? Fish!"

"Er, how much?"

"Oh, I dunno, seven-eight totes. There's more comin' in all the time."

I knew it was insanity to consider doing this. Nobody who liked me expected it of me, and this guy seemed to be laughing at me even as he asked me to do it. I had made quite a public thing of doubting fish farms and their works, and had every reason to abandon them to their smelly fates, as all the other truckers apparently had. I also didn't have a valid licence. I had a Class 5 licence for driving cars, pickups and mopeds like most people, but for a truck of the Dodge's size you needed a Class 3. I used to have a truck driving licence, back when it was called a "C" licence—I was very proud of the fact I took my original driver's test in my dad's ten-yard Dodge tandem when I was a sixteen-year-old kid, but when they went from letters to numbers I somehow got downshifted. I had pointed this out to the Superintendent of Motor Vehicles in numerous letters, claiming protection under the grandfather clause, but so far I was losing the argument. My partners kept telling me to smarten up and go get a new one, but it was a matter of principle for me. I had been stopped by cops once or twice and they hadn't noticed this technicality, but they could. The fine was $2,500, but the real penalty was getting written up in "This Week In Court." It was just another thing that might have tipped the scales toward saying no to the fish plant.

This was just the sort of deal I could never refuse.

"Yeah, I'll be there," I said.

And of course immediately panicked. What am I, nuts? I asked myself. You can't fill a gravel truck with rotten fish. The slime would leak out the crack around the tailgate. But my mind was running ahead of me, patching the holes. I could buy a roll of 6-mil poly and line the box with that, maybe a double layer of it. It still might squeeze out at the back where the crack was an inch wide. I could jam a two-by-four in there, under the poly. What if the tailgate unlatched under the weight and let ten tons of rotten fish out on the road? What would I say to my friends in the Save Our Scenery Society then? But if I pulled the chains tight, it would hold the gate shut even if the latch broke.

Conspiring with the enemy gave me a rare kind of thrill. I was a professional, and when a professional receives an honest request for his services, he answers the call. His personal politics stay out of it. There are limits of course—Eichmann went too far—but this little job wasn't going to affect the fish farm issue one way or another. I would come out of it a man with inside knowledge, a guy of substance—unlike the pencil-necks at soss. I would have the wisdom of Tiresias, the old seer with the dugs of a woman and the dork of a man, who lived both sides.

The truck started for me, and I made it up the twisty road to the fish plant only half an hour late.

"Hey—you came!" the foreman laughed. He was burly and bearded like an old antarctic whaler and obviously only half-expected me to show. "I'll back you in under the crane as soon as Fred gets unloaded." He met my eyes for the first time and his voice relaxed into a friendlier, fellow worker tone. "I...I guess loose fish will be okay in that truck, eh...?" It warmed my heart. I didn't expect to see him let his doubts show, not at this stage anyway, but seeing me standing there in front of him, nervous and weak from sweating, I guess it was too much for him. But I was on my way now, I didn't want sympathy.

"Oh yeah, I think so. I got a roll of poly and some boards to seal it up. Long as you don't fill me too full, most of it should stick." I don't think my breezy manner convinced him, but it gave him all the excuse he needed to go ahead. He broke into his tough grin again, and clapped me on the shoulder.

"That's the stuff! I knew you could handle it. Back that big bastard in there!"

I wasn't all that smooth with the truck because I had only driven it around The Bluff to blow the airhorn at the schoolkids. I'd never driven it loaded, and I'd never driven any diesel truck with a thirteen-speed transmission before. But I slid it back under the crane without grinding any gears or knocking over any sheds, and got out while they went about filling the Dodge's twelve-cubic-yard gravel box with rotten fish. I sweatily went over the checklist in my mind. I'd laid the board way across the back. I'd cut it two inches too short, but I'd jammed a square rock in the gap. I'd cinched up the chains as tight as I could. Must remember to unhook them before I dump. The poly was laid out and hanging over the sides, with dirt scattered around to hold it in place while they loaded me. I went upstairs for a coffee and leaned over the rail looking down on the operation, trying to look nonchalant. I was smart enough to know that if I hung around where the fish was, I'd end up with my hands in it. My goal was to get home without a single fish scale on me, or on the truck.

They had a bunch of broad-shouldered kids sluffing around, and the whaler fingered one up into the gravel box to handle the tote-dumping while he worked the crane. The totes were wooden boxes about a cubic yard big; and they lifted them with a sling around each side. They lowered them into the gravel box; then the kid would take the one sling off and they'd lift one side, spilling the tote over. At the first spill the kid doubled over and lost his breakfast. He crawled over the side, white in the face and refusing further service. The whaler looked around and picked another, bigger kid, a good-natured hulk I knew slightly who was on his first day. He slowly made his way up and got the spilled tote away, moving to a far corner of the box and fanning his nose between lifts. Then I saw why he'd been so slow to get in: he hadn't had time to buy gumboots and he was trying to get by the first day with flimsy plastic overshoes. It wasn't long before a look of horror came on his face and I looked down to see foamy pink fish juice pouring over the top of one overshoe.

He returned a sickly smile, then stepped right out of the shoe, plunging his white sock right into a pool of orange fish muck. He made a pathetic noise, and I put my fist to my forehead for him. I couldn't stand any more, so I went downstairs into the actual fish plant. It was just a big shed on the water's edge with totes piled up against one wall, a walk-in freezer, and across one whole end a long wetbench surrounded by about twenty-five slickered locals all hacking up fish with funny-looking blunt knives. I was surprised to see a lot of people who I knew to be strong critics of fish farms working there, including Cam Fisher, one of the table officers of soss.

Alexandra Burda Illustration

"I didn't know you worked here," I said, amazed.

"I didn't know you did either," she replied, haughty.

"I guess there's nothing wrong with taking money off them," I said.

"I don't eat their fish, if that's what you mean. You wouldn't catch me dead eating this garbage," she said loudly, her voice ringing around the tin building as she splatted down a ratty-looking jack spring and zipped it open without looking. "None of us do."

There were murmurs of shy agreement along the line. Being mostly old-timers, they felt salmon should be left the way God made them, and not squeezed into pens and force-fed like pâté de foie gras. When I saw Cam roaring at a forklift putting some boxes down in the wrong place, I realized she was actually inside foreman of the joint.

The truck was loaded with eight totes. I climbed up on top of the cab and looked at the damage. The whole gravel box was about half filled with dead fish, all lying this way and that. They didn't look that bad. It stank a bit, but it was the old smell of the coast. The load looked pretty stable. I folded the edges of the poly over the mess like a Christmas present and chucked some broken pallets on top to hold it down. There was a stream of pinkish juice the diameter of a pencil-lead draining out one corner of the box, but it looked like it was diminishing. There was nothing to do but put the truck in low gear and crawl up the steep driveway. I roared out of the yard and out of their lives into my own, carefully avoiding any jolts that might send dead fish sloshing over the tailgate. I took comfort in the fact this grade was probably the steepest I would have to handle on the trip, and the load made it up with no trouble. I pulled over every ten miles or so to see if anything was amiss, but nothing was. It might have been a load of clean drainrock I had in there. Even the little pencil-leak had disappeared.

It was going so well I decided to take it to the big dump in Sechelt, where it would be less noticeable than at the little Pender Harbour dump and also give me more truck time. It was a bit nervy driving that mess down the busy streets of Sechelt, right under the noses of fish farming's most dedicated opponents, but I slid through without a turned head, and up the hill to the dump. They had a special sump pit set aside for such unpleasantries, and I had gone to the trouble of clearing the load with the authorities, something nobody else bothered to do. I did this the night before, just in case I needed it. That's how good I was.

I even remembered to undo the chains holding the tailgate shut before I hoisted the dump up. I even fished the broken pallets out of the stew so they wouldn't go into the sump. Not that there would be any harm if they did, I just wanted to avoid even the chance of trouble. I wanted to be better than good. The exertion of lifting the pallets had me seeing red in a minute—reminding me for the first time I wasn't quite well—and I did get more than a few fish scales on me at last. But nothing serious. There was a man in a trench coat across the pit surreptitiously taking pictures of me, probably for the SOSS. I waved at him.

I made it home before 2 pm, hosed down the truck and went back to my thinking, feeling like a powerful instrument. Some sticky negotiations that had been holding up the fifty grand suddenly opened up for me, and I got on the phone to Ontario to close the deal before the people went out for the weekend, then phoned up the printer, got the price I was looking for from him, and set the deal in motion. I had been putting these closing moves off for weeks, but I'd come home from truck driving feeling the power.

The next day they called again. I was no less busy and felt no less ill, but agreed to go without hesitation. I made it on time this time. And went straight into the coffee room to wait for them to load. When I came out and looked down, I noticed two things. The truck was a lot fuller than the day before. And the stuff was a lot juicier. I only had about six inches of freeboard between the muck and the top edge of the gravel box. They had not only thrown in eight totes of very dead salmon from the farms; they had added six totes of offal—fish guts—from the processing plant. Old fish guts, which had been sitting around a week or more in warm weather. I didn't like it. They hadn't asked me. But what could I do now? Tell them to spoon it out? I should have stayed outside to watch, and stopped them half-full like the first time. I wrapped the plastic around, weighed it down like before, got in low gear and ground my way up the hill. I stopped at the top to look it over. Nothing had sloshed over the tailgate, although there were twin streams of pink fish juice the thickness of a cigarette squirting out each corner of the tailgate. I couldn't tell if they were diminishing or not, but I could tell they were really rank. This batch was much riper than the first one.

The old coast had never smelled liked this.

I worked my way over the twisty Egmont Road out to the highway and stopped for a look. The streams of fish juice were still squirting onto the road. The load itself seemed to have levelled off and kind of jelled. But it was all still there. I got underway, keeping a sharp eye behind me in the big side mirrors. A few miles down the highway, I began to notice little splashes of liquid flying out whenever I went around a corner. Then I began to notice it all the time, streamers of spray peeling off behind me as I motored along. A few cars passed the opposite way and I wondered what they saw. If someone came up behind me, they would probably get quite a surprise. I pulled over at the next wide spot.

The upper edges of the gravel box were glistening. The load looked wetter than it had when I started. The jostling of the road seemed to be breaking the stuff down. And somehow the poly had got pulled down into the soup so it was no longer sealing the big crack between the upper edge of the metal and the plank which made up the top eight inches of the gravel box, and every time the stuff surged a little going around a corner, it would splash out through the crack. Very gingerly I pulled myself up alongside the load and began trying to pull the poly back up where it belonged without getting any fish on me. I saw both of my knees turn dark as they touched the wetness. I inserted a couple fingers very delicately into the reeking muck, searching for the edge of the poly, but when I found it I couldn't get a grip. It was very slippery. I had to thrust both hands in to the wrist and rip hand-holds in the plastic. By the time I had it pulled up on both sides, my shirt front and my thighs were saturated with the oil and the stench of rotten fish. I spent a good many minutes scuffling in the dry grass on the side of the road trying to clean my shoes, but to little effect. When I climbed back into the cab, the smell was so strong I had to roll both windows down. It was so strong I soon lost the ability to smell anything, only a rawness in my nostrils and a fever on my brain.

Not ten miles farther on, I looked in the mirrors and saw ribbons of spillage once again trailing off behind me on both sides. My heart sank. I had to go back and put my hands in that rotten muck again. I looked for another wide shoulder and pulled over. The whole outside of the truck was now glistening with fish oil. The streams at the corners of the box had increased to the thickness of a cigar and had created sizable pools on the ground just in the first few minutes the truck was stopped.

I was starting to feel I would be lucky to get out of it this time around. I wished for the first time, but not the last, that I had turned off at the road to the Pender Harbour dump several miles back instead of making for Sechelt as before. I jumped up and plunged my arms into the gooey mess, no longer having anything to keep clean, and pulled the plastic cover up. When my eyes came to rest on the load of fish, I couldn't believe my eyes. When I had first started out, the load had looked mostly like fish. But as I drove and the rotting carcasses fell apart under the jostling of the road and mixed with the gooey offal, it came to look more like fish purée.

Now it looked like nothing I'd ever seen. I had to shake my head and blink my eyes. It was like a field of dandelions gone to seed. The entire fuming mass was bristling with little translucent globes. Hundreds of little pointy sacs waving in the breeze. It took me a minute to figure it out. These things were swim bladders. Each fish has this little bag it can fill with water to regulate its depth, and they're made out of some tough cellophany stuff that doesn't rot. As the rest of the fish parts broke down and went to mush, these little guys had become inflated with gas and floated to the top. It was a most hallucinatory sight, as if the load had suddenly burst into bloom. It disconcerted me. It heightened a sense of unreality that had already gone far enough.

I decided to get back on the road before the puddle of liquid fish under the truck got any bigger. As I drove I began to consider the implications of going through Sechelt with this steaming, dripping mess. Just waiting at the stoplight on Dolphin Street would result in a couple of gallons of rotten fish purée in the middle of the town's busiest intersection. The people in Pronto's restaurant would suddenly lose their appetite. The people in the office of the *Happy Shopper*, the pro–fish farm newspaper, would suddenly get a new perspective on the artificial fish issue. People would swarm round. It would be the event of the week.

The streamers of slime were out again. It was happening faster each time as the load became less and less stable. Going around one corner I glanced in the mirror and saw a little slosh of pink go over. If it kept getting looser, I might not be able to drive it at all pretty soon. I slowed down to 20 mph, 10 on corners. I might just make it to Sechelt in time to have it all go over the side—or suppose a pedestrian stepped in front of me and I had to make a hard stop. Tons of reeking pink glop would surge forward and go cascading up over the front of the truck, flattening the jaywalker and plugging every storm sewer for three blocks. The central core would be evacuated for days while cleanup crews worked overtime, all at my expense. Next week, banner headlines: Glop Truck Driver Had Wrong Licence. Court trials. Crippling expense. Disgrace. No one would ever talk to us again.

A car pulled up close behind me, then punched on its brakes and dropped back fifty yards or so.

I decided to turn around and take the load back to the Pender Harbour dump while I still could. It was no closer by this time, but it would save my having to go through any towns. The problem was to find a place on the narrow, twisting coast highway where I could swing this big bowl of jelly. It had to be level and wide, so I didn't spill the load…

Just then I came to the Election Section. The Election Section is a half-mile stretch of bad curves near Secret Cove, which the government has been promising to straighten for over ten years. Every election they give the local highways office a few thousand dollars to round up all the local contractors and make a show of doing something. Then on the day after the election they're all sent home, leaving the stakes to be torn out and the blasting holes to be silted up for another three years. At this point the Vander Zalm government was suffering at the polls so the Election Section was in business again. New clearings had been made on either side of the road, and a portable office trailer had been dragged in along with a water truck and a few government engineers in orange-and-white pickup trucks. To me it looked like a good place to turn around.

I geared the truck down and slowly reduced my speed to about 5 mph, then slowly eased the nose of the truck off the pavement into the clearing beside the office trailer. It bumped a little bit harder than I planned, but not very bad. I looked in the mirror and saw a flash of pink.

Lost a little juice, I thought. I'll get a hemlock branch and go brush off the pavement. I rolled gently to a stop, popped the maxi brake on and opened the door. There were a few fishtails and bits of flesh stuck to the side of the box, which I thought odd.

I walked around the rear end and looked behind.

My heart stopped.

For 100 feet the highway was covered with fish, fish heads, fish tails and bright orange mush. Both lanes were fully involved.

Some of the fish were whoppers.

And the little swim bladders were bobbing everywhere. Thousands of them, dancing, mocking me, in the hot sun. The car that had been following me at a safe distance was now stopped at the edge of the spill, and there was another behind it. I could see the driver shaking his head.

My heart was pounding like a runaway steam locomotive. I didn't know it, but the condition I had was giving me high blood pressure to start with. When I later had it diagnosed, I was solemnly warned to avoid excitement or sudden exertion lest I pop a blood vessel. This kind of stress was no doubt sending my reading off the scale. My ears were ringing. I was seeing red when I turned my head. But somehow I managed to stay upright. I waved the cars through, guiding them along the left-hand shoulder, clear of the mess. Then I got the shovel off the truck and started spooning the slop toward the ditch. I worked too fast and exhausted myself in seconds, making no discernible difference to the bubbling mass. Cars kept coming and interrupting me.

Alexandra Burda illustration

Then one of the government engineers showed up. He was a youngish chap wearing an orange plastic hard hat and carrying a clipboard. He had been over on the job-site somewhere, doing his best to put in hours without any crew or equipment to boss. He kept looking at the road, then at me, then at his clipboard, as if he hoped to get some guidance from it. He didn't know what to say. Nothing like this had ever come up in engineering school. But I could see that he was determined to be uncooperative.

"What are you stopping here for?" he said. "You can't leave that stuff here."

"I just pulled in to turn around and spilled a little. I'm on the way to the dump," I said.

"Well I'm going to have to get some information," he said, rolling up a new page on his clipboard. Just then cars came shooting around the corner from both directions, braking hard as the vista of salmon chowder opened before them. I ran out to flag them through, one at a time. When I finished and picked up my shovel again, the engineer caught up to me with his clipboard.

"I'm going to need some particulars," he said.

"Look," I said, "we're going to have an accident here if we don't get the road clear. Why don't you let me take care of that, then I'll give you all the particulars you want." Another three cars came squealing to a halt and I had to rush over to signal them through. The drivers all looked sour and shook their heads with disapproval at me. I was the focus of all their anti–fish farm feelings. What am I doing here, I wonder, I kept musing. I should be at home quietly clicking my word processor, whispering pleasant assurances to elderly lady poets over the telephone. Will I ever get back there? Will I escape from this mess alive? My blood pressure was setting a new Olympic record.

The engineer had now come up with a new idea, which was to surround the spill with about three dozen fluorescent orange traffic cones. He encircled the spill completely, blocking both lanes off, so that traffic actually had nowhere to go. This created a very dangerous situation, since he made no attempt to guide the traffic, and within minutes I had to run through the muck waving my shovel to prevent a head-on collision between a rusted-out Volkswagen Beetle and a 36-foot Winnebago-with-everything, both trying to slip by on the far shoulder.

I looked at the engineer. "This is a bit dangerous, don't you think?" I asked.

"I don't want people running through your garbage," he retorted hotly. "I *live* here."

I couldn't quite follow his logic. I guess he was making some oblique reference to the fact fish farmers were outsiders, a lot of them, missing the point I'd lived in the area for thirty-eight years myself. I reckoned if it came to a head-on collision, most people would probably prefer to swerve through the spill and get a little rotten fish on their tires, but I didn't have the breath to argue. I began looking for something better than the shovel because I wasn't getting anywhere with the cleanup. A snow shovel would have been better, or just a plank I could lay down and push like a bulldozer. Beside the engineer's office trailer I spotted a heavy wooden rectangle used as a base for portable road signs. I walked over and grabbed it.

"Hey!" the engineer hollered. "We use that. I don't want you getting your, your... stuff all over it."

It was like the word "fish" had suddenly become unmentionable to him.

"I'll clean it up after," I said, walking past him and banging it down on the road. It made a pretty good bulldozer. A little rusty car stopped on the shoulder and a burly kid got out. He walked over to me with a grin on his face.

"You need a hand?" he said.

I couldn't believe my ears.

"Do I ever," I said, "but it ain't very pretty."

"Ha-ha, little bit of rotten fish never killed anybody," he chortled and grabbed the shovel. Between us we soon had most of the big lumps pushed over into the ditch, leaving only a smeared layer of virulent orange mud over a lane and a half of the road.

"What are we going to do with that?" he asked.

"Dunno," I said. "Maybe we could slosh it off with water, if we had water." I remembered the tank-truck parked beside the office trailer and hollered at the engineer.

"What's the chance of getting some water out of that truck?"

"What for?" he said.

"To clean up your road here before this shit gets baked in and you end up breathing it for the rest of the year," I said. That got his attention. He shuffled over to the truck and opened up a hatch alongside the tank.

"What have you got to put it in?" he said dubiously, still clutching his clipboard.

I couldn't believe my eyes. Under the hatch was a high-volume fire pump hooked to a coil of hose.

"Does that pump *run?*" I shouted.

"Of course it runs," he said.

"Well for Chrissakes, start it up and hose this road off before somebody gets killed! We could have had this road open half an hour ago with that thing!"

Sulkily, he gave the starter a pull and a two-inch jet of high-pressure water burst from the hose. He kept it himself, not wanting to trust unlettered persons with the operation of a government water hose, and within a few minutes had the road gleaming as blackly as if it was freshly paved. While he was carefully spraying off the sign stand, I jumped back in the truck and was out on the road before he noticed. I could see him waving his clipboard in the rearview mirror as I geared into high range. I figured there had just been time for the first cars that had passed through to reach the police station in Sechelt. Now, if I made straight for the Bluff dump as fast as I could go without spilling any more, I might just make it in half an hour. That would give the cops just time to make it back to the spill—depending how long they spent taking a statement.

I should just be able to make it.

The Indy 500 never seemed so long as that fifteen miles. I had to gear the truck up furiously on every bit of straightaway, trying to make time, but brake with enormous care coming into any corners, tender as a waiter with a three-tiered tray full of beer. Another spill of any size would be game over. It didn't help that my hands were shaking with fever and my oily shoes kept wanting to slip off the clutch and brake pedals. I spent as much time looking behind me in the rearview mirrors as I did ahead at the snaking road.

After an eternity I crawled into the dump, drove straight toward the hole up at the far end I'd already picked out in my mind, and put the hoist in gear. The sopping mess slid out the rear into the ground. No constipated sperm whale ever felt greater relief. The evidence was off the truck!

I turned and began rolling down the grade toward the exit.

At that moment a police cruiser came flying into the dump at the head of a huge plume of dust, raring over the potholes like a bucking bronco. It shot past me without making any sort of signal, so I kept on rolling toward the highway and home. The cruiser bounded up to where I'd let off the load, spun around in the gravel, peeled back toward me and put on the siren. I pulled over, popped the maxi and climbed down onto the road.

I was strongly moved to fall down on the ground and pour my sick heart out in the dust, but a tiny voice in the back of my head, barely audible over the pounding of my temples, was whispering, "Don't give it away, don't volunteer anything, act cool, you never know…" The cop walked up looking mean, until he got a whiff of the truck box, which twisted his face up like a prune.

"Wow!" he yelped.

"Bears love it," I laughed. This was a lie, in fact. It was a peculiarity we'd all observed over the past months that the one kind of garbage the dump's considerable scab-ridden army of bears wouldn't go near was fish farm garbage. It was their only taboo.

"Did you just unload a truckload of fish waste in this landfill?" the cop intoned in his cop-like way.

"Can't deny it," I grinned, reeking. "Yes, I did."

"And are you authorized to do that?"

"Yeah, I am," I said. His eyes were watering, and I moved closer to him where the wavy lines coming up off my fish oil–soaked pants would go right up his nose.

"Oh. We were told you weren't…" he said, backing away.

"Well, you just phone the works superintendent at the Regional District and he'll fill you in," I said. I was like ice inside, dreading the next request. If he uttered the words "driver's licence," I would collapse in a heap, my life over. But the wavy lines did their work.

"Okay, well, sorry to bother you," the cop said and hustled back to the car. I let him go on ahead.

It didn't matter.

It was still the worst day of my life.

OLD WOMAN
by Anne Cameron

Old Woman
is working
gathering
the frayed ends of dreams
the ravelled edges of hopes
re-weaving
your soul
Her face
this pale moonlit night
is sharp and spare
her eyes
deep shadowed hollows
her mouth
pursed and wrinkled
and as she weaves
she hums a salt sea melody
that tells of cedar and rock
and the twisted
granite-wood arbutus
clinging tenaciously to cliff face
perched above the crashing waves
gnarled and bent by hail
She does not
waste her time
in recriminations
She does not
waste your time
with sympathy
She hums her song
her gnarled-root fingers
weaving your mind
making whole again
your fabric of being

From The Annie Poems *(1987), by Anne Cameron*

WHISTLING SHITHOUSES
Queen Charlotte Airlines' Stranraer Fleet

19

Excerpted from The Accidental Airline: Spilsbury's QCA *(1994),*
by Howard White and Jim Spilsbury

Of all the queer collection of aircraft we assembled in the course of our bargain-hunting for aircraft we could afford, it is clear to me the one we'll be most remembered for is the gangling Stranraer, the "whistling shithouses" we set beating their ungainly way up and down the fog-shrouded cliffs of the BC coast, loaded to the gunwales with Chinese second cooks and Finnish chokermen chewing snoose. This is the image that comes to my mind most strongly when I recall the company's salad days, and I am happy to have it as our epitaph.

In a way this is very ironic, because as time went on we were all rather embarrassed about the Strannies and were never so proud of ourselves as the day we finally graduated to DC-3s and left the old flying boats behind us. We thought wow, we're a real airline now. The whole office came out and rolled up their sleeves to help wash and wax the first DC-3; even the cipher girls from accounting got in on the act. But the DC-3s don't remember very well—they just made us like every other airline. The Strannies made us unique. Of all the planes we flew, they had the most personality by far.

We have all read about old-time sailors and their many beliefs and superstitions, and how almost human personalities were associated with the ships they sailed in.

Docking a Stranraer
was always a panicky
manoeuvre.
*University of British Columbia,
Rare Books and Special
Collections, Jim Spilsbury
fonds, box 24, plate 4-1*

Some ships were "lucky" ships and came through the worst storms and the worst battles unscathed. Other ships were not so lucky and were forever becoming involved in one or another type of marine disaster, not necessarily related to the competence of the crews involved. There were some ships cursed with such bad reputations that owners had difficulty in getting crews to man them.

This sort of thing is not normally associated with aircraft, probably because of the very nature of their operation, and the frequency with which the flight crews are changed. A modern aircraft flies almost continuously, but changes crews every few hours. It may fly halfway around the world and back, and take aboard six or eight different crews in the process. Things just don't have a chance to get that personal anymore.

But in the early days of Queen Charlotte Airlines it was different. Any given aircraft would be doing well to average four to five flying hours a day. The rest of the time it would be in the shop being serviced, so it was not unusual for an aircraft to have only one pilot for long periods of time. Pilots would come to have their favourite aircraft, to which they preferred to be assigned. This probably was particularly the case with the Stranraers, since they flew only in daylight, and their entire flight crew of captain, first officer and flight engineer would stay with the machine for weeks at a time. So individual Stranraers soon took on personalities that stayed with them. Most were good—some not so good. CF-BYJ was a case in point.

I seem to recall that CF-BYJ was the third of all the Stranraers we bought. We originally had two—CF-BYI and CF-BYL—which we were using on the run to the Queen Charlotte Islands and Prince Rupert.

When BYL was lost on a mercy flight from Stewart it left us short, so we got BYJ and immediately flew her back to Montreal for conversion to a passenger plane. It was on this, her first flight, that she got into her first real trouble. On arriving in Montreal and attempting to land in the St. Lawrence River at the Vickers aircraft plant, just above the Lachine Rapids, the pilot, in trying to avoid the broken ice packs in the river, which was very low, taxied her right onto a submerged rocky reef, taking part of the bottom of the hull out and sinking her in shallow water. What was to be a fairly simple conversion now developed into a two-month repair job. To start with, getting her through the ice pack and up on the shore was no simple task. A channel had to be cut through foot-thick ice with handsaws and, after getting her out, a large canvas and corrugated iron shelter had to be built over her so she could be thawed out and the hull rebuilt. Fortunately we were able to get our old friend Albert Racicot to do the job, and he had access to materials and spare parts. We also sent one of our crew chiefs, Curly Nairn, and another mechanic from Vancouver to oversee and assist.

The *Skeena Queen* (CF-BYL), last seen circling Prince Rupert on August 31, 1946.
Harbour Publishing Archives

Finally she was ready to go, and just like new. The ice had almost gone from the river and one of the local types undertook to pilot her out into the main channel. *Carunch!* and she had a new hole in her bottom. The French pilot waved his arms around and claimed that the river bottom was all changed since the thaw! Who knows, maybe he was right, but it took another three weeks to get her ready the second time, and she finally arrived in Vancouver after taking the Deep South route via Mississippi, Texas and California. Once out on the coast she was put right to work, and we bought two more Stranraers, BYM and BXO, just to make sure.

Incidentally BXO was the last of the Strannies left whole out of the lot. She was the only Strannie left whole in the whole world apparently, because in the 1970s when the Royal Air Force was looking for an intact copy to complete its collection of historical military aircraft at the Hendon air museum outside London, they came to BC and glommed BXO from a group of antique plane buffs and took her back to the old country in pieces. I visited her there in 1984, all painted in RAF colours as if she had never been built for the RCAF in Montreal or had a glorious career flying for QCA at all. I tried to bring this to the attention of the museum officials but they obviously didn't believe a word I said.

I felt badly about this, but I didn't say anything because who would understand? Here in the west we have a very tenuous sense of history, and even when we do end up staring it in the face we think it's just our own personal history, of no significance to the world. But it was surprising how many people came up to me and expressed indignation that the Brits had scooped the last living Stranraer on us and stuck it in their museum when it should have been in ours. Still, how could we really complain? A few of these flying history buffs, including the filmmaker and sometime TV weatherman

Bob Fortune, had tried to raise enough money to keep BXO here and hadn't been able to. As recently as the 1970s the awareness that this old plane might represent something worth saving still hadn't really developed in BC. For a number of years it just seemed we had been too slow off the mark and lost our chance to preserve what the Strannie represented, until BYJ changed that. But I'm getting ahead of my story.

After her second sinking in Montreal, BYJ got back home and flew the line relatively routinely for a few months. I say relatively because this plane couldn't seem to go two weeks together without throwing something at us. One hot summer day in 1947 the boys were welding up a crack in her exhaust ring just outside our rented TCA hangar on Sea Island when a spark went the wrong way and something started burning. In the time it took to grab the nearest fire extinguisher and hose down the flames, three wing panels had been destroyed, at a replacement cost of $12,500. The incident also convinced TCA we weren't the type of neighbour they wished to have sharing their classy digs and they threw us out, leaving us without adequate covered work space for several months. It was perhaps around this time BYJ got her nickname. We had been in the habit of naming all our aircraft "Something-or-other Queen." The *Skeena Queen*, the *Nimpkish Queen*, the *Haida Queen*, and so on. BYJ spent so much time in maintenance she was dubbed the *Hangar Queen*.

Then she encountered her third sinking, and this was a dilly.

It started as a regular scheduled flight from Vancouver to Zeballos, via Gold River,

Strannies CF-BYI and BXO docked at Sullivan Bay. *University of British Columbia, Rare Books and Special Collections, Jim Spilsbury fonds, box 20, QaCA-1*

Tahsis and Ceepeecee. Andy Anderson was the pilot with Bill Oliver, co-pilot, and "Boost" Coulombe, flight engineer, and there was one passenger aboard when she came in for a landing at Ceepeecee on a grey February morning, with reduced visibility in sleet and rain. The approach was normal, but right after touchdown she struck a partly submerged hemlock deadhead, with the top barely breaking water, ripping a five-foot gash in the bottom of the hull. The flight engineer saw what had happened and yelled at Andy to pour on the coal and keep her steaming for the closest beach. Andy opened the taps and bumped her as far as she would go up on the clam beach in front of the cannery, where she settled immediately in about five feet of water.

Andy said that locals appeared from behind every stump. Just before going up on the mud, they had passed a small boat with two people in it and had practically swamped it with the waves they made. It turned out that the boat contained our one outbound passenger, who had engaged an Indian dugout to take him out to the aircraft. When the plane roared right on by, the anxious passenger thought he was going to miss the flight and urged the oarsman to "Follow that plane." When the plane stopped, the passenger jumped right in through the open door with his suitcase and landed up to his waist in water inside the hull.

"It's okay, Mac," Andy said, "we're not going anywhere right now!"

Our inbound passenger didn't fare much better. He had been standing up in the aisle when the plane touched down, and when she hit the deadhead, a great stream of water and wood chips hit him square in the chest, filling his eyes and mouth and soaking him to the skin, but he took it all as part of his day's work. He was an official log scaler, employed by the BC Forest Service, on his way to the camp at Tahsis to scale some timber. According to the story our crew told, he just mopped his face off and spat out the water and wood chips, but he stopped to chew on a particularly large sliver of hemlock. Then he spat it out and shook his head, commenting to himself, "Just Number Two Common. Must be out of the cull boom."

The first word of the mishap reached us in Vancouver by radio, but the message was, of necessity, very meagre and completely lacking in detail. It just said BYJ suffered slight damage at Ceepeecee and suggested that our superintendent of maintenance, Charlie Banting, come over and take charge. We should have been better informed, but it was by now company policy to say as little as possible on the radio, since too many people were listening and if Carter Guest got hold of it there would be no end of complications. As it was, the mere suggestion of needing Charlie Banting confirmed our suspicion that all was not well.

It was quickly decided that John Hatch would fly over with a Norseman, taking Charlie Banting, another mechanic and lots of tools; Johnny thought I should go too—just in case there were any higher politics involved. We arrived the same afternoon. It was a dismal sight. The tide had come in to cover the entire hull and cockpit. Only the wings and tail structure were above water. There was still intermittent rain and snow.

Our first problem was to provide enough flotation to get the aircraft up on the beach as far as we could, so we could work on the hull when the tide dropped. There was a lot of talk about air bladders, which we didn't have, and oil drums, which are hard to harness. My contribution at this point was to visit the local logging camp and

After the crash at Ceepeecee, CF-BYJ was refloated with the aid of two logs. The photo at left shows the aircraft with the first log in place. The photo at right shows the aircraft with the second log in place. Ropes joining the two were used as a cradle to help float the hull.
University of British Columbia, Rare Books and Special Collections, Jim Spilsbury fonds, box 24, plate 7-2 (left) and 7-3 (right)

arrange to borrow two large spruce logs, which we got a fisherman to tow into the bay for us. Then we borrowed a lot of heavy rope from the fishing company. When the tide went down we floated these logs under the lower wings, one on each side, and then passed the rope over the logs and under the hull many times to make a sort of rope cradle. When the tide came in she gently raised off the bottom, and we were able to move her ashore so that on the next low tide she was high and dry on the beach. We of course released the rope slings and floated the logs out as the tide fell. Low tide was around midnight, and it gave us a total of about three hours to repair the hole in the hull. It was about five feet long and a foot wide.

At this critical moment in history we were joined by a very useful chap who was travelling for the Standard Oil Company, doing repair and maintenance work on their marine refuelling stations. He was a marine engineer by trade and had a wealth of experience in ship salvage work. He offered his help and we decided to go along with his suggestions. It was very simple: plug the hole with concrete. We didn't think it would set in time, but he had an answer for that. You mix caustic soda with Portland cement and use boiling water, and this would set up in half an hour, he said. The canners had both the caustic soda and the Portland cement, so we were in business. All we had to do was dig our way under the bottom of the hull and screw on a large sheet of galvanized iron to act as a retaining form while the concrete set. It all worked just like the man said, and the morning's high tide floated her off high and handsome. It never leaked a drop.

Telling about it now makes it sound so easy, but the undertaking had its moments. Bear in mind that the actual patching job was carried out at night with the aid of a borrowed Coleman gas lantern, and with a chilling mixture of rain and sleet coming down. Charlie Banting came from Manitoba, and he didn't mind cold weather or snow, but he hated rain. He was still wearing his prairie-style overcoat. It was very thick and heavy, came down to his ankles, and the collar turned up around his ears. But it was not rainproof, and during that night it must have taken on about twenty pounds of water. It sagged right to the ground like a tent, and Charlie could hardly move in it.

With her new concrete bottom, CF-BYJ is ready to fly once again.
University of British Columbia, Rare Books and Special Collections, Jim Spilsbury fonds, box 24, plate 7-1

The hem bulged out with water. Charlie was standing holding the lantern while Boost was lying on his back under the hull in a trench we had dug in the clam bed, working with a hand drill, fastening this large piece of galvanized iron to the hull with PK screws.

The trench was only about a foot deep and had filled with water, and Boost hardly had room to turn under there. Then I noticed something peculiar. Every now and again the steady stream of water running into the trench would suddenly swell to a subdued gush, and I noticed bits of paper mixed in with the dirty water. I began tracing this stream uphill with my eye, and a few feet up the beach I spotted the partly covered outlet of the cannery building sewer. Every time someone flushed a toilet, poor Boost got a soaking. It was running in the neck of his Mackinaw shirt and out his pant legs.

I pointed this out to Charlie and commented that we couldn't have picked out a worse spot on the whole beach. He looked things over slowly, with the rain running off the end of his nose, and then looked at me over the top of his glasses.

"Wahl," he drawled. "You cain't have everything *absolutely* perfect."

In the morning she was floating like a cork—no water coming in. All seats, floorboards and lining had been stripped out of her. All the wiring in the hull and all the instruments in the cockpit had been under water and ruined, but fortunately the engines in a Stranraer are mounted in the upper wing and this had been ten feet above water, so they were undamaged. The only question was how to start them. The wiring that ran the electric starters was out of commission and there was no way to crank the engines. This was no problem for our Charlie. He moored the Strannie alongside a log float. Then he got a fisherman's gumboot and made a fifty-foot length of rope fast to it. He had someone climb up and slip the boot over the upper propeller blade of the far-side engine. Then he commandeered four enthusiastic locals and got them on the other end of the rope. He signalled to Andy for prime, and "Switch-On," yelled "PULL YOU BASTARDS!" and they did. The old engine fired first pull, the process was repeated with the near-side engine and Andy was on his way back to the hangar and a third new bottom for BYJ.

Up to this point no one had been hurt in any of BYJ's tantrums, but a very definite pattern was emerging. In all three incidents sinking was involved, and in all cases snowy, icy weather was a factor. The fourth and final episode was true to form as far as sinking and snowy weather were concerned, but this time there was no happy ending. In retrospect, it was just as though old BYJ was trying to tell us something and we wouldn't listen, so finally she threw the book at us.

Jim Spilsbury aboard his yacht, *Blithe Spirit*, in his later years.
Harbour Publishing Archives

It was Christmas Eve 1949; the weather—reduced visibility in wet snow. Pilot Bill Peters was heading north from Sullivan Bay with four passengers. While landing in the little bay in Belize Inlet–Alison Sound where Oscar Johnson's floating logging camp was then located, something went wrong: just after touchdown, as Bill started his "round out" at about seventy-five miles per hour, the nose dug in, sheered sharply to the right and the big machine executed a complete cartwheel. The whole nose section of the hull broke off. Bill got thrown through a hatch but was fouled in the wreckage and dragged partway to the bottom before struggling free. Co-pilot Jack Steele and flight engineer Sig Hubenig were momentarily stunned but managed to recover in time to swim out through the break in the hull. Two passengers, Gordon Campbell and Gordon Squarebriggs, were able to save themselves but the other two, Ralph McBride and John Buckley, were pulled down and drowned. The ship sank in three minutes with only the very tip of the upper wing showing. Oscar and his crew were able to get a line round it, and dragged it to the surface with a boom-winch to remove the bodies of Buckley and McBride, who were still strapped into their seats. We theorized that they might have got out if their safety belts had not been fastened, and for this reason we generally advised seaplane and flying-boat passengers to leave their belts unfastened during takeoff and landing, but to secure them in flight in case of turbulent air. After this, Oscar lifted the wreck out with a logging donkey and A-frame, and piled it on the beach.

I am not a superstitious person, but by the time I was finished with BYJ I had almost become one. Her ghost lay quiet for thirty-five years.

In September 1981 I was taking an extended cruise up the BC coast with three friends, all of whom were already previously well acquainted with the coast but, like me, always willing to see more, so this was one of our "Voyages of Adventure and Discovery" in the good ship *Blithe Spirit*, which I had purchased after I left aviation. None of the other three had ever heard of BYJ, and I had no idea that there was anything left to see or on what part of the sixteen hundred miles of shoreline in the Seymour Inlet complex it might be.

We had been looking for a suitable spot to set our prawn traps, but after about twenty miles it was still too deep so we decided to find a spot to anchor for the night. The Seymour Inlet group had not yet been charted, so we were quite on our own. It was about 10 pm, and after crawling along with both echo sounders running we found our way into a narrow entrance. We felt our way through several right-angle turns, located a secluded bit of channel in which we were able to get our anchor down in a convenient twelve fathoms of water, and secured for the night. In the process of positioning the ship I had been sweeping the shoreline with the searchlight, and in doing so had picked up an unidentified object on the beach that might well have been the wreckage of an old building or something. In the morning I put the binoculars on this object and my spine just turned to ice. I launched the dinghy and rowed ashore before the others were up, and there it

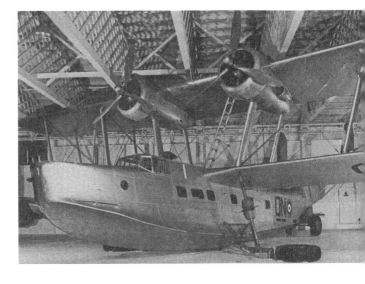

was: the remains of CF-BYJ, covered with moss and seaweed, but with part of the QCA speed-line and name still readable in black and yellow on the side of the hull. The spectre of Christmas Eve 1949 back to haunt me! Scavengers had been at it but, Belize Inlet being uncharted, it is not frequented by either pleasure boats or commercial fishermen, and the wreckage was still recognizable as a Stranraer. Some of the parts were remarkably well preserved.

In 1983 a tug, scow and crane owned by Bill Thompson of Pender Harbour picked up all that was left of BYJ with the intention of rebuilding it at the Canadian Museum of Flight in Langley, where Thompson was a founder.

Subsequent to the publication of this story, and due to a lack of storage space and funds at the museum, restoration efforts were stalled and the remains of BYJ languished at Bill Thompson's property for several decades. However, recently BYJ was moved to the Shearwater Aviation Museum in Nova Scotia, where volunteers are hoping to restore this historic aircraft. —Ed.

Former Queen Charlotte Airlines' ship CF-BXO on display at Hendon's Royal Air Force Museum in London, England. She is painted in Royal Air Force colours despite having been built for the Royal Canadian Air Force in Montreal and having enjoyed a glorious career flying for QCA.
Harbour Publishing Archives

20 CLOSE CALL WITH A GRIZZLY

Excerpted from Grizzlies & White Guys: The Stories of Clayton Mack *(1996),*
compiled and edited by Harvey Thommasen

I was home, in the house. My wife answer the phone. "There's a guy name Walmark who want to talk to you," she said. So I talk to him on the phone. I know the guy, I seen him before. He came here once before that. He said he had two guys who want to hunt grizzly bear in Kimsquit. "It's okay," I said. "Sure, come in."

They came in, fly in an airplane to Bella Coola. They get in my pickup. They get out a gun case. Nice gun case. They open it, there was a nice little gun in there. They said they didn't know how accurate it was or if it was any good for grizzly bear. I asked him, "What calibre is it?".350 Remington Magnum. Short rifle. That gun kick like hell. Uses shells that aren't very long, but they big around—thick. Them guys want me to use it, they want me to tell them how good it is for grizzly bear, and write down where I hit them grizzly bear. Then they want me to send them a report, tell them how good the gun is.

"Okay," I said. I asked him how much that gun was. "About seven hundred dollars in the store," he said. But it was special made for me. Short barrel, my name on shoulder mount: "First class guide—Clayton Mack."

I took them to Kimsquit. George Anderson, my son-in-law, came with me as my assistant guide. We took two hunters out the first day, got two grizzly bears. George got one, I got one. And then I took this guy, he was the youngest of the bunch. I took him quite a ways up the river. Lot of grizzly bear up there. Lot of fish spawning up there. And he shot at one grizzly bear. Gut-shot it, I guess, shot it through the stomach. We try and look for him, we see the blood all right, but we couldn't find him. George, he doesn't like guys like that, who gut-shoot the bears. He don't like to take them out. I try to tell George, "You take him out."

"No, you take him out," he said. "That bear was very close and he gut-shot him. Make the bear mad."

So we decided I would take that young guy out the next day. We finish skinnin' them two grizzly bears we got and then took the skins down to the boat. Spread them and salt them down.

We still got to get one more bear for this young guy. I took him up by myself the next day. I went up the Kimsquit River about a mile. There is a side stream, breaks in from the main river. Right close to the mountain. Trees are all small here, biggest about a foot through. I walked through some trees and came to a riverbed. A little water in there. A few fish in there, few dog salmons. I saw a bear go into the timber, I saw him walking. This young hunter was pretty clumsy. Noisy, clumsy, fall down and get his gun barrel stuck in the mud. You have to take that mud out of the barrel or else it blow

Clayton Mack at Kwatna in 1940.
Courtesy of Cliff Kopas

open. He don't seem to care. I tell him to be careful, he's going to ruin his gun. They told me later, "He has too much money, he doesn't give a damn what he does to his gun. Got so much money, he don't care." He was so clumsy I was worried he might get hurt.

There was a logjam. I put him in there. "You stay right here, I'll go back down and chase the bear up toward you. When he comes out of the woods there, shoot him," I said. I went down, walk down the river. I thought I was quite a bit below the bear now. That grizzly, he's behind me now I thought. So I went in the timber and started yelling like you chase cattle, *Ai, ai, ai!* I walk up, I don't see any sign of fresh bear track. Lot

Alistair Anderson illustration

of old tracks. I was about a hundred yards to the guys when I heard something behind me. *Woof, woof, woof.* Every jump she make, she made that noise.

I look back and saw a pretty good-sized grizzly bear coming toward me. I had this brand new gun. I stop and stand still. She keep coming, I didn't shoot right away. She stop about twenty, twenty-five feet away, and she stand up on her hind feet. About eight feet tall. Then she walk toward me on her hind feet. Look like she was gonna try and grab me up. I lift the gun up, try and shoot her in the chest. That gun slip. Barrel slide up her chest, and go off. Shot her under her chin, above her neck. She fell down, touched me a little bit on my leg. Dead. Big gun. I look at it. It was a sow, a female.

I stand there, and I hear sticks breaking, noises where this bear came from. Sound like a person blowin' their nose. He snorting. I look back, by God, I see another grizzly bear coming. Running toward me. This time I run. I run as fast as I can. There was a riverbed—ditch, like—about six feet deep. I jump down into it, I slide down on the bank, like, and hit the bottom. No water, dry riverbed.

I look up. It was a young grizzly bear, about four year old, I guess. Stand right there, right on top of his mother. He put his foot on her and he look at me. Pret' near as big as the other. Pretty big, too. I look beside me, there was a hole under the ground. It was a bank, overhanging bank. Flood, I guess, washed out quite a bit under the bank.

I look up and see that bear start circling around toward me. Joe Edgar told me that's a bad sign. Means he's a real bad bear. I shot the mother, you see, so he was mad at me. He wants to come after me. I thought, "He's gonna jump down." Gun loaded. I go under the bank. I hear the bear on the overhang, over my head. That bugger come right on top. That overhang roof about ten inch thick. I was afraid the overhang bank would break and bury me alive. The bear could smell me underneath here. I stayed in there looking up. Like a roof over me. I waited. If he comes down, I shoot. But he didn't, he was still on top of me, on the overhang.

He smell me, try and put his head down little bit once. Then he reach, try and put his hand down to feel for me. Then he came down with both front legs, try and feel for me underneath there. I see yellow jackets then, comin' out of his hair. They buzz all over me. The air was yellow with yellow jacket bees. I was scared to move too much. If I run that grizzly bear will get me; if I stay, I get stung. Then he came down, slide down, in an awkward way, like. He came down with his head down and then I see his jaw. I see his whole head is over toward me now. I shot him right between his jaw. I just about touch him, then I pull the trigger of that short .350 magnum rifle. *Bang!* He keep still there, I think I got him.

Talk about yellow jackets! Buzzing and flying all over. I came out of there, walked a little bit and climbed up the bank. I got on top of the bank and walked back toward the bear. I put my foot on the bear, spread the hair apart. He was just yellow inside the hairs. I guess he been raiding a yellow jacket nest. They like that, to eat the nest of yellow jackets. Lot of honey in that, and young yellow jackets.

I was standing there looking at all those yellow jackets in that bear when I heard something again, coming. I think, "Another bear coming. Must of had two young ones—two full-grown young bears." I started to yell at him, "Go on, beat it, I don't want to kill you." I went down little bit back to that clumsy guy. He asked, "What did you shoot?"

Clayton Mack with a grizzly bear, 1965.
Courtesy of Cliff Kopas

"Two grizzly bears," I said. "They try and get me. Come on, let's go look at 'em." He came over with me. That other third bear was still there. Sitting beside the mother. I heard my walkie-talkie, somebody talking on the walkie-talkie. They heard me shooting from the boat. They asking who shooting. I said, "A bear try and go after me." My son-in-law told me, "Better get out of there." We went down for the night.

We eat, had breakfast. Then went back up with the jet boat to skin them bears. We skin the mother, no yellow jackets on it. Just the young one. We try and skin the young one but you can't touch it. Not for the yellow jackets under the hair. They come fly in your face. So we drag that grizzly bear to the boat, sink him in the water to drown the yellow jackets, then we can skin him. I never seen anything like it. Just yellow inside the skin.

21 TRIANGLE ISLAND

Excerpted from Keepers of the Light *(1985, 1990), by Donald Graham*

While they watch winter winds scale shingles off their roofs, lighthouse keepers from Race Rocks to Green Island on Alaska's doorstep can always console themselves with the maxim: "It could always be worse, we could be at Triangle Island." Triangle Island light was the worst ever. In the annals of West Coast navigation the very name conjures up savage weather, disaster and death—complete and utter triumph of the elements over mankind. Established with a gush of enthusiasm under an ill omen in 1910, crowned with the worst calamity in the Department of Marine and Fisheries' history, Triangle would be abandoned as its costliest blunder ten years later.

Maritime events were always hot news in Victoria. When readers opened the *Colonist* or the *Times*, they first turned to the "Marine Notes" or "Shipping News" columns, which heralded arrivals and departures and served up lurid accounts of wrecks. Reporters were permanent fixtures in the outer offices of the marine agency down on Wharf Street, constantly hectoring the agent and his underlings for scraps to carry back to their editors. They could also be found at any time of day down on the docks, rubbing shoulders with burly stevedores, notebooks at the ready as they waited for ships' officers and crew to disembark.

Late in the afternoon of June 23, 1909, their patience paid off when the lighthouse tender *Quadra* lumbered up to the government pier, home at last from laying plans for the "ultimate lighthouse." H.C. Killeen, the man of the moment, came down her gangplank and regaled them with an account of how he had staked out a site on Triangle Island—forty-two miles northwest of Cape Scott, 650 feet above the sea—for a powerful first-order light which he was sure would "ultimately develop into one of the most important lighthouses on this coast." Rightfully predicting the "great development" of steamship traffic, the engineer declared that Triangle Island would serve as "a leading light which will be first picked up by the steamship captains and will give them their bearings whether they are bound for Puget Sound or Prince Rupert."

Triangle, as a special *Colonist* Sunday supplement exalted, stood out as "the furthermost western point of the Empire." It was the opposite bookend of British imperialism to Bombay's great gateway to India: a malevolent cone-shaped crag which had escaped the Ice Age, lurching out of the waves in flagrant, baiting challenge to the Marine Department's chief engineer, W.P. Anderson. After Anderson's heady architectural triumph at Estevan Point, there was nowhere to go but up. And what kudos might come from humbling that awesome outpost, five times higher, destined one day to become "the key to wireless communication on the Pacific"! Crowning it with one of his distinctive concrete phalli would surely propel him into the ranks of his heroes— Great Britain's Stevenson, Douglas and Halpin, the greatest lighthouse builders of all time, men who counted Eddystone and Skerryvore among their brainchildren. In a heated meeting on March 5, 1909, other members of the Lighthouse Board tried in vain to dissuade him, suggesting he build on Cape Scott, a more accessible site at the northern tip of Vancouver Island, instead. Their chairman was having none of that.

It was one thing to draw the plans but quite another to translate them into steel and concrete on the cutting edge of a ceaseless hurricane. Gales howling down the Hecate Strait and Queen Charlotte Sound linked arms with storms swirling in like dervishes from the open Pacific to collide with Triangle Island. Jet-force winds crashing up its steep flanks enveloped the summit in updrafts from every point on the compass at once. Straining at her anchor chains in the heaving grey sea, ss *Leebro* disgorged supplies and gangs of navvies in workboats that summer.

They laid a ton and a half of steel rails that climbed 1,820 feet up the rock face to a winch and donkey engine above.

The light station at the forbidding summit of Triangle Island.
Courtesy of the Canadian Coast Guard

During their off-hours the workers explored the island. Crawling into a cave near the shore one evening, they held up their lanterns and recoiled in horror from a skeleton sprawled against the dripping rock wall, leering back at them, clad in a battered lifebelt and gumboots. No one ever uncovered the identity of the hapless "sentinel of Triangle Island," only that he was a white man who had somehow made his way ashore years before. After an eerie lamplit ceremony, Captain Freeman of the halibut vessel *Flamingo* interred his bones in the cavern, but not before a radio operator with a grotesque sense of humour tucked the skull under his arm as a souvenir.

Up on top of Triangle, the crouching workers dug, drilled and blasted water cisterns, and framed a duplex dwelling and wireless shack. Fierce winds pried shingles and siding off almost as fast as the men nailed them down. Carpenters harnessed in safety belts hammered up forms for the tower, then mixed, poured and tamped the concrete. Once stripped, the tower stood forty-six feet tall. For three months they battled the shrieking gales to haul up and wrestle fifty-two half-inch-thick curved panes into place around the huge beacon room. Some days the battering wind vibrated putty out of the frames faster than it could set. The iron lantern chamber was braced inside with stout beams, and anchored by cables and turnbuckles to the rock.

The first decade of this century seemed to promise that all Nature would be subjugated, bent to man's will through an enlightened partnership of labour, capital and technology. Encyclopedias of the day portrayed a universe understood in all its complexity. This was the age of the *Titanic*, after all, the crowning era of steam and steel. In November 1910, the *Colonist* proclaimed in shouting capitals "TRIANGLE LIGHT IS SHOWN NOW," echoing Killeen's confidence in "the largest and most powerful of North Pacific Coast lights." And so it was. Its gargantuan lens, an identical twin to Estevan's, with outer prisms nine feet in circumference, rumbled around on a tub filled with nine hundred pounds of shimmering mercury, and focused a million-candlepower light from the kerosene wick through its bull's eye in a slender cone that stretched fifty miles out toward Japan.

Back on Triangle, however, huddling out of the barbarous winds' reach, lightkeepers and radio operators looked down in disbelief upon the furrowed banks of cloud and fog, while mariners underneath searched in vain for the mighty flash in the night. The light was too high. As ugly rumours piled up, Colonel Anderson came west to inspect Pachena, Estevan and Triangle, all built since his last tour of inspection. If he had any reservations about Triangle, he kept them carefully to himself.

Life soon became unbearable for the tiny colony, which inherited the dubious concrete achievement of Anderson's obsession. James Davies took over the station in July 1910 with his wife and three daughters. His assistant, A. Holmes, and the two wireless operators, Jack Bowerman and Alex Sutherland, doubled as schoolteachers.

Every hour after dark, Holmes or one of the Davies family had to climb the tower and wind up the counterweights, which spun the monster lens until they hit the floor. Sleep was often impossible thanks to the shrieking gales and the constant "evil lament of the huge sealions." Seven-foot deposits of guano rendered Triangle's soil so caustic that it burned like lye and rotted leather boots. Occasional halibut, dropped off by sympathetic fishermen, were the only relief from their monotonous fare of canned food,

The tramway at Triangle looked like the world's worst roller coaster.
Courtesy of the Canadian Coast Guard

but approaching and landing at Triangle was always a perilous venture. Davies once tried to enhance his family's diet by ordering a large consignment of apples, oranges, bananas and vegetables. When the *Leebro* unloaded, the precious cargo oozed out from under thirty tons of coal. Two apples and half a banana survived. They tried keeping chickens and a cow, but the animals were driven over the cliff by the wind.

Since isolation magnifies trivia to gigantic proportions, it was hardly surprising that men confined under such abysmal conditions would turn upon each other, snarling like rats in an overcrowded laboratory. A dispute over a ton of coal soon escalated, on that wind-scoured outpost, to fisticuffs. When word of the rumpus reached Victoria, an exasperated Captain Robertson, the new marine agent, issued standing orders to Davies: "You and your family...have no communication whatever with the wireless Station on Triangle Island, except when business necessitates it." The navy's Radio Telegram Branch reinforced the shaky truce with similar instructions to their men, so the people manning the very nerve centre of Pacific communications lived next door to one another, incommunicado.

In February, James Davies called next door "on business" and sullenly handed the operators a message for Victoria: "MRS. DAVIES DANGEROUSLY ILL SOME TIME PAST, BAD HAEMORRHAGE CANNOT STOP, ESTEEM IT A FAVOUR IF VESSEL SENT DIRECT AS MATTER IS SERIOUS." Captain Robertson wired his superintendent of lights aboard the tender *Newington*. Gordon Halkett in turn ordered Captain Barnes "to proceed with all despatch to the station."

As she plied her way full speed toward Triangle, a freak wave overtook the *Newington*, poured over her fantail, filled her decks to the rails, twisted and wrenched out steam pipes, and swept away all the deck cargo. Cringing in terror, the crew clutched

The supply ship *Newington* almost sank as the result of a freak wave during an emergency evacuation at Triangle.
City of Vancouver Archives, BO P397

railing and bulkheads, and held its collective breath as water rose chest-high. The ship shuddered, then rose groaning from her grave under tons of the North Pacific.

Once at Triangle, Halkett leaped from the workboat, scaled the tramway and found Violet Davies up at the house, "very weak from loss of blood." The deckhands lashed her to a mattress and lowered her down to the beach. They had a tough time hoisting her up the side and over the rails "owing to the *Newington* rolling badly." Halkett brought a doctor aboard at Alert Bay and he urged the superintendent to waste no time getting her to hospital. Fifty-six hours later, an operator came across to Davies' house to tell him his wife had arrived safely in Victoria.

After signing on for two-month stints at Triangle, radio operators were often marooned, still living out of their suitcases a year later, bitterly complaining they had been "shanghaied." Even when, at long last, a ship came smoking over the horizon, weeks would slip by while the crew gambled their wages away, waiting for safe landing conditions. While their mother ship cut lazy circles offshore, workboats often stood little chance of abetting the islanders' escape, swamping in the surf and beating their way back to the tender.

The buildings atop Triangle looked like shrivelled bugs, snared and sucked dry in a spider's web of cables and turnbuckles fastened into deadeyes grouted into the rocks. All the buildings were linked by cables—lifelines with burrs that sliced cruelly into fingers and palms. Even so, the dwellings teetered and swayed on their foundations so violently that their occupants became seasick. Windows bulged inward like lenses before they shattered. As a matter of routine, no one ever opened a door alone. Men grovelled along on hands and knees between the buildings. To vacuum her house,

Left: The huge first-order light shone in vain above Triangle's fog.
Courtesy of the Canadian Coast Guard

Above: The telegraph operator's dwelling with makeshift bracing against Triangle's hurricane-force winds.
Courtesy of the Canadian Coast Guard

Violet Davies needed only to open a window. The wind barged down chimneys and through walls to snuff out fires and spew billowing clouds of soot through the houses. Everything on the station stood poised to rush over the cliffs to the raging sea 608 feet below.

On October 22, 1912, the anemometer registered 120 miles per hour before the wind, furious at having its temper recorded, ripped it from its mounts, then assaulted the buildings, cleaving off six brick and iron chimneys at the roofline. A shed leapt off its foundation next to the tower and fled, somersaulting end-over-end over the side into the sea. The wireless mast snapped like a straw, cutting off all communications. Down on the beach the raging surf reduced two storehouses to kindling. The two-ton donkey engine for the tramway crawled several feet away from its base.

Praying and shouting encouragement to one another, the two radio operators crouched in their dwelling like lunatics sharing a padded cell, becoming hysterical when the gale bashed in their windows and yanked the flapping doors off their hinges. The house shuddered and split in two. The attic water tank ruptured, flooding all the rooms. Preferring James Davies' company to the prospect of staying to be crushed, they inched along the walkway to the keeper's house, chins scraping the ground. And his dwelling "absolutely rocked in gale," he wrote, "not safe to be inside."

While the gales caught their breath out at sea between storms, Triangle's stark terrain held other dangers. Frank Dawson, another radio operator, went for a hike and tumbled two hundred feet over a cliff to a rock ledge. He had nearly screamed himself hoarse before a search party discovered his perch and hauled him up by rope.

By December 1912 Davies had clearly had enough. He begged Robertson for a transfer from this pest-hole of fear to "more congenial surroundings" as a reward for nineteen years' service. "Triangle is very hard on our nerves and a great strain on our constitutions," the former keeper of Egg Island confessed. Only two years old, his dwelling was already "unfit for habitation." Rain driven horizontally by the incessant gales "swamps us out," he complained, "as the building leaks, and it is an utter impossibility to keep a fire, as the place gets smoked out and we have sometimes to go a week at a stretch without a warm meal." Three winters at Triangle were too many; Davies wanted off before a fourth. "The way the wind circles around the buildings in whirlwinds makes keeping a fire out of the question," he told Robertson, "and you can imagine what a trial it is to myself and mine."

Davies escaped with his family in March. In late January 1914 his successor, Thomas Watkins, sent a message off to Victoria, reporting that a gale had flattened the storage shed on the beach again, strewing 450 oil cans and five kegs of nails along the shore. "The roof is blown about 300 feet along the beach," he reported, "Sides & Floor about 150 feet from original position." Both dwellings "got a severe shaking"—the door of the spare house blew off its hinges and the chimneys were scattered all over the ground again. By March there were only "two habitable rooms, a bedroom and a kitchen," in Watkins' house. That October the keeper was eager to transfer to a new station planned for Bonilla Island up north in Hecate Strait—a "much more suitable place for a man with a wife and young children than Triangle is."

Watkins was succeeded in his turn by Michael O'Brien, who had spent five years down in the hold of the Sand Heads lightship, where he had contracted rheumatism "owing to the confinement and dampness." He was "very desirous of being exchanged to Triangle Island" where he could live with his wife and family.

Triangle Island light may have been a nightmare for its keepers, but when the verdict came in on Anderson's accomplishment, his peers were unanimous. In 1913 F.A. Talbot published his definitive *Lightships and Lighthouses*, an ambitious study of the world's leading lighthouses, the latest and best survey of the state of the art. "Probably the most important light and certainly the loftiest on the Pacific seacoast north of the equator is that on the summit of Triangle Island, British Columbia," Talbot reckoned. He also lavished praise on the "Engineer-in-Chief of the Lighthouse Authority of the Canadian Government" for Estevan Point, placed in "a most romantic setting," and told how Anderson had laid a tramway through a "grand primeval forest" to haul concrete to the site.

The two lights confirmed Anderson's revolutionary reinforced-concrete designs, with their ornate and functional buttresses, as "the last word in lighthouse building." Naturally neither could compare with Eddystone or Skerryvore as engineering feats, yet there was no denying that Anderson's "most powerful beacons" were of "commanding character, representing as they do the latest and best in coast lighting." Never one to rest on his laurels, Anderson altered Triangle's plan, stretching the tower out to twice its height and tapering the central column, for a master plan to build new towers at Point Atkinson and Sheringham Point, each offering easy access for an appreciative public.

The nine years after Triangle Island first captured the public's imagination were nine years of war for its keepers and nine years of exquisite agony for its creator. For all his official preening, Anderson must have seen that Triangle's light was too high when he inspected his masterpiece the very first time, when he watched the shed on the beach slowly shrink to the size of one of his prized stamps as he rode up on the tramway. The chief engineer may even have ascended through the grey stratus that clung like cotton candy to the top two hundred feet of the eyrie most of the year. Surely he knew his mistake. The cardinal rule of lighthouse construction—never build higher than 150 feet—could be read on blackboards and in notebooks in every first-year engineering course in Canada. In his own annual report for 1906, only three years before he unrolled the plans for Triangle Island light, Anderson had reiterated, "*They should not be placed at an elevation exceeding 150 feet above the level of the sea on account of the prevalence of fog.*" So what must he have felt when all the praise pouring in was poisoned by rumblings and (even worse) derision in wheelhouses and shipping offices from Shanghai to San Francisco?

No one will ever know. Any complaints had to be put on paper and mailed off to the chairman of the Lighthouse Board of Canada. There was, of course, an endless barrage on every conceivable subject during Anderson's tenure. Petitions "praying" for new lights, complaints about existing ones, requests for foghorns, beacons, buoys, lifeboats, sema-

The patrol vessel *Galiano*, just prior to its sinking in 1918.
National Defence/Canadian Navy Heritage E-46568

phore stations, and suggestions for changing characteristics of lights—handwritten pleas from lowly fishermen's co-operatives, or demands typed under the imposing letterheads of the world's most prestigious shipping lines—all piled into that in-tray in Ottawa, each one numbered and placed by harried secretaries on the Lighthouse Board's agenda. But there was not one letter about Triangle Island.

Whatever the explanation for the absence of any reference to the blind cyclops in the Board's minutes, Triangle Island was about to loom up and confront them all as the naval patrol vessel *Galiano* dropped anchor off the station shortly after noon on October 29, 1918, and sent off her workboat with supplies. It should have been a long-awaited day of deliverance for the radio operators. Sid Elliot was ecstatic—he was scheduled to "come off." Jack Neary would see his brother Michael, serving as a radio operator on the *Galiano*. For the lightkeepers there would be a sack of mail. But no one was permitted to go aboard or stay ashore since eight crew members had been left behind at Esquimalt, laid low by the dreaded Spanish flu running rampant in Victoria. Crestfallen, Sid learned that his stint would be continued; he plodded back up the thousand steps "home" while Jack caught up on news of friends and family.

By 1:30 that afternoon, southwest winds began to muster their forces for another assault. The shore party hurriedly transferred cargo while clouds piled up on an ominous, dirty black anvil on the horizon. As the storm struck, Jack and Mike Neary quickly embraced and shook hands goodbye. Seamen dumped the remaining cargo onto the beach, snatched up Miss Brunton, a housekeeper who had been teaching the O'Brien children, thrust her into the workboat and bucked the roller-coaster swells back to their ship. *Galiano* wasted no time hoisting her anchors. As she steamed away, the keepers piled freight on the tram, then climbed home to open their mail.

No one will ever know why the *Galiano* headed for the open sea rather than seeking shelter in Shushartie Bay. She was a "cranky bitch" at best in foul weather, with decks and alleyways always awash when the wind was on her quarter. Her crew had long complained about their captain's inscrutable preference for riding out storms at sea, tempting fate.

Two hours later Art Green, the radio operator on watch, jerked upright in his chair, clamped his headset tightly to his ear and grabbed for a pencil to scribble her last feeble message: HOLD FULL OF WATER. SEND HELP. He called Sid Elliot over and both took turns signalling till sunrise. There was no reply. Art looked over at Jack Neary snoring on his cot. "Shall I wake up Jack?" he asked. "No, let him sleep," Sid advised. Why wake him up to a nightmare? No one ever learned the *Galiano*'s fate. Fishermen on the halibut steamer *George Foster* gaffed Wilfred Ebbs's body out of the water with a pike pole two days later; two other bodies were later found drifting two hundred miles away, east of Cape St. James.

Michael O'Brien left that winter to keep his own appointment with tragedy at Entrance Island light, and Alex Dingwell came down from Green Island to preside at the dismantling of Anderson's monumental mistake. In 1920 the Department of Marine grudgingly conceded defeat to Nature's fury and human error, a decade after the *Colonist*'s editor had gloated, "Triangle Island is at last to be put to the uses for which Nature apparently designed it from the beginning of things." Many of the same men who had bolted the beacon room together scaled it again to wrench off the rusted nuts. Piece by piece the curved glass panels, the nine-foot lens crystals, iron frame, copper sheeting, clockworks and pails of mercury went down the tramway and out to a ship's hold. Some deckhand-photographer with a keen sense of history documented the surrender, capturing the last boat on its way out from Triangle Island.

The hulking lantern from the West Coast's "leading light" has been resurrected upon the tarmac at the new Canada Coast Guard base in Victoria, where it dwarfs tourists on Coast Guard Day. And way up in that punishing corner of nowhere, Colonel Anderson's squat monument still stands above the clouds, futile and permanent, a twentieth-century Tower of Babel waiting to intrigue archeologists a thousand years hence. Who would have built it there, and why?

REMEMBERING GWYN GRAY HILL
Legendary Coastal Sailor

22

Excerpted from The Inlet: Memoirs of a Modern Pioneer *(2001),*
by Helen Piddington

There are all manner of ways of travelling this coast by sea. Fishermen head north in flotillas nose to tail, often without charts, following the leader. We hear them talking, sometimes, to keep themselves awake, almost incoherent with weariness. Tugs too keep in touch with their buddies travelling at snail's pace, usually alone but sometimes in procession, sharing good tides through rapids. Locals dart across these southeast-northwest paths in and out the inlets to Vancouver Island. Most have small, fast boats and no time for chat. The coast guard and police have large sleek vessels and travel alone, silently, at speed. They zoom up inlets, then down again in minutes, mission accomplished. It makes you wonder what could have been so serious or so easily solved?

Tourists often travel in clumps, chatting non-stop about engine speed, the weather, their next meal at the next resort. We hear them on the radio, days before they get to us, if indeed they sidetrack off the main route north. Most go straight between marinas and resorts, concerned only with creature comforts: food, drink, water, garbage disposal, showers and laundry. If they notice the country they are passing through it is rarely, if ever, mentioned. Many come fully provisioned from home base. Why bother with perishable local produce like prawns or crab that requires cleaning or cooking? Or, horror of horrors, organic lettuce that might contain slugs!

The largest boats, with anxious skippers or well-paid crew, go solo. So large, some of them, that when they make fast to our wharf, the boat shed and auxiliary wharves strain so much their moorings are almost torn free.

Those who sail the coast usually avoid resorts and anchor out, preferring to be alone. This group does its own fishing, buys less than powerboats but is more apt to ask us aboard for a drink or a meal.

Over the years, people from all these groups have become dear friends. We look forward to their annual appearance north and south. Some make us their destination, "the highlight of their summer." We hear their triumphs and disasters, their illnesses and hopes. How sad when boats are sold and friends stop travelling.

There is another group again, and these I call "explorers." They come off-season, as early as April, as late as October. More welcome then because we are less busy. They may stay a day or two, taking part in what's going on ashore—glad to stretch limbs and be of use. Some we've known since our sailing days, encountered first in some remote northern anchorage. Their visits weave warm patterns through our lives. They seem like family and as important in our children's lives. This group is self-sufficient, ignores resorts, always anchors out unless visiting. Travelling perhaps half the year they keep in touch with world affairs. They have opinions. They read. They know and love this coast, can handle her many moods— her hazards—enjoy the scenery, the wildlife and the birds. And they venture inland, always on the lookout for clues to local history. This is the group we left when we became landlubbers and so are the ones we understand most easily.

Gwyn Gray Hill's yawl, *Cherie*, at Boussole Bay, Alaska, in 1976. His yawl was painted with aluminum undercoat and, if annoyed, he'd crank up his oil stove to produce clouds of black smoke. Some called him "General Smuts."

Courtesy of Helen Piddington

And of this group there was one very special person: a Welshman by the name of Gwyn Gray Hill. Our paths had crossed often while cruising, and once we settled here he came faithfully twice a year on his trips north and south. He would arrive, a cloud of black smoke on his yawl *Cherie*, painted with aluminum undercoat so she would blend in. Though nearly blind he missed nothing. Would call out as he approached: "I can't see—I can't see!" then comment on some obscure, minute detail. Apparently the thick lenses looped to his ears with strips of black inner tube showed him what others missed. Or he'd begin questioning: "What about Colonel So-and-So who vanished at the head of Loughborough in '28? Have you heard any more about him? And what about Bill Baker? Did he actually drown? Was his body ever found?" All this was ancient history—well before our time and sometimes his. But to Gray Hill the past was as precious as the present,

to be pondered over, sorted through, treasured. And if there was no mystery then one must be found.

Gray Hill gave different versions of his past. Some say he grew up in a castle in Wales, was taught at home by private tutors. Others claim he was actually English and went to boarding school in Switzerland or Germany. Some are convinced he was a remittance man, an only son paid to stay away from home, or the illegitimate son of his "sister." Who knows? But one thing was sure—he led a charmed life. As a lad he survived that famous Scottish botulism case of 1922. His father had taken him fishing at Loch Maree and requested something other than pressed duck for their lunches. Eight people who ate the duck became ill and died.

Whatever the other details, it is known that Gray Hill arrived in Victoria in 1931, a young man with means. He tried commercial fishing with a family connection out of Comox but did not enjoy it. Then lads like the Rodd brothers, interested in boats and the sea, became his friends and he spent the next few years with them in wild adolescent fun.

Gradually these lads grew up, became concerned with work, careers, their wives and children. But Gray Hill, with no responsibilities and no need to earn a living, did not develop. Wanting always to carouse, he became an aggravating nuisance—then a recluse.

His first boat was *Charmer,* a lifeboat from a vessel of that name. On *Cape St. Elias,* his second boat, he began what became annual cruises up this coast. As his sight was poor and getting worse, he memorized the outline of the entire landmass between Maple Bay and Alaska.

Benita Sanders and I heard about Gwyn Gray Hill on our first trip to the Charlottes

Above: Gray Hill's *Cherie,* as illustrated in *Character Boats of the BC Coast: Series 1*, by Stephen Jackson (Harbour, 1973).

Above left: Some say Gray Hill grew up in a castle in Wales; others claim he was actually English and went to boarding school in Switzerland or Germany. Some are convinced he was a remittance man or an only son paid to stay away from home. Who knows?
Courtesy of Helen Piddington

To the left is the massive 4-inch by 14-inch by 15-foot beam that the tiny Gray Hill helped raise and hold in place until it was secured.

Courtesy of Helen Piddington

in 1968. One day, struggling along the shore to Kaisun, we caught sight of *Cape St. Elias* underway in the distance and never for one minute imagined that either of us would meet him—much less be friends.

After some fifty years of sailing, when he could no longer distinguish between land and sky, he gave up travel and lived aboard *Cherie* at Maple Bay. Eventually he moved to a rest home in Duncan and was put next to the Rodd brother who disliked him most. But at this point both were too old to realize or to care.

During all those years he visited countless people whose meals, I'm sure, kept him alive. For between stops he survived on a liquid diet, or so he claimed. And while his questions were repetitive and sometimes annoying, we were always pleased to see him. Nothing fazed him, everything intrigued him—the weirder the better. And when he came, wolves sang from the hills across the inlet.

Gray Hill liked the shape and size of our son Adam as an infant. Felt him a perfect candidate for the Northumbrian pipes. He had given his pipes to Peter Rodd, another baby he'd admired, but now it was imperative that our child fall asleep to pipe music, to get it into his system early. Thus one evening after Adam was tucked in, Dane turned on the generator so the vacuum cleaner could provide air for Gray Hill's chanter. The noise was extraordinary. Adam slept on. He has yet to try the pipes.

I've claimed elsewhere that we got scant help from anyone. Gray Hill was the exception. During our first summer Dane realized the kitchen ceiling was sagging dangerously. So he cut a beam 4 inches by 14 inches by 15 feet. One end fitted easily into a slot in a central wall but the other was the problem: How could he raise and position it alone? It was enormously heavy. A young, strong inlet dweller who came by that morning was asked to help but refused. His back, he said, might get hurt; he could not take that risk. Then up came Gray Hill from the wharf. A tiny man, who appeared to have little or no strength, he saw the solution immediately. Taking a stout timber some five feet long, he raised the beam with Dane then held it upright—fingers interlaced, back and arms straight, knees bent—supporting the entire weight of that beam while Dane edged it in place. I have photos of him holding it and others of him resting afterwards, unscathed.

Gray Hill was as grubby as his boat—greasy, sooty and reeking of fuel. When he came up for meals I longed to pop him in a hot bath. He would arrive at table empty-handed, unthinkable on this coast, but with his own sharp penknife, like a European peasant. And always he teased me about our spoons and forks—knowing full well their history and provenance. It was just one of his rituals. Then he would keep us up, entranced, till all hours. When he left I would give him jam—"Oh, yes please. Rhubarb—I love it!"—bread, cakes, fruit and vegetables until we discovered he gave it all away at his next port of call.

Gray Hill gave everyone on this coast a nickname. After we got the wild boar we became the Piggwigglingtons or variations on that theme. And between visits, while he could still see, he would write long letters to each of us in his beautiful copperplate script, changing his own name from Gray Hill to J.W. Roast to Rost and back again at whim. He never married but fell in love with other men's wives—the tall slender ones, especially, and all along the coast he promised his mother's rings. The one to get them deserved both rings and boat, for when his cruising days were over she fed him, washed him, drove him where he needed to go and kept him comfortable.

The last time we saw him was very sad. He was seated on a clean boat, in clean clothes, his skin pink and fresh, almost unrecognizable. But his mind was vague and blurry.

Sure he was aggravating, time-consuming and sometimes downright rude—as when pristine yachts pulled up behind him he'd sully them with puffs of soot—but he was also endearing and endlessly entertaining and we miss him very much. Gwyn Gray Hill will always be part of our lives, part of this coast, part of Loughborough and her mysteries.

HERON

by Russell Thornton

In the deep-cut, swerving ravine
the hour before dawn. Creek more spirit than water
pouring white down the bouldery creek path
at arm's length toward me and past.
                                              Out of the grey dark
a heron rises, a grey lopsided bundle,
a tent suddenly assembling itself and, in a split-instant,
collapsing and assembling itself again in mid-air.
There it is, opening its near-creek-spanning wings,
trailing its long thin legs, carrying its neck
in an S-shape, head held back: silent heron
flying away farther up the ravine.
                                      Is it the same heron
I saw once before—the slender, sensitive-still,
blue-grey mystery alone in front of me in bright daylight?
I watched it until the houses, people, streets and cars
faded into the fringes of the light,
faded, and reappeared along with this same creek
spilling out of a pipe and flowing for a block
through old backyards and into another pipe—
and then saw the still one gone. The entire creek unbroken
could be the heron's home, these waters
of the snowmelt and rain that gather and surge
and twist their way down to the sea.
                                        The heron
alights somewhere, disappears, and lifts again
as I come around a turn—and I see it again. And now
I see it at the shallow creek-edge, in an eddy
where the current swings out around a boulder and is lost—
all calm attention standing there, searching
through the creek waters' sunless rays.
                                          It finds a fish—
the fish swims quick into the poised long bill.
The heron lifts, the dark tasting itself, the ravine
flying through the ravine—living sign,
secret heron of the beginning, morning bird.

From House Built of Rain *(2003), by Russell Thornton*

THE SAD SAGA OF COCKATRICE BAY

23

Excerpted from Full Moon, Flood Tide: Bill Proctor's Raincoast *(2003),*
by Bill Proctor and Yvonne Maximchuk

Cockatrice Bay is located on south Broughton Island on Queen Charlotte Strait, north of the entrance to Fife Sound. The bay was well known for its run of big coho salmon, some weighing as much as twenty pounds.

In 1951 a logger named Art McIntyre came to Cockatrice looking for timber, and he found what he was looking for around May Lake. Art, being a man who liked to dam creeks and use water to move logs, liked what he saw. He had already dammed Scott Cove Creek and Marion Creek in Tsibass Lagoon. To Art, this was just another creek.

Cockatrice Creek is 1,980 feet long and it drains Phyllis Lake. There is a swamp between Phyllis Lake and May Lake, 2,310 feet in length. The idea was to build a dam at the tail-out of Phyllis Lake to raise the level of the swamp so logs could be towed from May Lake to Phyllis Lake. Once the dam was built, the level of Phyllis Lake rose fourteen feet. When the dam was completed, Art built an incline railway to the beach.

The remains of the log cradle and railway at Cockatrice Bay. It is believed that the upside-down boat, fitted with an Easthope 10/14, was used to tow logs across Phyllis Lake when Art McIntyre was logging there. When they were finished, it was put on the railway and abandoned at Cockatrice Bay.

Bill Proctor photo

An incline railway has only one car, which is pulled by a winch, in this case a steam winch. The car would go right into the lake, the boom man would shove the load of logs onto the car, and the winch would pull the load up out of the lake to the top of the hill and from there downhill to the beach. The car, loaded with logs, would go right out into the sea and the logs would float off. Then the winch would pull the car back up the hill and down to the lake for another load of logs.

Art logged this way for five years. Needless to say, that was the end of the big coho of Cockatrice Bay. When Art moved away in 1956 he left the dam in place, and also the railway and the steam winch. The railroad was 1,980 feet long and built on cedar logs, so there were a lot of logs, plus there were a few loads of big logs that had spilled on the way to the sea and been left to rot.

In 1964 a man named Ed Brandon, a shake cutter, came to Cockatrice Bay with his old boat, *Fearless*, and saw all the big logs. Ed was an old loner for the most part but he could see that this was too big a job for one man, so he went to Vancouver to find someone to help him, and he came back with a man named Bob Savage, an Englishman who had never been out in the woods. Bob was forty years old and had a good job in town, but he quit his job and bought a gas-powered winch for $2,000, and some power saws, and came to Cockatrice to make his fortune.

The two men got the winch ashore and tried to drag the logs down to the beach, but the logs were too big. They cut them into short lengths, but this made the work too slow because the short logs were always hanging up on something.

At about this time Ed hired another man, a shake cutter named Joe Walters. Joe was seventy years old and all he knew was how to split shakes by hand. When Joe arrived

These are the remains of the dam on the creek at Cockatrice Bay. The dam killed large runs of coho, and though the creek has been cleaned and restocked, the salmon runs have never returned to their historic levels.
Bill Proctor photo

he built a nice little cabin on the shore by the mouth of the creek, and while Bob and Ed were still trying to get logs to the beach, Old Joe was splitting up a storm. Bob could say to Joe that splitting by hand was too slow, but all Bob and Ed had to show for two months of work was a lot of broken cable and a few blocks. Old Joe had built a cabin and split ten cords of beautiful shakes.

Now Ed took off and went to Vancouver to buy a barge to haul the shakes and blocks and also the rails from the old railroad. Ed was gone for three weeks and all Bob and Joe had was a rowboat, which neither of them could row very well. Both of them chewed snuff, and while Ed was gone they ran out of snuff. It was right at this time that I went to Cockatrice to fish. I got there in the evening, dropped the anchor and was cooking supper when this man came rowing out and circled my boat. I went out on deck and invited him to come on board.

He looked like a wild man and seemed scared but he came and sat in the cabin and I gave him a cup of tea. He said his name was Bob Savage. Then he told me all the things that had gone wrong, all about Old Joe and the snuff, and apparently three nights before I came along, Joe had said to Bob, "We only have a half box of snuff left so there is none for you tomorrow." They got in a fight and Joe had arms like an ape and Bob ended up out in the bush, and that's where he had slept for three nights.

Bob asked me if I would take him to Alert Bay because he was leaving for good. As it happened, I planned to go to Alert Bay to see my wife, Yvonne, who was there waiting for our second baby to be born. So the next day Bob loaded all his stuff aboard and I took him to Alert Bay, and that was the last I ever saw of him. He gave me a seven-foot plywood rowboat for taking him in and left Joe the big rowboat.

About the time Bob left, Ed came back with an old sailing schooner, the *Joan G*, originally the *Maid of Orleans*. (The 129-foot-long ship had a long and interesting history. Built in 1882 in San Francisco, she served as a slave ship and went seal hunting in the Arctic, where she spent two winters locked in the ice. She was used in the fur trade by the Hudson's Bay Company, served as a rumrunner, towed logs here on the coast and worked as a herring packer.)

No sooner had Ed come back than he fell and broke his leg and had to go back to Vancouver, leaving Old Joe there all alone.

I thought about Old Joe a lot, and then one day I got a letter from Bob asking me to go and take Joe to Alert Bay. He sent me fifty dollars with the letter. When I got there, Joe seemed to know I was coming. He had everything packed and ready to go and he had even had a shave that morning. Joe was a nice man and a hard worker, but he left Cockatrice Bay with nothing to show for ten months' work. He had no way to get all his shakes out and he did not even own them, for everything was in Bob's name.

Now there was no one at Cockatrice Bay, but there were tools, chainsaws and lots of other good stuff: blocks, drums of gas, the winch and the old *Joan G*. I brought home what I could pack and wrote to Bob, telling him I had a lot of his stuff in my shop and that when he came back I would bring it out to him. At the very same time, he wrote to me and told me to take possession of everything: all he wanted was his chainsaw and a few odds and ends. I took the letter to the police and they told me to go ahead and take everything and store it, but if Bob came back I would have to return it to him. I thought maybe I could buy it all from him, so I made him an offer of $500 for everything and he accepted it.

I went out and beachcombed some logs and lashed them into a float, then moved the winch and all the other gear aboard. I thought that was the end of it, but I had no sooner got home than I got another letter from Bob wanting me to buy the *Joan G*. It was Bob who had paid for it and it was anchored up at the head of Cockatrice Bay. It seemed that Ed thought he

The remains of the historic *Joan G* (originally the *Maid of Orleans*) can still be seen at Cockatrice Bay. *Harbour Publishing Archives*

owned it, but Bob had paid $3,000 for it and he sent me a copy of the bill of sale. Bob wanted me to buy it for $1,000 and take it home and look after it.

So I went back again and took a look at it, but wondered what the hell I would do with it. It did not leak and it was a bit of coastal history, so I left it where it was.

Sometime shortly after that, DFO [Department of Fisheries and Oceans] hired a man with a skidder to go in and pull the dam out of the creek. To do this he had to build a road in to the lake. He got within about 300 feet of the lake when the funds ran out. Ten thousand dollars already spent just on the road, but the dam was still in place. Then DFO went in with a powder man and they blew one big log out of the centre of the dam. This brought down the level of the lake some, but there was still no way a fish could get up. There were no fish anyway, so it didn't really matter.

Then Ed came back and found the DFO road there, so now he could get the logs out.

He went back to Vancouver and bought a small tractor and found another partner, Ken Olsen, who had an old tug named *Pacific Foam*. The two men got the tractor ashore and loaded the old *Fearless* with shake blocks. Then they began loading the rails on *Joan G*. They piled all of them—about a hundred—on the deck, which made the *Joan G* top heavy. They were going to load the hatch with shake blocks but the tractor broke down, so Ed loaded it aboard *Fearless* and went to Vancouver, leaving Ken in Cockatrice.

Ed never came back for two years. Ken finally left, and the *Joan G* washed ashore during the winter of 1967. All the rails slid to one side and she rolled right upside down and sank.

In the spring of 1968 two men came from San Francisco to see me, to find out whether the *Joan G* could be refloated and repaired and towed to San Francisco, but by then she was too far gone to do anything with. The men had wanted her for the San Francisco museum and they offered me $5,000 if I could save her. I sure wished then that I had bought her from Bob for $1,000.

For two years nothing further happened in Cockatrice Bay, but then some shake cutters came and started to split shakes up the creek. They took a load out and left a hell of a mess right in the creek. Then Ed came back once again and poked around looking for some junk. Sometimes he would find a bit, before it was lost forever.

On the stern of the *Joan G* there were two big bronze rudder plates that weighed about a ton each. At low tide Ed put a cable around them and a stick of dynamite inside and blew the stern off. The old boat can still be seen lying there, but time and tide are taking their toll on what the people have left.

In 1973 two men with a tug and a skidder came to Cockatrice. They put the skidder ashore, planning to pull out all the remaining logs. The fact was that they had no salvage sale, so the Forest Service ran them out.

Then all that was left at Cockatrice Bay was a few logs, a hell of a mess and a little cabin by the creek. Someone shot the windows out and then someone burned the whole thing down. The mess and the remains of the dam were still there.

In 1987 DFO and all the patrolmen in the area and myself went and worked in the creek to clear a bit of a channel. In the spring of 1988 the Mainland Enhancement of Salmonid Species Society hatchery planted 25,000 coho fry into May Lake. We did the same thing every year for four years until there were coho coming back every year.

There were still two problems: a big log in the creek, and the tail-out of Phyllis Lake. In the summer of 1996 a group of sportsmen from Sullivan Bay hired Don Wilson to clean out the mess once and for all.

Now Cockatrice Creek is cleaned and restocked, and all that remains to be seen is whether the salmon run will rebuild to historic levels.

24 OYSTERS AND ST. VALENTINE

Excerpted from Notes from the Netshed *(1997), by Mrs. Amor de Cosmos*

They say it was a brave man who ate the first oyster. But I know that once he ate it, he ate many more. Say what you will, they are delicious molluscs. I have eaten them smoked, fried, raw, stewed and even baked in a loaf of French bread.

I thought about all this as I went on the ferry from Horseshoe Bay to the Sechelt Peninsula, or as the locals like to call it, the Sunshine Coast. The sun wasn't shining but that didn't bother me. I knew I was in for a good time visiting my cousin Leroy on his oyster farm.

Okay, his name isn't really Leroy and he's not exactly my cousin. The name Leroy was of his own choosing. As a kid he found it meant "the king" in French, so he chose to switch over, finding Leroy much more regal than the name "George" that his mother had given him. He always felt himself to be a self-made individual, so why not a self-made name? As for Leroy being my cousin—well, he is actually more like a shirt-tail relative by marriage, but it's kind of a long story so I just call him my cousin.

Leroy is always interesting to be around. He has a personality beyond the ordinary, and somewhere he has picked up an education to match. But more than that, he has one of the sharpest wits I've ever met. Unfortunately, he started his career as a fisherman, and as a fisherman he was a bust. On a troller he tended to get seasick. On a gillnetter he exerted a peculiar magnetism that could attract the only drift log for miles around, and sea lions were his constant companions. As soon as he stepped aboard a seiner, either all the fish in the neighbourhood disappeared or the engine broke down, or both. Once, in the middle of a particularly bad season, he told me that he was going to take an oar out of his skiff and start walking, and as soon as he got far enough inland that people would start asking him what that thing was he was packing, he would stop and settle down. Evidently that's how he got to the Sunshine Coast. It's not exactly inland, but at least oysters don't swim. Leroy felt he could cope with species that stayed in one place.

After some years labouring in the oyster business, Leroy had bought his own oyster farm. I was going to set up his books for him, and he would explain the world of oysters to me.

I took the ferry over to see him on St. Valentine's Day—the day set aside for lovers. Oysters, of course, have a connection with that amorous saint, as they are considered an aphrodisiac. Everyone seems to know this, although none, including companions I have shared oysters with, has ever offered me any actual proof.

Tidal flats at Oyster Bay at the head of Pender Harbour on the Sunshine Coast. It was here where early oyster cultivating experiments proved a runaway success.
Harbour Publishing Archives

Leroy met me at the ferry and we drove to his "farm." An oyster farm is really only a lease from the province to grow oysters on a piece of shoreline. As such it is mostly out of sight, at least at high tide. On the shore there will be a small shack to store tools and trays and stuff, and somewhere there is a skiff to go out to the floats from which are hung strings. In Leroy's case, he also had an old herring punt with an outboard.

At Leroy's place we set up his books. The finances of an oyster farm are not too complex. The capital equipment is the skiff and the outboard and the floats. The oyster spat (the "seed") is quite cheap. You can get into the oyster business with only a few bucks, but the trick is to make money at it. From what I could see, what with harvesting and so on, the business is highly labour intensive. For this reason oyster farms are usually family owned. Nobody gets rich, but then nobody starves either. Leroy's analysis was short and sweet: Buy a farm and you buy a job for life.

Leroy brought me up to date on the salmon farmers, who are now mostly gone. In the 1980s a bunch of salmon farms started up, but for once the Sunshine Coast lived up to its name. Each summer, the sunshine brought with it a plankton bloom in the water that wiped out many of the salmon farmers. This did not affect the oysters, although the oyster farmers have had their share of problems with the red tide. Most of them survived because their operations were small and they had already found ways to diversify their income, so they could stand a season with little or no cash. If the red tide came, Leroy would find something else to do until it passed. Small can be beautiful, if you find beauty in positive cash flow.

When we were done with the books we went to the local pub and I met some of Leroy's fellow oyster men. On the whole they were not like Leroy. They were older and somewhat slower. If you asked them how they were, they thought the question all the way through before replying. I guess the occupation attracts a certain type.

But the oyster farmers were not dull, and because it was St. Valentine's Day the jokes about love and oysters were flying fast and furious. I got them going a bit by noting that the oysters they grew were not the true BC oyster, but imports from Japan. One guy countered with the comment that, like most people, I knew next to nothing about oysters. He was right, but whenever anyone says this about any subject I simply dare them to enlighten me.

Did you know that an oyster will not die of a broken heart? The reason being that they can and do change their sex. They start as females, become males and then go back to being females again. This would be a boon to some people I know. If you're unsuccessful in one area, no problem—just go over to the other side. Apparently European oysters can change their sex indefinitely, but the big BC ones, the Japanese imports, get only two chances. That's still one more than you and me. I think if I were an oyster, St. Valentine would be my patron saint.

BEACH OYSTERS AND FANCY OYSTER STEW

25

Excerpted from One-Pot Wonders: James Barber's Recipes for Land and Sea *(2006), by James Barber*

On a low tide and a rocky beach almost anywhere north of Lasqueti Island, you should find beach oysters. They're not the little ones you slurp raw in fancy restaurants; they're big and they need to be cooked.

The simplest way is put them on the barbecue, flat side of the shell up, and cook until the shell opens. Sprinkle with Tabasco sauce or lemon juice or mayonnaise or sesame oil or Scotch, and eat either with a knife and fork or stuffed between two slices of bread. Messy but nice.

Kim La Fave illustration

Or you can fry them. Opening beach oysters onboard can be very bad for decks, so be careful. I suggest you put them on the barbecue until the shells open just a little bit, when you can pop in a kitchen knife and sever the muscle.

Fry them in butter over medium heat, sprinkle with pepper and lemon juice or soy sauce or teriyaki sauce or Tabasco sauce or Worcestershire sauce, and eat.

Fancy Oyster Stew
Serves 4

An oyster stew made of beach oysters is a wondrous thing on a cold winter's day. It sounds a bit complicated, but it's dead easy. You've read the tide tables, you know where you're going to find the oysters (this is a winter trip, an occasion well worth advance planning) and you have bought a couple of extra ingredients, like a small carton of cream, some fresh dill and a decent loaf of bread. I've also taken (at various times) gin, champagne, Jack Daniel's and Captain Morgan rum, and one Christmas in Heriot Bay, when the guests missed their plane and didn't arrive with the cooked turkey they'd promised, we ate this stew, with a bottle of Scotch, for Christmas dinner.

> 4 or 5 big beach oysters (or a 1 lb/500 mL tub if you don't want to take the boat out)
> 2 Tbsp (30 mL) butter
> 1 large onion, chopped
> 1 stalk celery, chopped fine
> 1 clove garlic, chopped fine
> 1 large potato, diced ½ inch (1 cm)
> 1 sweet red pepper, diced
> ½ tsp (2 mL) salt
> ½ tsp (2 mL) pepper
> 1 tsp (5 mL) paprika
> ½ cup (125 mL) white wine *or* water *or* canned clam juice
> 1 cup (250 mL) milk
> 1 tsp (5 mL) Worcestershire sauce *or* Asian fish sauce
> ½ cup (125 mL) half-and-half cream (or, if you're desperate, evaporated milk)
> juice of 1 lemon

Open the oysters while you heat the butter in a pot over medium heat. Fry the onion, celery and garlic 5 minutes. Add the potato, red pepper, salt, pepper, paprika and wine. Cover and cook 10 minutes. Cut the oysters into 3 or 4 pieces and add them to the pan with their juices. Cook 4 minutes. Add milk and Worcestershire sauce, heat through almost to the boil, lower heat and stir in cream for no more than 30 seconds (boiling will make it curdle), and remove from heat immediately. Sprinkle with lemon juice and eat.

Once you've made a good oyster stew, you'll want to do it again.

PADDLEWHEELS ON THE PACIFIC

26

Excerpted from Fishing for a Living *(1993), by Alan Haig-Brown*

In 1977 the international community of nations recognized a new convention granting coastal states exclusive fishing and other rights to the 200 miles of water directly off their shores. While this rule reserved the 200 miles off the west coasts of Haida Gwaii (formerly the Queen Charlotte Islands) and Vancouver Island for Canadian fishermen, it limited their access in the Gulf of Alaska and Bering Sea where many, like Edgar Arnet, had built their careers and their boats on the rich halibut grounds.

"Going out west" had a long tradition among Canadian fishermen. When the boats loaded ice and left Prince Rupert for the halibut grounds, they steered a course westward from Dixon Entrance across the huge, open expanse of the Gulf of Alaska. Alone on these very cold, rolling seas without radar or satellite positioning, the crews survived monster waves, frozen rigging and breakdowns. With little chance of outside help, they relied on their creativity, courage and calm. Perhaps the most famous tale is the account of Edgar Arnet's paddlewheels—a story still told around galley tables and anywhere fishermen gather.

The *Cape Beale* leaving for a trip to the halibut grounds, January 1957. *Courtesy of Edna (Arnet) Simpson*

By 1924 Edgar Arnet had decided to build his own boat. With a partner, John Berg, he had a Norwegian immigrant draw up a set of plans and make a model for a halibut boat. Because the boats must often work in heavy seas to haul the longlines to which the short gangen (lines) with their hooks are attached, the sea-keeping qualities of the boat are all important. After some debate with the builder over the best design for the stern, they went ahead with the construction of a classic halibut boat. A small cabin was set well back from the bow, but in a departure from tradition the cabin was ahead of the hatch. The long propeller shaft was in two parts; the main shaft, which ran through a series of bearings under the floor of the fish hold, was coupled to the tail shaft, which extended out through a stuffing box and the heavy timbers that formed the keel and stern post. A steel shoe ran out from the end of the wooden keel to hold the bottom of the rudder in place.

The *Cape Beale,* as it looked in its early years. *Courtesy of Edna (Arnet) Simpson*

The boat was built in a rented Vancouver shipyard near what is now the north end of the Burrard Street Bridge. By the end of February 1925, they had the hull planked, caulked and painted. The deck beams were in place, although the deck hadn't yet been laid. After launching, they towed her around to Coal Harbour and rented space at Andy Linton's boatyard, where they completed the decking, built the house and rigged the boat in time to leave for the Alaskan halibut grounds on June 3. They picked up crew, ice and bait in Prince Rupert and headed out to fish around Kodiak Island, Portlock Bank and Yakutat. John Berg, who had made a couple of trips to these waters on a small Seattle boat, served as skipper.

The following summer, in what was to become a familiar pattern, they got work for the boat packing salmon before going out to fish halibut again. Halibut could be fished virtually year-round with a ten-day layover between trips. John Berg died in 1927, so it was Edgar running the boat on that fateful trip in 1928.

They had been fishing out around Kodiak Island. Fishing had been good and when time came to deliver the trip, Edgar set a course directly across the Gulf of Alaska for Dixon Entrance at the top of the Queen Charlotte Islands. "We were just about in the middle of the Gulf of Alaska, over 250 miles from the nearest land. The darn thing broke right in the shaft log where you couldn't get hold of it. The propeller slid back from the speed that we were making and jammed up against the rudder. The rudder was useless. So then I thought of this side-wheeler. I talked it over with the crew and they thought I had something wrong upstairs.

"We were seven men, some of the crew were in favour of trying to work out something. So we started to make this side-wheeler. Three of the crew wanted to take off in the dory and row for land. We objected to that, so they couldn't. We worked on this jury-rig. It took us about two-and-a-half days until we finally got it going.

"By golly, we were making about two miles an hour. This winch we had, you could turn it so that the heads were fore and aft or athwartships. This made it a lot easier. We used a rope messenger from the winch head to a drum in the middle of the boom, which we had laid across the gunwale to use for the shaft with paddlewheels on each end. We took a couple of turns of rope around the drum and the winch with an end-less rope. Well, the darn ropes couldn't last forever. A couple of hours and they were all chaffed up. It was our tie-up lines that we were using.

"When they were all gone we took the cable off the anchor winch. It was quite flexible, not too stiff, so we rigged that up with a couple of turns around the drum and the same on the winch with a tightener up the mast for the slack. This was just a snatch block on the end of a line for the cable to run through. The line ran through another block at the top of the mast and could be tightened from the deck.

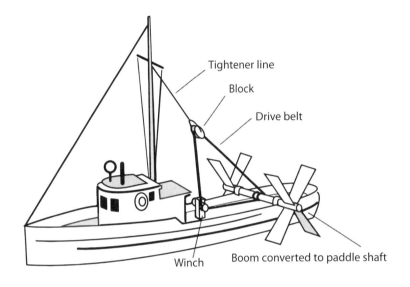

Tightener line

Block

Drive belt

Winch   Boom converted to paddle shaft

"It worked fine, but then it started to chew up the wood on the boom that we were using for the paddle shaft. We saw that wouldn't last very long so we thought of the funnel that the exhaust pipe went through. It was about two feet in diameter. It wasn't welded, it was riveted, so it wasn't hard to knock the rivets out and wrap the sheet metal on the drum. That went fine, but the steel cable would wear the eighth-inch metal, so we would move it over. In a couple of days there was no more funnel left, it was all chewed up.

"We had a bunch of fishing anchors with one-inch stocks. We took these and lashed them about four or five inches apart, like a Jacob's ladder. We wrapped that around the drum and it worked fine. You could go a couple of days before moving the anchor stops.

"We had tried to make course for Dixon Entrance but the darn wind was against us and was pushing us up into the Gulf, so we decided to make for Sitka. We still had a southeaster, and one day it was blowing about thirty or thirty-five miles an hour. It got quite rough and, with the boat rolling, the paddles would dig way down in the water. On one roll that she took, the boom that we had made for the paddles broke off on some cross grain. So we had to put our dory overboard and fetch it back. We managed to bolt it and tie it together. The paddles were too big so we cut them down to half the size.

"The winds were still taking us up the Gulf and we couldn't make Sitka. On the seventh or eighth day we saw the top of some mountains so then we knew we were

Above: Edgar giving instructions aboard a halibut boat, likely the *Cape Beale,* with skates of halibut gear behind him. *Courtesy of Edna (Arnet) Simpson*

Top right: Edgar (second from left) and one of his early halibut crews. *Courtesy of Edna (Arnet) Simpson*

Right: The *Cape Beale* with her steadying sail raised. *Courtesy of Edna (Arnet) Simpson*

getting close to the east side of the Gulf. In the evening we saw a boat in the distance. The tide and wind were taking us right for him. We got there before dark, launched our dory and rowed over to him. It was an American boat from Petersburg called the *Baltic.* They'd had a good day's fishing and had gone to bed. The skipper got up and I told him what went wrong. 'Well,' he said, 'there's a passenger boat coming down the coast tomorrow.'

"But I didn't figure he'd stop for us so I asked the skipper of the *Baltic* if he would tow us to the first cannery down the coast. This was the Libby, McNeill and Libby cannery, about a hundred miles south and just in from Cape Spencer. He agreed so we dismantled the paddlewheels and he put a line on us. I thought we would get one of the cannery tenders to tow us up to Juneau, which is only about seventy miles. But the

Edgar at the outside steering station of an early pilchard or salmon seiner.
Courtesy of Edna (Arnet) Simpson

Edgar built the steel-hulled *Attu* in 1959, well before the 200-mile limit, and named her for the island in the Aleutians.
Alan Haig-Brown photo

cannery manager said no way he was going to let any of his tenders go as he was too busy getting his traps set. So I talked the skipper of the *Baltic* into towing us up. He was reluctant because he was on good fishing. But I told him the insurance would pay.

"In Juneau we sold what fish we had—we had a fair trip—and contacted the insurance. They allowed us to have a new shaft installed and aid for the tow. They didn't pay for a new boom or funnel. The newspaper people in Juneau got wind of our trip and wanted us to rig the paddlewheels up again so they could take pictures of it. But we had taken it all apart. After a week in the shipyard we were ready to head back out to the Kodiak grounds.

"On the trip when we broke the shaft, we were fishing alongside an American boat called the *Grant*. The skipper of that boat always sold his trip in Rupert. When we left

Three generations of
Arnets. Left to right:
Edgar's grandson Russ,
Edgar Arnet and Edgar's
son, George.
Courtesy of Edna (Arnet)
Simpson

the fishing grounds and set course for Prince Rupert we figured he'd be leaving the same day, but we never saw him after we broke the shaft. He could have passed just a few miles away and we wouldn't have seen him.

"Twenty-five years later, about 1952 or 1953, the same skipper on the same boat was fishing off Kodiak Island. He was setting a course for Dixon Entrance. When he was halfway across, just about where we snapped our tail shaft, he came on the air with a Mayday call. His crankshaft had broken. The US Coast Guard came on the air right away. The skipper of the *Grant* gave his loran position and within twenty-four hours the Coast Guard had come, put a line on him and towed him into Sitka or Ketchikan. We didn't even have phones in the 1920s. It's a lot different today."

Edgar went on to a long and successful career in the fishing industry. He built the combination seine boat–longliner Attu *with a steel hull and aluminum cabin in 1959. One of the first steel seiners built with an aluminum house, she was fished for many years by Edgar's son, George Arnet, and is now being managed by Edgar's grandson Russ Arnet. But when halibut stories are told in the galley, one of the favourites will always be the tale of Edgar's paddlewheels.*

THE SECRET VICE OF FERRY-WATCHING

27

Excerpted from *When Nature Calls: Life at a Gulf Island Cottage* (1999), by Eric Nicol

This story shows that there have always been plenty of things about ferry travel for people to poke fun at, whether the rising fares, fuel surcharges, cuts in service, delayed sailings, CEOs with fat salaries, poor management, and so on that currently frustrate travellers on BC Ferries or the issues that affected Eric Nicol and others when he penned this piece. —Ed.

It is Polynesia North, but first you have to get to it, which isn't easy. The southern Gulf Islands are a jigsaw puzzle kicked over by a falling angel. Because they are off the reasonably straight line that would be the shortest distance between the two points—Vancouver and Victoria—reaching them can require the taking of several ferries of diminishing size and schizoid schedule.

A couple of the Gulf Islands have been threatened with the building of a bridge to help connect the Mainland with the Big Island. None of the plans has got past the planning stage, because the planners have had crosses burned on their lawns by delegates from whichever island doesn't welcome becoming a viaduct for motor traffic. It is part of the mystique of every island that the island is the sublime destination, not part of a highway system.

Peter Lynde illustration

You come, you stay until fulfilled, you leave. No one-night stand in a motel. You *marry* the island, sir, if you know what's good for you.

This commitment is particularly firm for Saturnans. The permanent residents of Saturna Island almost relish the plight of us Mainlanders who try to have an affair with the island that lasts less than a lifetime. The need to transfer from a large ferry to a smaller ferry, to sit for hours in various transfer compounds, baking in sun or peering through rain for the vessel delayed by any one of the many afflictions to which the BC Ferry Corporation is prone—these circumstances do much to keep Saturna free of the uncommitted.

There have been case-hardened men who have chosen the French Foreign Legion over signing on for Saturna.

So we summer cottagers are obliged to see the Ferry Experience as a major part of the pleasure—a bizarre type of masochism—or a character builder, in the same class as World War Two.

It begins with my having to make a reservation for my car. To do this with any hope at all of retaining a shred of sanity, I must have the current ferry schedule. In my judgment, a large part of the Ferry Corporation's thousands of employees is devoted entirely to changing the ferry schedule. The changes are made after consultation with the Oracle of Victoria, which predicts the seasonal ebb and flow of traffic, with consideration of the influence of the Japanese Current and hunches drawn from a hat.

The obvious place for a person to obtain a copy of the ferry schedule is aboard a ferry. Having to board a ferry in order to obtain the ferry schedule needed to make a reservation to access the ferry: this is how the Ferry Corporation discourages triflers and people who are already hysterical.

In addition—and this may be only a personal observation flawed by paranoia—the schedule pamphlets are placed in parts of the ship not normally seen by the passenger searching for one: in the engine room, under lifeboats, et cetera.

For further backup against its leaking information, as soon as the Ferry Corporation senses that too many would-be passengers are getting hold of the current schedule, it issues a new schedule, with previously unknown constellations of asterisks to ensure that no two days of the week have exactly the same timetable. This schedule is then hidden in new places on the vessels.

The only constant in the car-ferry scheduling is the requirement that your vehicle arrive at the check-in booth at least forty minutes before departure time, which is the stuff of whimsy. Tardiness may be punished by relegation to "standby status," a vehicular kind of Purgatory from which few attain salvation. Whereas the ferry rarely apologizes for leaving late unless summer has turned to fall, the loading crew have little patience with drivers who plead being delayed by gridlock, or a medical emergency such as donating a kidney. In this they have the full support of those of us who have arrived well ahead of the deadline and sit in our cars until turned to stone.

Because of these vagaries of the long wait, it is easy for me, the driver, to doze off, with my hand poised over the ignition key. Not until I jerk awake to see that the cars ahead of me in the line have been waved onto the ferry, hear a public-address voice blaring "Will the small red Honda please proceed?" and note an attendant gesture me forward with an expression of total exasperation, do I panic. I reverse instead of go forward, release wind rather than the brake, try to lower the radio antenna by opening the hood and, at last, lurch forward through a gauntlet of faces clearly not glad to be helping the mentally handicapped.

Barrelling, I catch up with the cars entering the maw of the ferry, just as we hit the speed bumps. These steel ridges rise and fall with the tide, phases of the moon that can neuter a car's suspension system. Watching vehicles try to take the bump too fast— sparks spraying as metal grinds on metal—is one of the more dependable sources of entertainment for the car-deck ferry crew. I've drawn applause more than once.

Now, however, I've learned to traverse the deadly rise as if anticipating the sudden uplift of a tsunami. Disappointment is obvious on the countenances of the crew, but I'm accustomed to being no fun at a party.

Then it's into darkness. I know how Jonah felt, being swallowed into the belly of the whale. Such is your entry into the ferry's car deck. You follow the jittery brake lights of the car ahead, round and round, chancy as the ball in the roulette wheel.

I suspect the Ferry Corporation has me secretly listed as dangerous cargo. Why else would the crew always park me beside a colossal tanker filled with enough propane gas to blow the ship, and possibly me with it, to smithereens?

That highly flammable presence inches from my door persuades me not to remain in my car in company with the dogs and cats and livestock not allowed up on the

Adrian Raeside illustration

passenger decks. But the decision to abandon the den isn't made lightly. Reason: It is incredibly easy to be unable to find the car again when it comes time to disembark and partake of an even more frantic panic than that inspired by boarding.

They—the ferry people—hide certain cars, you know. While certain drivers are upstairs, trustingly looking for a schedule pamphlet, they somehow move a car that was parked on Deck 3B up to Deck 2B. That's why I find myself trying to run crazed up a down escalator crowded with other passengers—an aerobic exercise with few redeeming features.

So I write the number of my car deck on the palm of my hand to improve my chances of ever seeing my car again. This means not washing my hands during the voyage. Going to the washroom must be carefully thought out, therefore, if not avoided altogether. It may seem overcautious, wearing Pampers in order to find an automobile, but the sea can be a stern mistress.

This fact is briefly forgotten in the excitement of seeing that the ferry is at last moving out of the jetty. She hoots, sharing my surprise at actual movement. Gazing out the lounge window, on the side that will sun-dry me when the ship, giggling, turns around, I'm moved to capture the moment in verse:

Time cannot pale,
nor custom dull,
the oft-told tale
of buoy meets gull.

Thus are some of us stirred by the drama of the ship's leave-taking. More, however, head for the cafeteria. It isn't good form for passengers to bring their own grub onboard to save money. That shows no spirit of adventure. It's like packing a chastity belt for a cruise on the Love Boat.

The ferry cafeteria provides a unique experience akin to losing your virginity. You enter this labyrinth whose minotaur is the cashier and file past a spare buffet of sandwiches, muffins and other delicacies, all wrapped for freshness and, indeed, forever. Trying to extract one of these goodies from its plastic carapace helps to pass the time for most of the crossing of the strait.

It also gives you something to do with your hands while you observe other passengers—a fascinating cross-section of escapees from urbanization. Most of us read, or pretend to. This way we avoid making eye contact with someone who turns out to be someone we know. Or should know. Like a former lover. Or our proctologist. Someone we ought to care about enough to be able to recognize the moustache.

Passengers who have forgotten to bring the survival kit of books or crossword puzzles may be forced to stand on an outside deck, pretending to be fascinated by a passing deadhead.

I have resorted to this escape manoeuvre myself, inhaling both funnel smoke and that from nicotine addicts obliged to puff outside and fume in more ways than one. To be free of all annoyance, you may be required to stand at the bow of the ship, leaning into the wind until your eyebrows blow off.

For me, having my vision impaired by salt spray makes it harder to interpret the symbols on the doors of the ferry's restrooms. These have been designed to minimize any appearance of gender discrimination. The female symbol (skirted) and the male symbol (panted) are barely distinguishable, especially if the ship is rolling. Yet I dare not loiter at the door, peering at a hieroglyphic. Guys have been arrested for harassing the Ladies, which is why I pause only briefly and may run several laps around the deck for confirmative glimpses before actually entering the washroom.

Once in, I hate to leave it. But how many times can a guy comb his hair?

Then, hey, we're there! Arriving at the island! Moment of climax! We sit in our cars, waiting for the ecstasy to begin. For, truly, 'tis better to have felt your ferry dock than never to have loved at all...the penetration of bow 'twixt pilings...the erection of the landing platform...the repeated impact that gives release to our hand brake...then, ejaculation! One last bump and grind up the ramp and we are off to the womb of our island home.

Ferry delayed? Think of it as coitus interruptus. Euphoria is only a ship's whistle away.

28 CLAM CHOWDER THE TRADITIONAL WAY

Excerpted from The Raincoast Kitchen: Coastal Cuisine with a Dash of History *(1997), from the Campbell River Museum Society*

"This traditional preparation was taught to me by my father, one of the pioneering Pidcocks at Quathiaski Cove."—Ruth Barnett

Don gumboots and warm clothing. Armed with shovel and pail, make for a clam bed at low tide. Butter clams thrive in sand-gravel beaches mainly in the lower third of the tidal range, where they may be found at least 12 inches (30.5 cm) deep. Unlike oysters, clams are at their best when preparing to spawn in summer, and at their least tasty immediately after spawning. Dig up a bucketful, wash them and drop into your pail of sea water. If the clam is fat, its shells may not be tightly closed. Take home and set pail in a cool place, after sprinkling oatmeal into it to deal with any sand.

Ready to make clam chowder?

In a large pot, sauté ½ cup (125 mL) chopped bacon until fat is clear. Add 1 cup (250 mL) diced onion, 2 cups (500 mL) diced potato and sufficient water to boil the mixture.

Above a large bowl, open clams with a dull knife, cutting through the muscles on either side of the clam's hinge. Open each clam using the knife to loosen the clam from its shells. Drop into the bowl in order to keep all the clam liquor. Pull away the

clam's spout (or siphon) and the attached membrane and discard. If desired, chop up clam into smaller pieces and return to bowl.

When potatoes are done, add clams and set pot on a low boil for no more than 10 to 15 minutes. Then add a large tin of evaporated milk, reheat and serve. Of course amounts may be varied to taste. I often add celery and thyme.

A satisfying meal for a cold stormy day.

Working at a clam cannery in Winter Harbour, ca. 1907.
Museum at Campbell River 19410

> *"Things were tough going in Depression days. We just survived. I ate so many clams I'd swear my stomach started to go in and out with the tide."*
> —*Willie Granlund, Campbell River Museum oral history project*

A READ ISLAND MURDER MYSTERY

Excerpted and revised from Tidal Passages: A History of the Discovery Islands *(2008), by Jeanette Taylor*

When breakfast was cleared away and the children had gone to school, Laura Smith packed her husband's lunch, rifle and bedding. John was heading off in his dugout canoe to hunt for a few days—and they needed the food. It had been another tough summer for the Smiths. John had lost his log boom to the tides, leaving the family destitute. Fortunately Hattie and Edgar Wylie helped out with gifts of salted salmon and venison. The Wylies, their closest neighbours on this remote stretch of the BC coast, could afford to be generous. They had a busy store, a small hotel/boarding house and a bar frequented by the many loggers of the region.

Laura probably watched with some concern as her husband set off on that early fall morning in 1894. She didn't love John anymore and their marriage was just a token. Out on the water, the waves were bunching up into whitecaps and driving against the island's rocky shores. A storm was brewing.

When Laura returned to the house she probably set a coal-oil lamp in the window as a signal to her lover Chris Benson, to let him know her husband was away. Chris Benson was Laura's current favourite, bringing groceries in exchange for her favours. His visits were no secret to anyone in the family, but Chris had become reckless of late, stopping by two or three times a week. Tongues were wagging, which bruised John's pride. One night in bed, John had told Laura she must stop seeing Chris. If she didn't, the children had overheard him say, he'd "deal with him." Laura probably

Edgar Wilmot Wylie was a charismatic fellow who attracted a small community to his remote home on Read Island. Many of them—including Chris Benson and John Smith—were friends from North Dakota, where Edgar had been chief of police before he fled under suspicious circumstances. Edgar died in 1908, leaving his beggared estate to his housekeeper. *Museum at Campbell River 10332*

didn't respond. What was the point? They needed the food Chris brought them and, after all, John was no angel himself. Sometime before this he had pulled their neighbour Hattie Wylie into their bed, where Laura lay sick, to have "immoral relations."

Laura's circumstances were complex and abusive. Her first lover, Henry Lang, was, like Chris Benson, a boarder at the Wylies', but he quit visiting Laura after she gave birth to his child, Daisy. That's when Chris Benson, a business partner of the Wylies, started coming around.

Laura's husband had immigrated to Canada with Edgar Wylie, a rotund man with liquid blue eyes. Edgar had risen to the rank of chief of police back home in North Dakota in 1888, when he ran afoul of the law in some grain deal gone wrong. He and John lit out for Canada, where Edgar lived under an alias for a time on remote Read Island. It proved the perfect spot, so both men sent for their families and settled on adjacent homesteads. Edgar may have had some investments to draw on, or perhaps it was his adept hand at cards that bankrolled his businesses. He was soon financing loggers, including John Smith, through credit at his store. In less than a decade, he was ready to build a new hotel on a bluff with a fine prospect, on a corner of John Smith's land.

While the Wylies' fortunes had flourished, the Smiths were barely able to feed their family of four by that fall day in 1894 when John set off hunting with his dogs. Laura stood on the shore to see him off, with the baby on her hip, and then walked up the boulder beach to their cabin. About an hour later she heard the clatter of boots on the front verandah—or so I picture this scene, based on the account she and her daughters gave in a trial a year later. She must have swung around with an expectant smile, but it wasn't Chris at the door. John was back. His dogs had run off, he said, so he'd had to cancel his hunting trip.

The three older children came home for lunch that day, fighting the wind along the rock bluff that separated their cabin from the Wylies' place, where school was held in the hotel parlour. Later John followed the children back to school, to see Edgar Wylie, and he was still away when Laura spotted Chris Benson's double-ended rowboat headed across the channel. Chris veered off to the south, going to a little cove out of sight of the hotel, and Laura was waiting for him when he bounded up the front steps of the cabin. Chris was a big man, who would have had to duck his head, removing his straw hat, to step inside.

"'We're all alone now, ain't we,'" Laura later quoted him as saying.

"'Yes, but the old man did not go off this a.m.,'" she said.

According to Laura's testimony, Chris agreed not to stay long, but somehow one thing had led to another. The baby was probably down for her afternoon nap and the house was quiet, so they had slipped into Laura's bedroom. They were up again and standing in each other's arms in the open bedroom door, with Chris's suspenders hanging loose from his shoulders, when John crept inside with a wooden shake mallet. Laura stepped aside just as John levelled a powerful blow that struck Chris on the left side of his head.

"'Oh, Smith, you've hurt me,'" Chris groaned before he slumped to the floor at the foot of the bed.

"'Damn you,'" John said. "'I'll fix you. You won't come see a woman of mine again.'"

Laura had backed into the kitchen, where she heard John deliver a few more blows. When he joined her, he told Laura not to say a word about what had happened or he'd shoot her. He locked both the outside doors, and in the hour that ticked by until the children drifted home from school, Laura heard the occasional moan from her bedroom.

Ten-year-old Myrtle got home at about 4 pm. She was puzzled by the locked doors but she went to play by the little creek near the house until Laura called her to help

Hattie Wylie was the daughter of a well-known doctor associated with the Mayo Clinic. She helped her father and later served as a midwife and nurse for Discovery Islanders. Hattie left her husband following John Smith's sensational murder trial because, as she said, life on Read Island had become too wild.
Courtesy of Jeanette Taylor

Edgar and Hattie Wylie built a second hotel/boarding house on a bluff on John and Laura Smith's land, which adjoined their property in Burdwood Bay, on the east coast of Read Island. There is a hint in John Smith's murder trial that Edgar Wylie paid for John Smith's legal costs. This was denied, but following the trial Edgar got title to the Smiths' land.

Photo from Lukin Johnston's Beyond the Rockies

gather wood shavings and firewood. They were lighting the cookstove when Myrtle heard a low moan from behind her parents' bedroom door. She drew closer to listen but her father told her to go back outside. When the child was gone, Laura slipped into the bedroom to feel Chris's hands. On a last check, just before the other two children came home at about 5 pm, his hands had begun to go cold.

Laura served the family supper as usual that night, just as dusk began to settle. And though it was getting dark, she urged the children to take the baby and go play among the trees on the hillside behind the house.

"'Let's take this body out to the boat,'" John said when the children were gone.

Laura was shocked by this, but the situation was a "drowned hog," as she later put it. John hefted Chris's lifeless shoulders, and Laura took his feet. They dragged him down to his little skiff in its hidden bay and lay him inside on his back. Then, in the growing darkness, John towed the boat south, letting it blow with the southeast wind into a bay. He hoped that when the boat was found it would appear Chris had fallen in the storm and hit his head. The problem was that John was not a man for details. He left the body in an unlikely position in the boat, where there was no blood to suggest a site of impact. And then there were Chris's clothes. What fool would be out in such foul weather dressed only in his shirt and unfastened trousers?

The next morning Hattie Wylie came to the Smiths', as she often did, and John took her into his confidence. She helped in a futile attempt to scrub Chris's blood from the bedroom floor and she took away a pile of Laura's blood-splattered clothes from beneath the bed. Before she left, Hattie admonished Laura not to talk about what had happened, later adding that if John was sentenced to hang, Laura would have to watch.

It was nearly three weeks before a high tide lifted Chris Benson's boat off a beach

Opposite left: Mike Manson, a longstanding MLA for the northern part of Vancouver Island, was also a justice of the peace with the authority to inquire into legal matters. Mike had the savvy— backed by rumours of love triangles on Read Island— to suspect foul play when Chris Benson was found dead in his boat. He arranged for a boarder at the Wylies' hotel to pose as a lover to Laura Smith to extract a confession.
Museum at Campbell River
13648

and set it adrift in the channel, where loggers found it and towed it to Wylie's Hotel. They sent for Justice of the Peace Mike Manson, who examined the body and made enquiries. Its circumstances and rumours afloat about love triangles made him suspicious, so he shipped the body to Vancouver and sent for the police. When the coroner's report arrived, it confirmed that Chris Benson had died as a result of a massive blow from a blunt instrument. Laura heard the details and later told John the coroner thought Chris may have lived for up to twelve hours after he was struck.

"'He didn't either,'" the children heard their father say, "'because he got a devil of a pounding.'"

John Smith seems to have been the police's prime suspect from the outset but it was hard to get concrete evidence so they arranged for one of the Wylies' boarders to become Laura Smith's next lover. The man was paid what was then a handsome sum, at $125, to extract a confession. He must have feared for his own safety in this tender trap, but Laura's husband turned a blind eye to his visits. The food he brought was much needed.

At first Laura said she knew nothing, but as the weeks passed, with her lover pretending to be very sweet on her, the story emerged. Two months later, Laura gave a full written confession that led to John Smith's arrest. Thereafter, Mike Manson took Laura and the children into his family's care on Cortes Island, and fourteen-year-old Cora and her younger sister Myrtle agreed to testify against their father. They'd heard and seen enough to convince them he had murdered Chris Benson.

The case came to trial in Vancouver about a year later, and though John Smith was impoverished, he was represented by the best lawyer in the province. With the death penalty looming, John stared off into vacant space through the four long days of his trial. Laura described the details of their lives with candour, corroborated by her daughters' evidence. John's chief witnesses were Edgar Wylie and a boarder, who said John spent that day with them, butchering a deer. Later he took a haunch home, which—they proposed—explained the bloodstains on the bedroom floorboards.

The Crown Council prodded Edgar Wylie, wondering if he'd paid John's legal fees, based upon a letter given as evidence. Council also noted that most of John's witnesses were in Edgar's debt. He was fishing, it appears, for a hint that Edgar was an accessory to this crime, but Edgar's steady denials ended this line of inquiry. It was not, after all, Edgar Wylie who was on trial.

When the last of the witnesses had testified, John's lawyer summed up his client's situation in a long, impassioned defence that earned him a round of applause from the packed courtroom. His colleagues later said this was one of the most eloquent appeals ever addressed to a Vancouver jury.

The Crown Council gave a concise but clear summation of the case, followed by a forceful address from the judge. He reminded the jury of their duty and the legal distinctions between murder, homicide and manslaughter. He then gave them his view of the case. He was convinced, he said, that Laura Smith and her children had told the truth. He found it odd that neither Hattie Wylie nor John Smith had testified. The latter, his lawyer had claimed, was in too nervous a state to speak. The judge also questioned the reliability of Edgar Wylie as a defence witness, with his checkered past and

a recent conviction for bootlegging to aboriginal people. The other key witness, the judge reminded the jury, had initially said he didn't remember where John Smith was on that day—but on the stand he claimed John was with him and Edgar. These same friends, said the judge, had tried to discredit Laura because she engaged in lewd conversation, but as he pointed out, Laura had made no attempt to hide any of the seamy details of her life. The jury's chief difficulty, as the judge saw it, would be whether to convict John Smith of manslaughter or murder.

The jury filed out of the courtroom and returned one and a half hours later. The courthouse hallways were packed, and when the folding doors were opened a throng of spectators had to be restrained by the police as they made a mad dash for seats. "The prisoner was conducted to the dock and sat with a frightened, hunted look in his eyes," said a newspaper.

"'Do you find the prisoner guilty or not guilty?'" asked the judge.

"As the words 'not guilty' dropped from the foreman's lips," said the newspaper, "a swelling torrent of applause had to be checked by the judge." With the court once again in order, the judge thanked the jury. He did not agree with their verdict, he told them, but he must accept it.

"'You are acquitted, owing to considerable extent, no doubt, because you had a bad woman for a wife,'" said the judge. He warned John not to hurt Laura because

Above: Laura Smith's youngest child, Daisy, is seen here with her natural father, Henry Lang. After the murder trial, Laura took Daisy north to Port Neville, where they lived for a time with Henry. Daisy was sent to a Vancouver orphanage when she was about eight, and though she likely never saw her mother again, she remained in contact with her father.
Courtesy of Jeanette Taylor

he would not get off a second time. "'You can go,'" he said, and a jubilant John Smith stepped out the courthouse doors and into the fresh, cold air of a winter night on the Vancouver streets.

John Smith got off on this murder charge because of gender bias and Victorian mores. The all-male jury, swayed by an eloquent lawyer, were in sympathy with a man who had been cuckolded by his wife.

The lives of all these people twisted into a vortex after this trial, which continued to spin into the next generation. Hattie left Edgar Wylie shortly thereafter because the life-style on Read Island was too wild, as she later told her children. A year later, Edgar Wylie was the one on trial, after an aboriginal woman died as a result of his bootleg whiskey. And though Edgar got title to John Smith's land—and his hotel site—perhaps for debts owed, he lost it in a card game.

Laura and John also separated, and the three older children remained with John. Within the year, fifteen-year-old Cora married a Cortes Islander, taking her little brother. Myrtle, whose testimony corroborated her mother's claims, disappeared completely from public records thereafter. As for Laura, she and Daisy lived with the child's natural father for a time, in a logging community to the north. But when Daisy was about eight, she was placed in an orphanage in Vancouver, where her father sometimes visited. Laura moved to the remote mid-coast, where she remarried and lived out her long life in this final relationship. She and Daisy may not have ever met again. As an adult, this separation suited Daisy, who obscured her past by saying that her mother's name was "Hattie" Smith and that she had died in childbirth.

Over a century later, when Daisy's granddaughters began genealogy research, they had few details to work with, save a prideful boast that Daisy was the first white child born on Read Island. That clue led them to my book Tidal Passages, *and eventually to stories of their Irish immigrant ancestors who came to the United States three centuries ago.*

"I have wondered many times how our grandmother would feel," wrote Daisy's grand-daughter Lois Wade, "if she knew we have discovered many of her secrets. I feel a little like we have disturbed the dead. But I am also very happy to give her a story, a childhood and a family. I find myself thinking about [Laura] much more than I would have imagined," says Lois. "Was she good to Grandma? Did she sing to her? Is this where Grandma learned her Irish ditties?"

DANCE OF THE WHALES 30

Excerpted from Whalers No More *(1986), by W.A. Hagelund*

The author was born in BC in 1924 and went to sea at the age of sixteen, whaling and working on coastal tugs. He collected stories of whales and whaling lore and added to this his very personal history of whaling on the West Coast. —Ed.

Speaking of whales, there was one favourite story my boys often asked me to tell as they settled in to go to sleep. With a certain literary licence on my part, our boys knew it as "The Dance of the Whales." Few people have seen this phenomenon, and never have I seen accounts of it written, but it was perhaps the most thrilling sight I have ever seen. If I were a painter, I could paint its details in stark shades of colour, for the picture of it is still etched in my mind.

It was during the latter part of the afternoon watch, on a day that had been wet and squally, and I was cold and miserable as I stood my trick on the wheel. Finn John, smoking his old stubby pipe and wearing his brown Indian sweater and his battered old brown fedora, scanned the ocean as we rolled along on an outward sweep, skirting a northerly storm front that had kept us in its frigid grip all day. My eyes automatically came up from checking the compass to search the horizon opposite the direction the mate had swung his head. I snapped alert as my weary eyes spotted a strangeness there that warranted greater concentration.

To the southwest, the storm clouds were lifting and breaking apart as the wind backed around to that quarter. Fingers of sunlight poked down through these rents in the clouds to illuminate the grey, heaving sea, turning the cresting waves a translucent green, and their foaming tops a milky white. Between these shafts of warm yellow were the dark curtains of rain squalls sloping down to the sea. What had caught my eye were small dark shapes that appeared and disappeared in those dark areas of the rain squalls. Undoubtedly fish-shaped, they were so far away that only once in a while could I actually see their tails. This placed them well over five miles away, and the only fish I knew that could be seen five miles off were whales. But I'd never seen whales behaving like this before. Almost a hundred feet in length and as many tons, they were propelling themselves up, completely out of the water.

Alexandra Burda illustration

I cannot recall what sort of hail I made to get Finn John's attention, but when he turned to look, they were gone. He looked back at me, a little bemused, after scanning the area for a good five minutes through his binoculars without sighting a thing; even the sunbeams had disappeared. But he showed respect for my judgment and keen eyesight by hauling the ship around to a heading I indicated and, still at cruising speed, we moved toward that distant spot where the two winds came together.

Twenty minutes later we were among the rain squalls, and the wind tore the clouds apart with a fury that rent the silence with several long rolls of thunder. It was like the beat of drums, signalling that the curtains were rolling back and the play beginning. Sunbeams poked down onto the sea ahead of us with a brilliance that caused my eyes to water, the dark vertical lines of the rain squalls retreated northward, and the heaving, cresting sea came alive with colour. Then, before us, not more than ten or fifteen cables off, the surface of the sea erupted as sleek black whales nearly as big as our ship hurled themselves up out of the water, some standing as high as our mast, their tails beating the surface into a frothy foam to maintain their momentary posture.

Never had I seen anything like it. Finn John got so excited he literally jumped up and down. Pulling his pipe out of his mouth, and tearing off his hat, he beat it against the weather dodger of the bridge as he roared at me, "Jesus Christ, God almighty! Will you look at those goddamn sulphur bottoms yump and dance!"

He rang down for slow speed, but there was no need to call anyone up; the noise made by the whales had brought them all out from the supper table. There must have been a dozen or more whales in sight at any one moment, and as they dropped back into the sea, others took their places. God only knows how many whales were there, perhaps a hundred. Some of the smaller ones leaped so far out of the water I could see the horizon under their tails, and they terminated their leap in a curve that brought them back to the surface in a thunderous fountain of spray as they landed full length. Sometimes they would rise together in pairs, facing one another, and pause like two huge dancers before our startled eyes, their tails beating the sea into a froth that rumbled louder than any propeller rising to the surface.

Bounding up to the bridge, Louis scowled over at the whales like a tiger held at bay, his jowls quivering, his mouth opening and closing, and his hands clenching and unclenching on the handle of the telegraph. His gunner's instinct to let fly with a couple of harpoons warred with his master mariner's regard for our old ship's aging gear.

Caution won out and, ordering John to skirt the pod of blue whales, he began looking for more suitable whales for our taking. The display lasted less than fifteen minutes; then the sea became strangely silent. Before anyone could retire, however, we sighted several humpbacks breaching to starboard, and pounced on them so swiftly they were lashed alongside before we went to our supper. On our way into the station, we heard that the crew of the *Black* had not resisted the temptation when the pod of blues had surfaced near her, and they were now returning to repair her windlass and replace the whole length of her mainline. There was no doubt they rued their impulsiveness.

During supper, Finn John attempted to explain the phenomenon we had seen by stating the whales were merely throwing themselves out of the water to create an impact of sufficient force to dislodge the encrustations and parasites they hosted on their skin. He said these parasites became more active and worrisome to the whale the farther inshore, to the warmer and less salty waters, they came.

But Jacques-Yves Cousteau, in *The Whale: Mighty Monarch of the Sea*, states that both finback and blue whales couple by facing together like humans, and, to achieve this, they swim up from the depths together, trying to achieve penetration and climax before reaching the surface. I believe that what we had seen was the grand finale, after climax had been achieved, and the inertia of their swift passage upward rocketed them above the surface, where the tail wagging was a burst of ecstasy, signalling fulfillment of this great desire.

Perhaps someday the dance of the whales will be performed within range of a camera, and this amazing spectacle will be recorded for all to behold. Nothing less would convey the true magnificence of these great creatures.

INDEX

RAINCOAST
Chronicles

RAINCOAST CHRONICLES
FIRST FIVE
Collector's Edition
Edited by Howard White
978-0-920080-04-7
$28.95

RAINCOAST CHRONICLES
SIX/TEN
Edited by Howard White
978-1-55017-067-2
$28.95

RAINCOAST CHRONICLES
ELEVEN UP
Edited by Howard White
978-1-55017-105-1
$39.95

RAINCOAST CHRONICLES
FOURTH FIVE
Edited by Howard White
978-1-55017-594-3
$29.95

Also available in this series:

RAINCOAST CHRONICLES 12
Edited by Howard White
978-1-55017-028-3 • $16.95

RAINCOAST CHRONICLES 13
Edited by Howard White
978-1-55017-052-8 • $16.95

RAINCOAST CHRONICLES 16
Time & Tide: A History of Telegraph Cove
By Pat Wastell Norris
978-1-55017-121-1 • $16.95

RAINCOAST CHRONICLES 17
Edited by Howard White
978-1-55017-142-6 • $16.95

RAINCOAST CHRONICLES 18
Edited by Howard White
978-1-55017-171-6 • $16.95

RAINCOAST CHRONICLES 20
Lilies and Fireweed: Frontier Women
of British Columbia
By Stephen Hume
978-1-55017-313-0 • $19.95

RAINCOAST CHRONICLES 21
West Coast Wrecks and Other Maritime Tales
By Rick James
978-1-55017-545-5 • $24.95

RAINCOAST CHRONICLES 22
Saving Salmon, Sailors and Souls:
Stories of Service on the BC Coast
Edited by David R. Conn
978-1-55017-626-1 • $24.95

RAINCOAST CHRONICLES
Collector's Edition
Edited by Howard White
978-1-55017-527-1 • $100.00
AVAIL. DIRECT FROM PUBLISHER ONLY

Available from your local bookstore or from:

HARBOUR PUBLISHING
P.O. Box 219, Madeira Park, BC, V0N 2H0
Toll-free order line: 1-800-667-2988
www.harbourpublishing.com